DOVER
BEACH

The Last P.I. Series

Book One

Richard Bowker

Book design by eBook Prep
www.ebookprep.com

Cover design by Jim McManus
Complexstories.com

October, 2017
ISBN: 978-1-947833-12-8

ePublishing Works!
www.epublishingworks.com

DEDICATION

For Robert and Helen Collins

CHAPTER 1

It was one of those gray December days that freeze the soul as well as the body. The stack of unread books grew smaller; the fire in the wood stove was dying; I was thinking (not for the first time) that I was in the wrong line of work. Then I looked out my window and noticed the stranger standing in the slush below.

I quickly looked away. Didn't want to scare him off. I imagined him staring at the sign in the window and wondering whether to come up; it wasn't a very good sign, after all. I put the book down and waited. I heard the downstairs door creak open, then slam shut. I heard slow footsteps on the stairs; it was dark out there. The footsteps stopped outside my frosted-glass door. There was a pause, then a loud rapping.

I took out my .38 caliber Smith and Wesson automatic and aimed it at the door. You can't be too careful nowadays. "It's open," I called out pleasantly.

The stranger stepped inside. He stared at the gun. I stared at him.

Tough to make out very much in the semidarkness, except that he was well dressed—absurdly well dressed. "Mr. Sands?" he inquired nervously. The accent was

Southern; he managed to make two syllables out of my name.

"That's right."

"The private investigator?"

"That's right."

"I may have a case for you."

I motioned to a seat across the desk from me, and I put the gun away. The man sat down. I lit the oil lamp on my desk, and we took a good look at each other.

Straight black hair, eyes the color of my stove. Sloping jaw, good skin—tanned. He was about my age, but I had a feeling the similarity ended there. The hands he was rubbing together were well manicured; the overcoat he wore looked new.

"Now, what can I do for you, Mister…"

"Winfield. *Doctor* Charles Winfield."

"Ah."

Having taken stock of me, his dark eyes darted away and took in my well-appointed office. They glanced meaningfully for a moment at the wood stove, but I didn't feel like taking the hint. He kept rubbing his hands. "I saw your ad in the *Globe,*" he said finally.

"Ah."

"Why don't you have a telephone? This would have been much easier over the phone."

"Phones don't work very well around here," I said.

"Oh." He was silent again. He looked as though he wanted to pace, but there wasn't room. "It's an absurd profession—private investigator," he said after a moment. "I can't imagine there's any demand for your services."

"You're here," I pointed out.

"I don't really know why," he said.

"That makes two of us."

He glanced at me, then quickly looked away. "Someone tried to kill me yesterday," he said.

"Ah."

"But that's only part of it—that's not really even why…"

"If you're willing to start from the beginning," I said, "I'm willing to listen."

He nodded. "I'm twenty-two, Mr. Sands."

My turn to nod. My age. The magic age.

"I was raised in Florida. I never knew my father, and my mother never said much about him. I naturally assumed—" He waved his hand.

"Naturally."

He took a breath, then plunged ahead. "It was only when my mother was dying that she explained anything, but it didn't really make much sense to me at the time. She said she had been living up here in Cambridge—she was a graduate student, I guess. She underwent some kind of experimental procedure at MIT that involved making her pregnant. But then, apparently, she left for Florida. Tensions were high, I suppose, and she wanted to go home. I don't know. She never went back to MIT."

"Not much of MIT to come back to," I remarked.

"Yes, I noticed." He paused. "I never tried to make any sense out of what my mother told me until I was in medical school—until a classmate showed me this." Dr. Winfield reached into an inner pocket and removed a sheet of paper. He carefully unfolded it and passed it to me.

It was an article from an old magazine. More than twenty-two years old. The title of the article was: "Controversial New Cloning Technique Defended." It consisted mainly of an interview with one Robert Cornwall, professor of genetics and cell biology at the Massachusetts Institute of Technology. There was a photograph of Professor Cornwall.

He looked remarkably like Dr. Winfield.

"Do you know what a clone is, Mr. Sands?"

"No," I lied.

"It is a genetically identical copy of a living organism. Many plants generate clones as a normal form of reproduction. Biologists used to know how to clone other species in the laboratory. They did it for bacteria and frogs and such. Techniques for cloning mammals were just being developed back then."

"You think you're a clone, Dr. Winfield?"

"Look at the photograph."

I looked some more. "Uh-huh," I said noncommittally.

He reached out and took the article back. "One can't go through life not knowing who—or what—one is. Don't you agree?"

"Yes," I lied.

"I had no way of finding out while I was in medical school down in Fort Lauderdale. I had to wait until I was a doctor, until I had some freedom and some money."

"They let doctors out down there?"

Winfield shrugged. "Of course. They know we'll come back. It's letting people *in* that they won't do."

"So you came to Boston to track down Professor Cornwall and uncover the secret of your past?"

"That's right."

"And you want some professional help?"

He nodded.

I pressed my hands together and leaned back in my chair. "Well, it's my professional opinion that you'd be wasting your money, Dr. Winfield. He's not here. He's dead, and everything that constituted his life has been scattered to the winds. That's the way it is."

"Then why," Winfield asked, "is someone trying to kill me?"

I rocked a little in my chair. "Oh," I said. "Right. Tell me more."

"I arrived here two days ago and immediately went to the Registry. Cornwall is not in their records as being confirmed alive or dead. There was also no record of his prior existence here—he wasn't in the old phone books they had, for example."

"None of which means very much."

"Of course not. So yesterday I went and took a look at MIT. Scattered to the winds, as you say. So what would a professional private investigator do next?"

"Go to someplace that isn't scattered to the winds," I suggested. "Like Northeastern. See if anyone there remembers Cornwall."

Winfield nodded. "Exactly what I did. It was late in the day, however, and there weren't many people to talk to. So I started back to my hotel. On the way, someone shot at me. Two shots. Both just missed. I ran all the way to the hotel and didn't venture out of my room. Today I got a newspaper from room service and saw your ad, so I decided to risk a visit. And here I am."

"I see. It was after dark when you were shot at?"

"Twilight—almost dark."

"And this was near Northeastern?"

"Yes. Some side street off—what is it?—Huntington Avenue?"

I stopped rocking my chair and leaned forward. Winfield's face flickered in the lamplight. He started rubbing his hands again. "Dr. Winfield, this is not the South, I'm afraid. We lead difficult lives in a difficult world, and sometimes people get shot at—not because they're looking for their father or whatever, but because they're wearing a new coat."

Winfield's gaze shifted away from me. His nervousness seemed to turn to excitement. "That's a possibility, I grant you. But here is a more interesting possibility: 'controversial new cloning technique,' Mr. Sands. The technique makes it possible to clone *people.* That's quite an important skill, given our birthrate nowadays. What if someone doesn't want it known that the person who possesses this skill is still alive?"

"Who?"

"Well, for example, our present government, such as it is."

I half smiled, wondering if that was a joke. Dr. Winfield didn't smile back. "You mean cloning people to increase the population, rebuild the country?" I said. "Excuse me, but I'm not persuaded. The government would never be interested in that."

"All right, maybe so. Maybe some other group has Cornwall, and wants to keep the government from finding out."

My expression was apparently sufficient response.

"You can think it's farfetched, if you like," Winfield said. "You don't have to believe my theory to do your job—if I hire you."

"True." I fingered my gun. "You want a bodyguard?"

"Yes. And I want you to find out what happened to Cornwall, and who is trying to kill me."

"Two new dollars an hour, plus expenses," I said. "Ten dollars in advance."

Winfield gazed at the gun. "How do I know you're any good?" he asked. "You're just a name in the newspaper. You've got a crumby office, and you've got a gun. That's it. Any references? Any satisfied customers?"

I considered. "Forget about the ten dollars in advance," I said. "I'll work on the case tomorrow. If you're not satisfied with my progress, you can fire me—no charge."

Winfield considered in turn. What was there for him to consider? "All right," he said finally. "Why don't you escort me back to the hotel? You can report to me there tomorrow night."

"Okay. Fifty cents to escort you to the hotel. Refundable if you're killed on the way."

Winfield laughed. "You people are tough up here."

"Gotta be." I stood up and put on my ratty old parka. I picked up my gun, put out the light, and we left my office. Lower Washington Street was dark and deserted; the ancient, abandoned strip joints seemed to shiver in the chill air. Winfield looked around nervously. "Aren't there better neighborhoods for your office?" he asked.

"I like the rent. Where are you staying?"

"The Ritz."

"Ah." I walked Dr. Winfield to the Ritz. We didn't say much. No one tried to kill him. He handed over the fifty cents when we reached his room. "Tomorrow night," he said. "Find out for me about Cornwall."

"Tomorrow night," I agreed.

Winfield suddenly smiled. "I bet it will be something amazing." His gaze hovered somewhere above my left shoulder, and then he disappeared inside his room.

The Ritz was warm. I hung around the lobby for a few minutes, then left before I wore out my welcome. There was no sense in going back to the office. I wandered over to Charles Street, and on an impulse spent my fifty cents on some bacon. You only live once. Then I walked through the Common to Park Street and waited for the train to come in.

I was a little early. A few people were standing around in the slush. A casual acquaintance nodded to me. "How's business, Walter?"

"A bit slow there for a while, but it's picking up now."

"Good, good." He had no idea what my business was.

Over by the old cemetery, Ground Zero was sitting on a milk crate, playing the accordion. He was an ancient black man with a keloid-scarred face; I never cared to ask him how he got his name. I went over to him. "Howdy, Ground Zero."

He nodded. "Howdy, Mithter Thandth." He lisped.

I rooted around in my pockets and found a penny. I tossed it into his cap. "Know any private-eye songs, Ground Zero?"

He considered. "How 'bout a TV theme?"

"Great."

His hands moved over the accordion keys for a few seconds, and then he started in. "Theventy-theven Thunthet Thtrip." He banged the side of the accordion twice. "Theventy-theven Thunthet Thtrip."

He was a better accordion player than singer. I threw another penny into his cap. "Just play it, Ground Zero. I'll imagine the words."

He shrugged, disappointed, and went on with the instrumental version. It didn't sound like a very good song, but who am I to judge? He was still playing it when I heard the rumble that meant the train was pulling into the subway station below. I waved to Ground Zero and wandered back to the station's entrance.

The commuters were straggling out the door. Gwen was one of the last of them. Her face lit up when she saw me. "Walter," she said. "Hi."

She tilted her head and looked at me for a moment, then took hold of my arm. We started walking. "What's in the bag?" she asked finally.

"Oh, just some bacon."

We stopped, and she looked at me again. I tried to keep from grinning. "Bacon?" she repeated.

"I got a case today. Time I started bringing home the bacon."

Gwen smiled. That's about the most you could get out of Gwen. "Congratulations," she said. She squeezed my arm.

"Wanna hear about it?"

"Tell us at dinner. I can't wait to see Linc's face."

I nodded. "Life's small pleasures."

She leaned against me for a moment, and that was indeed one of life's pleasures. Then we walked on through the slush, while I thought about my case.

CHAPTER 2

It was Stretch's turn to cook supper. The familiar aroma of his stew hit us as soon as we walked in the front door. Gwen and I looked at each other and smiled. We hung our coats on the rack in the front hall and went back to the kitchen.

Stretch was at the stove, stirring the stew. Linc was slumped in a chair at the table, propped up by a couple of pillows. "Hi, all," I said, and I dropped the bacon onto the stove. "Why don't you cook this up, Stretch?"

Stretch looked at it. "Bacon? What's the occasion?"

"Walter got his first case today," Gwen announced.

Linc applauded. "The Sandman comes through. We all knew you would."

"Gee, you did a great job of keeping it to yourselves," I said.

"We didn't want you to get a swelled head."

"Well, you were entirely successful." I poured myself a glass of cider and sat down next to Linc. He was wearing two or three sweaters and a pair of gloves. His eyes glittered out of his pale, unshaven face like jewels dropped in old snow. "So how's it going?" I asked him.

He managed a smile. "Never better. I think the climate's agreeing with me. There's something about slush—I guess it's just good for what ails you. But enough of that. Tell us about your case."

I was glad to comply. I told them the story of the mysterious Southern doctor and his supposed clone while Stretch cooked the bacon and set the meal in front of us. "It was one of those gray December days..."

But somehow it didn't sound quite as exciting in the retelling. By the time I had finished, Gwen and Linc were studying their stew, and Stretch was looking at me with a puzzled expression. "Wait a minute," he said. "This guy Cornwall has been missing for—well, for twenty-two years—and you're trying to track him down for free?"

"Um, well, yeah, I guess so."

"But that's stupid, Walter. You're never going to get anywhere. And do you really think someone other than your average hood is trying to kill this doctor?"

I shrugged. As usual, Stretch was missing the point. "It's a case," I said. "I run an ad in the paper, and everyone laughs at me, but I get a case. And the guy paid me fifty cents," I pointed out. I grabbed a piece of bacon self-righteously.

"It's probably worth a try," Linc said.

"It might be good experience," Gwen said.

"Yeah. Good experience." I chewed my bacon.

"Besides, it could be worse," Linc said. "You could be working for the government."

Linc knew when to change the subject. The government was always good for an argument. Stretch worked for the government.

"The government's okay," I said.

"How can you say that?" Linc demanded. "You probably break a dozen laws every day."

"I'm glad the laws exist, even if I break them."

"Do you know how idiotic that sounds, Walter?"

I grinned. "I'm a private eye, not a philosopher."

Stretch ladled out more stew. I noticed that Linc had barely touched his. "The government is all that keeps us from chaos," Stretch said.

"Oh, bullshit," Linc replied. "I've seen what governments can do. Give me chaos any day."

"This government is different," Stretch said.

Linc rolled his eyes. "The only way this government is different is that it's less powerful. And that's by necessity, not by choice."

"I saw what things were like before we had the government," Stretch said quietly. "I'm proud to be a part of it."

Linc sighed. When Stretch started talking about pride, the argument was over. We ate in silence for a while. Linc looked very tired. "I think I'm gonna go take a nap," he said. "Maybe dream about truth, justice, and the American way."

"You should try to eat more," Gwen said.

He smiled. "Why? Did someone pass a law?" But he obediently gulped a couple of spoonfuls of stew before he got up from the table. He patted me on the shoulder as he made his way past. We listened silently to his slow footsteps on the stairs. Stretch took Linc's bowl and scraped the remaining stew back into the pot. "Linc isn't feeling well," he murmured.

I ate another piece of bacon. I didn't want to think about Linc, so I changed the subject. "What'd you write about today, Gwen? Anything exciting gonna show up in tomorrow's *Globe?*"

"Fuel aid," she said.

"We get any?"

"Nope." Gwen wasn't the world's most talkative writer. I noticed that she was staring at me in that soul-dissecting way of hers, her head slightly tilted, her eyes half closed, appraising. It was not the kind of stare that made you feel very comfortable. I waited nervously for the result of the appraisal. "I guess you're a full-fledged private eye now, Walter," she said softly.

"I guess so," I replied, no longer able to look at her.

"Does that mean you don't have to go out with Bobby tonight?"

"Bobby! Jesus, I forgot. I'll be late."

Her head remained tilted.

"Look, it's not that big a deal," I said. "We just drive up to New Hampshire, he does his business, and we come back. He just needs me because Doctor J has to stay behind and guard the warehouse."

"It's illegal," Stretch noted.

I ignored Stretch. "Nothing's gonna happen, Gwen. Honest."

"You told me those Charlestown people weren't going to be very happy."

"Yeah, but they can't *do* anything about it. They don't want to get this guy Fitch angry at them by messing with one of his suppliers. I'm more worried about the snow than I am about them."

Gwen looked down at her stew and said nothing. Her appraisal of me was complete. I sighed and finished off the bacon. Then I stood up. "Great supper, Stretch." Gwen stood up too.

"Walter, you be careful out there," Stretch said. "And thanks for the bacon."

"Sure thing." Gwen and I walked out to the front hall. Stretch stayed behind to do the dishes.

I put on my parka and my knitted cap, and we gazed at each other for a moment. Gwen isn't very good-looking, I guess. Chin too pointed, cheeks too hollow. Her old black trousers and bulky sweater didn't do much for her figure. But then, none of us is going to win any beauty contests. And anyway, her brown hair looked beautiful by candlelight; her dark gaze could be exciting as well as nerve-wracking; and when you managed to make her happy, her smile made your life seem worthwhile.

"Linc isn't going to last the winter," she said finally.

"I know."

"I worry," she said. "About all of us."

"I know. It'll be all right. Trust me."

She looked at me, and I knew that she didn't trust me, didn't trust anything or anyone in this world—had no reason to. But there was nothing she could do about it, so she had to give in. "I'll wait up for you," she said.

We held each other for a moment, and then I walked out into the night.

CHAPTER 3

The road barely existed anymore. Hunched over the wheel, Mickey stared out through the snow and swerved constantly to miss the rocks and potholes and assorted debris. A broken axle up here would not be a good idea.

Bobby was nervous. When he's nervous, he talks too much. "So she says, 'Oh, it's so hod to pot with all this. It's been in the family for generations, you know. We godded it all through the Frenzy and now things are settling down, but what am I to do? One must eat, mustn't one?'

"'Oh, certainly one must,' I says. Jesus, they all make you feel like they're doin' you a favor, handing over their firstborn or something. But I'm not the one that's starving. You know what I'm saying? Jesus, this snow's a bitch." Bobby leaned forward and peered out at an abandoned house. He doesn't see very well. "I hate bein' outside the city. I mean, the city is dangerous, but at least you know what's goin' on. There are rules, sort of. Who the fuck knows what's goin' on up here?"

Bobby sat in the middle, between Mickey and me. A shotgun rested between my legs. I held its smooth barrel in my right hand. The van's heater was turned up full blast, and it felt great. I wished Bobby weren't so nervous. He was making me nervous too.

We were off the highway now, passing by cold white fields and scrawny trees and rocks. Bobby was right: we didn't belong here. Still, something stirred inside me— wisps of memories that were better left unremembered. "How much further, Mickey?" I asked.

"Not far," he said. Mickey was about as talkative as Gwen.

Bobby drummed his fingers on his thighs. "This guy is so fuckin' weird, Wally, you won't believe it. It's being stuck up here in the boonies, if you ask me. You got no human interaction, you know what I'm sayin'?"

"He has you. And O'Malley's people."

"O'Malley's people. Shit. Talking to one of them's like talking to a tree. This guy is so weird. Christ, I wish I could see something."

Mickey was going even slower now. Eventually there was a light in the distance. "That's it," he said. We aimed for the light, and came to a stop in front of a large gate. The light shone down at us from behind the gate like a beacon from heaven. A dog was barking. I don't like dogs.

"Get out with your hands up," an amplified voice ordered. It sounded like God.

I looked at Bobby. "So fuckin' weird," he said, shaking his head. He motioned to me to get out. I left the shotgun behind and climbed down into the snow with my hands over my head. Bobby and Mickey did the same.

The gate swung open, and two figures appeared out of a shack. One stayed behind and trained a shotgun on us. The other moved forward. He had a revolver in one hand, a Doberman on a leash in the other; the Doberman was about the size of the van. The figure was wearing a knitted cap and a homemade sheepskin coat. He was about twelve.

He searched us. The Doberman growled when it was my turn. Good doggie. I kept my hands up. The boy found my Smith and Wesson and pocketed it. He found the shotgun in the van and gave it, and the Doberman, to the figure waiting by the gate.

The boy returned to us. "Okay," he said. We all got into the van. The boy kept the revolver trained on Mickey, who drove slowly through the open gate. We passed the other figure, standing by the shack and restraining the Doberman. It was a girl, maybe a little younger than the boy. The Doberman kept barking. The gate clanged shut behind us. I felt as if I had crossed a border.

Here is a survival skill I have learned. Generally, when you come upon an isolated farm surrounded by barbed wire, with searchlights and Dobermans and shotguns in evidence, it is a good idea to move on. Quickly. Not tonight, however.

"So how do you like this snow?" Bobby asked the boy.

The boy didn't reply.

"I don't think there was this much snow in the old days," Bobby went on. "Of course, they say that about a lot of things. But I think maybe they're right about the snow. A lot more snow than there used to be."

Bobby was nervous. I wished he would shut up.

The land extended flat and unbroken on both sides until it disappeared in the darkness. The road along which we were traveling was plowed and newly paved. We were headed for a sprawling house that blazed with light about a half mile in front of us. Several smaller buildings were scattered like seedlings around it. There was a large barn and a silo off to one side, and in the distance a windmill loomed like a creature from a fairytale.

"Stop," the boy said when we had reached the house.

Mickey pulled up by the front porch.

Another figure stood by the door, holding another shotgun. The boy got out and waved, and the figure motioned for us to come in.

"Here goes," Bobby muttered. We got out and crunched across the snow to the open door.

"Wipe your feet," the figure commanded.

We wiped our feet and walked inside.

"Come with me." The figure took off her cap—it was a girl with a misshapen face. We followed her while our senses reeled. Warmth: the house was warmer than the van, warmer than the Ritz; a month's supply of logs blazed in a fireplace. Light: electric lights, shining out from chandeliers and sconces, reflecting off mirrors and polished mahogany furniture. Smells: the sharp sweet scent of burning birch, the rich aroma of something sweet being baked. Apple pie? Strudel?

Somewhere close by a piano was playing, children were laughing. I felt as if I had stepped into a storybook.

The deformed girl led us into a long dark room lit only by a coal fire. The room had a vaulted ceiling, tapestries on the wall, a Persian carpet on the floor. At the far end of an oak table sat a man with a gray beard and deep-set, glittering eyes. He was wearing a flowing white robe. Maybe I hadn't stepped into a storybook; maybe I had stepped into the Bible. Maybe *he* was God.

"You may return to your post, Lavinia," the man said in a deep, God-like voice.

The girl silently left the room. The man's gaze turned to us: three travelers from a distant land, bearing gifts.

Not much to look at. Bobby is the only fat man I know— but it isn't a healthy fat, a storybook fat. And his eyes are clouded, and his teeth are rotten. Mickey is short and has a shriveled arm. And I—well, I am reasonably normal, which means reasonably scrawny, reasonably scarred by life. I don't think I look like a private eye.

"Please sit," the man said.

We sat.

"I trust your drive was uneventful."

"Wasn't bad, Mr. Fitch," Bobby said. "But the snow didn't help matters much."

"Ah, yes, the snow." Mr. Fitch paused. "'When blood is nipp'd and ways be foul.'" He fell silent then, as if he had exhausted his supply of sociability, or forgotten the next line. He looked as if he didn't have much need for sociability. He sat straight and stiff as a pine tree, his hands folded on the table in front of him. His skin was leathery, his mouth hard. He scared me.

"We brought some very good merchandise," Bobby said. "You'd be surprised at how much is still out there, if you know the right people."

Mr. Fitch nodded, unsurprised. "I'll take a look."

"Want us to bring it right in here?"

Mr. Fitch unfolded a hand and gestured at the empty table.

Bobby stood up. "Great. Come on, boys."

Mickey and I followed him back out to the van. Lavinia kept a careful watch on us from the front porch. "What'd I tell you about that guy, huh?" Bobby asked as Mickey opened the doors and jumped inside. "He's got maybe thirty kids and half a dozen wives and he goes around lookin' like the goddamn Lord of the Universe. Watch that stuff, Mickey, okay? It's fucking fragile."

I did most of the lugging. Mickey couldn't help much because of his arm, and Bobby preferred talking to lifting. After a few trips back and forth we had covered the table with our stuff, and Bobby started his sales pitch. "Look at this china, Mr. Fitch. Rose Medallion. Service for six, plus assorted other pieces—almost perfect condition. See this portrait? Look at the signature: John Singer Sargent. He was famous. Ever see his murals in the Boston Public Library? That tea set is sterling silver. And you said you liked books, right? A complete set of Dickens—leather bindings, acid-free paper. I don't think anyone ever opened them. Isn't that something?"

Mr. Fitch examined everything while Bobby rattled on. He unwrapped every piece of china and stared at it. He took the painting out into the hall to study it in better light. I noticed he was wearing hiking boots under his biblical robe. Bobby was sweating. Mickey and I stood by the fire and waited.

"All right," Mr. Fitch said eventually. "Come with me." He strode outside and signaled to Lavinia, who fell in step behind us. We crossed to a long, narrow structure off to one side of the main house. He took out a key and opened the padlocked door, then went inside and flipped on an electric light. We followed him in.

It was a storage building—shelf after shelf of cartons jammed against the walls, a narrow aisle down the middle. Amazingly, the place was heated. We stood awkwardly in the aisle while Lavinia waited outside, her shotgun cradled in her arms.

"PC?" Mr. Fitch asked.

"Right," Bobby said.

Mr. Fitch reached up and took down a small box. He opened it. The object inside was covered with bubbly plastic stuff. He unwrapped it.

It was not as beautiful as the china, but Bobby was not interested in beauty. He took it from Mr. Fitch and hefted it approvingly. It was a hard drive, I knew. Not that I cared. "How many?" he asked.

"I'll give you twenty-five."

"Are you crazy? I need fifty, or no deal."

Mr. Fitch shrugged. "I haven't got fifty."

"Well, what else do you have? Got any ammo?"

Mr. Fitch stiffened. "I don't deal in weaponry."

"Okay, okay. How 'bout software? And printers. How about them?"

Mr. Fitch and Bobby started dickering. I was impressed by how forceful Bobby was, considering that his entire future was on the line, and a girl stood ten feet away holding a shotgun she was clearly prepared to use. He knew what he was doing, at any rate, because after a few tough minutes they had struck a deal, and I found myself lugging the precious equipment out to the van.

"Nice work," I said to Bobby when he came to inspect.

"Thanks. He's weird, but he's a Yankee, and that means you can do business with him. Jesus, I could use a drink. Let's go inside."

I followed him back into the house, carefully wiping my feet before I entered.

Our merchandise had been cleared from the table. One of the Rose Medallion plates was piled high with pieces of cake. A solidly built woman with gray hair was pouring cups of tea, using the sterling silver tea set. I sat down next to Mickey, who was eyeing the cake with considerable interest.

"Can I get you anything else?" the woman asked when the tea had been poured.

Bobby cleared his throat. "I was wondering if there might be anything stronger than tea in the house. To celebrate our new business relationship, you understand."

The woman looked at Mr. Fitch. He paused a moment, then banged his fist on the table. "'What?'" he thundered. "'Dost thou think because thou art virtuous there shall be no more cakes and ale?'"

She smiled and left the room. In a moment she returned with a green bottle, which Bobby gazed at with something approaching religious ecstasy. She poured an inch of the amber liquid into a glass and gave it to Bobby, then did the same for Mr. Fitch. She offered the bottle to Mickey and me next, but we refused. We were tea people.

Bobby toasted Mr. Fitch. "Here's to many more nights like this," he said.

Mr. Fitch nodded his agreement.

The cake was delicious. Bobby drank half his whiskey. "You must come to Boston and let me return your hospitality," he said.

Mr. Fitch's face darkened. He set his glass down. "I will not go to Boston, Mr. Gallagher. I lost a child there once. Killed by the brigands who inhabit that place."

"Well, it's really a lot better than it used to be," Bobby said, a little uneasily.

"'Dost thou not perceive that it is a wilderness of tigers?'" Mr. Fitch roared. "Tigers must prey, and Boston offers no prey but me and mine."

Tigers? Bobby scratched his head, for once at a loss for words. I reached for another piece of cake. "'How happy are thou, then,'" I remarked, "'from these devourers to be banished.'"

Mr. Fitch stared at me. "You know *Titus Andronicus?*"

I raised an eyebrow. "Doesn't everyone?"

He smiled and drank his whiskey. "Maybe this world has a future after all," he murmured.

Bobby looked at me as if I had just caused the blind to see and the dumb to speak.

Mickey poured himself another cup of tea.

"Boy, was that something. Boy, was that ever something. That guy is so *weird*. But we showed him, huh, Wally? Hey, when did you learn that—whatever it was?"

I shrugged. "You know me. I just sort of pick things up."

"Sure impressed the hell out of Fitch, anyway. Boy, was that something. He liked the set of Dickens too. I wasn't gonna take it from the lady, you know, but then I remembered how he likes books."

"What does he do with all that stuff?"

"He keeps what he wants and trades the rest. Drives up to Maine and dickers with the border guards. They're corrupt as hell, thank God. Imagine, all the problems we've got, and the government bans the sale of computer equipment. What a world."

"Why don't you go up to Maine yourself—eliminate the middleman?"

"Because Fitch'd kill me. Also, I'm nervous enough just going to New Hampshire. What was it he called Boston?"

"A wilderness of tigers."

"Yeah. That goes double for fucking Maine."

I smiled, suppressing a memory or two. The snow had tapered off, but progress was still slow along what was left of the highway. We had it all to ourselves.

"God, 93 used to be such a good road," Bobby murmured. "I remember leaving MIT early on Fridays and whipping up north to go skiing. Imagine *wanting* to be out in the snow."

"You used to work at MIT, Bobby?"

"Yeah, in the business office. Why?"

"Did you happen to know a professor named Robert Cornwall?"

Bobby looked at me as if I were crazy. "Why do you wanna know something like that?"

"I got a case today. Somebody's looking for Robert Cornwall."

"Who's looking for him?"

"His, uh, son. Did you know Cornwall?"

Bobby slowly shook his head. "I didn't really pal around with the professors, Wally. I was just a local kid tryin' to make a few bucks. Jesus, what makes the guy's kid think he can find him after all these years?"

"He's been down South. It's the first chance he's had to look."

"Sounds like a waste of time to me."

I didn't reply. I'd heard that before.

"I'd lay any odds he's dead," Bobby went on. "Hundred things could've killed him, from typhoid to starvation— well, to the goddamn Brits. People are starting to forget about the Brits, you know, now that we're supposed to be such good friends. But Jesus, did they ever fuck us over. We were just starting to get back on our feet around here, and they come in and screw everything up. Said they were doing us a favor. They did the Irish a favor too, I suppose. Fuck their favors. They should've left us alone."

"Okay, Bobby," I said softly. The Brits were his favorite subject, and he could veer into it from the strangest angles. We both fell silent. We weren't far from the city now. I started thinking about home. I started thinking about my case.

"Trouble," Mickey said. He pointed back over his shoulder. A police car was behind us, flashing its red and blue beacon.

"What the hell do they want?" Bobby muttered. "I pay off enough people around here."

"Should I stop?" Mickey asked. "Probably can't outrun em."

"Yeah, I guess so. Dammit."

Mickey stopped the van. The police car pulled up behind us.

"Let me do the talking," Bobby said. "Maybe they're just killing time."

I got out and let Bobby clamber down into the slush. I stayed next to the van and looked back at the police car. A cop was walking toward Bobby. Another cop sat on the passenger's side and watched. I turned back to Mickey. "One cop usually in a cop car, right?" I asked.

"Right," he said. "Maybe it's a special patrol. Looking for smugglers."

"Sure."

The cop came up to Bobby and glanced at me and Mickey. He was tall and skinny. His cap perched precariously on top of his head; a well-aimed rock would've knocked it off. "You got a permit to be driving this thing outside the city limits?" he asked Bobby.

"Officer, I think we should have a little talk," Bobby said.

"No permit? What's in the back?"

"Now, Officer, I'm sure that we can come to a meeting of the minds about—"

"Open it up, asshole." The cop reached out and pushed Bobby toward the back of the van. I saw a lot of wrist and forearm.

"The goddamn uniform doesn't fit," I said to Mickey. The cop still sitting in the car made a movement. I saw a glint of metal. I reached back into the van, picked up the shotgun, and blasted out the windshield.

The tall cop and Bobby fell to the ground. The other cop made a move as if to slide across the front seat to the driver's side. I aimed a little above him and shot again. He lay still.

The tall cop had grabbed Bobby and was struggling to get the gun out of his holster. I got down from the van, ran through the slush, and clubbed him with the butt of the shotgun. He fell back with a howl of pain and let Bobby go. I reached down and took his gun.

"The other one's getting away," Mickey called out.

I looked up. The other cop had gotten out of the car and was running with difficulty, bobbing and weaving close to the ground. "Let him go," I said.

Bobby staggered to his feet and looked at me with a mixture of fear and astonishment. "What the fuck are you doin', Wally?"

"They're not cops," I said. "They must've stolen the car. Or maybe it's a fake." I poked the tall guy lying at my feet. "Who sent you? O'Malley?"

He rubbed his jaw where I had clubbed him, and he didn't reply. I undid the safety of his revolver and fired a bullet into the ground three inches to the left of his jaw. He looked up at me, shotgun in one hand, his revolver in the other, Smith and Wesson bulging in my pocket. He was a little afraid. "Yeah," he gasped. "O'Malley. He just wanted to hassle you, that's all. We weren't gonna do nothin'."

I looked at Bobby. He was shaking. "Kill him," he said. "He was gonna kill *us*, right?"

I shrugged and kicked the guy. "Tell your boss not to mess with Bobby Gallagher," I said. "Now get lost."

The guy studied me for an instant to see if it was a trick; then he scrambled to his feet and raced off after his buddy.

"I told you to kill him," Bobby screamed at me.

"Oh, give it a rest, Bobby," I said. "You wouldn't have killed him either." I walked back to the van. Bobby followed. Mickey went over to the police car and silently started draining the oil and gas from it and removing the more useful parts.

"Sometimes we gotta do things we don't want to do," Bobby said to me. "We can't let O'Malley think we're soft."

"I don't kill people," I said. "Too many people have died."

"Ah, shit," he replied. But he couldn't seem to think of anything else to add, and he was silent for a while. When he finally spoke, it was on an entirely different topic. "How long you been back from the army, Wally?"

"A couple of months, I guess."

"And you finally got your first case today?"

"Well, I've only been running the ad for a week or two."

"I've been thinking maybe you should give up on this private-eye business and come to work for me full-time. I mean, being a private eye's a cute idea and all, but you know and I know it's not going anywhere. You've just been reading too many books. You're too smart to waste your time dreaming. I could use some more help, especially if I'm gonna be dealing with Fitch. Toughen you up a little bit and you'll be great at it."

"Thanks, Bobby, but I don't think so."

"Oh, come on, you really think you can be a private eye like those guys in the books? Maybe you're not as smart as you look."

"Maybe. But anyway, I've got a case now, and I figure I should see it through."

Bobby shook his head. "Waste of time," he said softly.

Mickey got into the van. "Ready," he said.

Bobby looked at him. "What do you think of this private-eye shit?"

Mickey grinned. "Wally'd get my business." He tossed me something. "Besides, now he's official."

I looked at Mickey's gift. It was a badge.

Bobby shook his head some more. "Too many books," he muttered. "Let's go."

I put the badge in my pocket. Mickey started up the van, and we were silent as we made our way back to the sleeping city.

CHAPTER 4

Gwen was waiting for me in the front parlor when I arrived. She was wearing her patched blue robe and a couple pairs of woolen socks. "How did it go?" she asked.

"Oh, fine."

"No problems?"

I shook my head. "I think I'll have a glass of cider." We went out to the kitchen. With Gwen, I was never sure if my lies were successful. I always had the feeling that she understood everything, and that sometimes she just decided to let me get away with one.

She poured us each some cider, and we sat at the table. I told her all about the farm and Lavinia and Mr. Fitch and the electric lights and the tapestries on the wall. And then I remembered something. "I brought you a present." I reached into my pocket and took out a piece of cake I had grabbed from the Rose Medallion plate.

"Oh, Walter. Thank you."

"It was either this or a hard disk, and I figured you had more use for cake."

She smiled and ate the cake.

"Bobby wants me to go to work for him full-time," I said.

I waited for a response, but none came. She looked at me and sipped her cider.

"I told him to forget it. I'm a private eye now. No time for stuff like that."

She nodded, "You must feel good about getting that case."

"Yeah. Well." No sense going into it. She knew how good I felt. I finished my cider and stood up. "You should get some sleep," I said.

Gwen stood up too. She took the lamp in one hand, and my hand in the other, and we went upstairs. We paused as we passed Linc's bedroom. He was breathing heavily; he muttered something unintelligible in his sleep. Gwen's hand squeezed mine. We went into our bedroom.

She set the lamp on the night table and pulled the bedcovers down. I took off my shoes. We got into bed, and she put out the lamp.

The darkness was total. We pulled up the covers. I put my arm around Gwen, and she snuggled into the crook of my shoulder. "Do you feel like it?" I asked.

"I guess not," she said.

"Okay."

We were silent for a while. The darkness became less total. I could make out the looming bulk of the dresser, the elegant curves of the escritoire, the useless outline of the useless radiator.

"I'm glad you're safe," Gwen said.

"So am I," I said. Glad to see the dresser and the escritoire for another day. Glad to see her. Across the hall, Linc snorted and groaned.

"Someday," I murmured, "sleep will come easy."

"And dreams will come true," Gwen replied.

"Someday."

We didn't say anything then. I stroked her hair, and we breathed together, and eventually her breathing became deep and regular. I listened to it for a long while, and then carefully pulled my arm from beneath her head. She settled herself onto the pillow, still asleep. I got out of bed, groped for the lamp, found it, and made my way out into the hall. I was an old hand at this. I lit the lamp in the darkness and walked slowly up the creaking stairs to the third floor. The lamp threw spooky shadows against the walls. I wasn't afraid of spooks, though; there was too much else to be afraid of in this world. At the top of the stairs, I turned right. More shadows, more spooks, beckoning to me in the dim light, writhing in their lust for life, for freedom. The room reeked of the past, overpowered me with the musty odor of lives lived, of genius spent. It was an odor as exciting as any perfume. I entered the room.

Too many books, Bobby had said. An accusation.

Guilty. I stared at them:

Confess, Fletch
The Dreadful Lemon Sky
The Good-bye Look
Ten Little Indians
The Case of the Amorous Aunt

Green with mildew, brown and brittle with age, dying but not dead yet. Not dead yet.

It occurred to me that I needed a title. What good was a case without a title? *Confess, Clone. The Case of the Confused Clone.* I was new at this.

The Godwulf Manuscript
God Save the Child
Early Autumn

In those books Spenser was still alive. Still working out at the health club, drinking beer, listening to the Red Sox. Ah, would that it were not fiction. *That way madness lies,* as Mr. Fitch would say. But maybe you had to be mad to stay alive nowadays. *God Save the Clone. Early Winter.* No, try again.

Farewell, My Lovely
The Maltese Falcon
Penance for Jerry Kennedy
The Big Sleep
Trent's Last Case

Trent's Last Case. An old, old British mystery with a couple of twists at the end. I took it off the shelf and glanced through it. Private eyes were nowhere to be found, although I liked the first sentence.

Sands's First Case. The possessive sounded ugly. Sandman. That was Linc's nickname for me. I didn't like it. The Sandman went around putting people to sleep, and I— I only did that for Gwen.

I smiled.

The Sandman's First Case.

It would have to do, until I came up with something better.

I rummaged through a rotting carton of textbooks until I found one on cellular biology. I took it out, sat in my old, overstuffed armchair, and read by lamplight until dawn. Then I tiptoed back downstairs and got back into the warm bed beside Gwen.

I shut my eyes and snuggled up to Gwen, and after a while sleep came for the Sandman—short and troubled as always, but enough to let him make it through another day.

CHAPTER 5

Stretch and Gwen left for work early. Linc stayed home. He had a job at the Salvage Market downtown, but he had been showing up less and less lately. He sat at the kitchen table and watched with amusement as I prepared to go out into the cold cruel world.

"So the Sandman starts his case," he said. "Is he nervous?"

"A private eye is never nervous," I replied.

"Should I wish him luck?" he asked. "Or do private eyes not need luck?"

"A little luck never hurt anyone."

"Good luck, then."

"Thanks, Linc."

He came and stood at the door as I carried my bicycle down the front steps and wobbled off.

The day was crisp and clear for a change, and Louisburg Square glistened in the sunlight. As was my custom, I stopped off at the north side of the square and said hello to the statue of Christopher Columbus, which by some absurd historical irony had managed to survive everything unscathed.

"Discovered any new worlds recently?" I asked it.

As usual, it didn't deign to reply.

"Well, if you do, let me know. I'm always interested in hearing about new worlds."

The statue had nothing to tell me, so I continued my journey.

It wasn't a very good day for bicycling, but I had a feeling I might be covering a lot of ground, so I decided to risk a fall or two onto the ice. I took a right on Mount Vernon Street and coasted down to Charles; then left on Charles, past the Garden and the Common, and right on Boylston. There were no cars, and only a couple of other brave souls on bicycles. Everyone else was on foot, hurrying to jobs in buildings that were scarcely warmer than the outside air. Another day, another new dollar.

I turned left by the empty shell of the Public Library, then right onto Huntington. A mile or so south on Huntington was Northeastern University.

Odd what the Frenzy got and what it missed. The library, of course, but why Symphony Hall? MIT, certainly, but why not Northeastern? People said the Frenzy was antilearning, antiscience. But maybe, I thought, it had more to do with power. When the people went crazy on those awful nights, maybe they just ransacked the places that somehow symbolized to them the power of the old world. The forces that ran the old world also ran MIT, ran the Symphony, ran Harvard. They were the forces that had to be destroyed.

Northeastern? Well, Northeastern was different. Northeastern produced engineers, but they were working-class engineers, struggling to make tuition payments and pass calculus. They were victims as much as anyone else. So Northeastern survived to become a power in the new world that had been created.

Just a theory, of course. Probably ascribed too much rationality to what was the ultimate irrational act. I thought of all the books in the Public Library that were now ashes. The new world could have used those books.

An ancient man was guarding the bicycles in the quadrangle outside the main building. I parked my bike at the end of the row and tossed him a penny. He tipped his cap.

I went into the main building. It wasn't warm, but there was heat coming from somewhere. I took off my cap. After a little searching I found the cafeteria. Students were moving in and out, lounging at tables, reading bulletin boards. I looked at them, searching for a familiar face.

None at the moment. I wouldn't have to wait long, I was sure.

The faces I saw seemed happy and full of adolescent high spirits. Strange. Perhaps they knew something I didn't. I bought a *Globe* from a blind guy huddled in a corner and sat at an empty table near the door. I read "Garrick Petitions South for Winter Fuel Aid" by Gwendolyn Phillips very carefully, and I skimmed the rest. After a while I heard someone call my name.

"Walter Sands! What are you doing here?"

I looked up. It was Cindy Tappen. She seemed a lot more, well, *mature* than I remembered—her body had filled out nicely, and the once scruffy hair was now short and curled. She had on tight, faded jeans, leg warmers, and an ancient leather jacket. She was even wearing lipstick. What was this younger generation coming to? "Hi, Cindy. Can I buy you some cider?"

"No, that's okay." She sat next to me and gave my arm a squeeze. "So how're you doing, Walter? When did you get back into town?"

"A couple of months ago."

"In the army, right? What were you up to?"

"Guarding the salvagers down in Washington."

"Oh, wow. I bet that was exciting."

"Pretty boring, actually. And depressing."

"Oh, well, sorry to hear it. Back with Gwen and those folks?"

I nodded. "I've been meaning to look you up, but—"

Cindy smiled. "Yeah, yeah. So now what? Thinking of school?"

"Not really. I've got some other, um, angles I'm working on."

She reached out and covered my hand with hers. "You should come to school, Walter. Honestly. A person with your brains—do it for your country."

I shrugged. "That's what Stretch keeps saying. Tell you what I'll do for my country, Cindy—I'll help you make strong, smart babies. The country needs your babies more than it needs my brains."

Cindy grinned. "Tell you what. You come to school, and I'll let you help me make babies."

"This is blackmail. I won't hear of it."

"Suit yourself. So what brings you to Northeastern, if you don't want an education?"

"I'd like to ask a favor."

"Okay. Watcha want?"

I didn't particularly care to hear any more comments about my new profession, so I prevaricated. "I met this guy from down South in the army. His folks were separated, back in the old days. His father was a biology professor at MIT, and my friend never learned for sure what happened to him. So I promised to find out what I could."

Cindy made a face. "Sounds like a waste of time, Walter. How can I help?"

"Well, I was wondering if you knew of any professors from MIT that are still teaching here—someone who might have known this guy's father."

Cindy removed her hand from mine and considered. "I don't know who taught where in the old days, Walter. But I could introduce you to the chairman of the bio department. I took a course from him last semester. He's sort of yucky, but he's old, so maybe he'd know something."

"That sounds great, Cindy. I'd appreciate it."

She stood up and held out her hand. "No time like the present. Let's go. Maybe *he* can talk you into coming to school."

* * *

Cindy led me through a maze of cinder-block corridors to a frosted-glass door. A hand-lettered sign had been taped to it:

R. Costigan
Chman. Bio. Dept.

She opened the door and we walked inside.

We were in a small reception area filled with cartons and broken-looking equipment. From the office to our right a man's voice was speaking, loudly: "Yes? Yes? I'm sorry, I can't—What?" We moved into the man's line of sight. He gestured for us to wait while he continued to talk into the phone. "I'm having difficulty…. Could you speak a little…What?" Finally he shook his head and replaced the receiver. "Not worth the effort," he muttered. He looked at Cindy. "Um, Sally, is it?"

We moved into his office. It was as messy as the reception area. "Cindy. Cindy Tappen, Professor. I had you last semester."

"Ah, yes. Cindy." He looked at me.

"And this is my friend Walter Sands," she said.

"Ah. How do you do." He stood up, and we shook hands. He was a tall man, with a shock of sandy hair and jug ears. He was wearing a tweed jacket, tattersall vest, dingy white shirt, and a stained woolen tie. The clothes hung limply on him. They were his own, I figured. He had held on to them a long time. He sat back down and folded his hands. "What can I, ah, do for you, then?"

"Walter's looking for information about someone who used to teach at MIT," Cindy explained. "I thought maybe he could ask you. Is that okay?"

"Certainly, certainly. Glad to help." He paused, and then smiled, as if he suddenly remembered that it was expected of him. There was a certain vagueness about the man that I found a little irritating; maybe I hadn't hung around professors enough.

"Thanks, Professor," Cindy said. "Well, I've got a class, so I'll leave you two alone. Tell Walter how great Northeastern is, Professor. He needs an education."

"I'll be happy to, Sal—uh, Cindy."

Cindy squeezed my arm and left me alone with Professor Costigan.

I smiled at him. He smiled back. I took a breath and launched into the story I had told Cindy. He nodded vaguely as I told it, as if he had heard it all before, or perhaps didn't understand a word of it. "…So you see, Professor, any information you could give me would be greatly appreciated."

He nodded some more. "Indeed," he said. "Professor Cornwall is certainly not with us now, of course."

"Have you ever heard of him?"

"Well, no, not precisely."

What did that mean? "Perhaps there are records around somewhere that might mention him."

"Records? Oh, yes, there might be records." He paused, and then realized he was expected to look for said records, or at least give me more information about them. He stood up. "I have some documents from the early days in one of these cartons here. I think perhaps MIT is…" His voice trailed off as he wandered over to a carton and started poking around in it. After a while he gave that up and went to a battered green filing cabinet. "Cornwall…The name seems vaguely…"

He tried another cabinet, a desk drawer, a mound of computer printouts in a bookcase. It became clear soon enough that he had no idea where to find the records he was muttering about, and that he was going to keep searching until I told him to stop. "That's okay, sir. Really."

"What? Oh, well, I can't seem to…" He sat back down and smiled uncertainly.

How have you survived? I wanted to ask him next. But I forced myself to stick to the issue. "Perhaps you might know of someone else who might remember him— someone who taught at MIT, for example."

"Ah." He brightened. "George Hemphill, of course." He extracted a slim notebook from the inner pocket of his tweed jacket and began perusing it.

"Who is George Hemphill, sir?"

Costigan looked up. "Oh. He's in my department. Used to be at MIT in the old days. Quite good, but a bit, um, you know." He made an indecipherable gesture. "He teaches a seminar for our advanced students, but we can't seem to persuade him to..." His gaze returned to the notebook. "Ah. Here he is. I remember now, he lives out in Cambridge for some reason. Three-sixty Fenton Avenue. Perhaps you'd want to wait until he comes back here. He only comes in on Tuesdays, I think, and today is—what? Thursday? Friday?"

"I don't mind going to Cambridge," I said. There. That hadn't been hard. Was it worth trying for anything more? Nothing to lose. "My friend told me his father was a specialist in cloning. Would you know anything about that?"

"Cloning? Oh, of course." He smiled.

"Well, perhaps you could tell me something about it. For example, could they clone human beings, back in the old days?"

"Ah. Interesting question." He crossed his legs and leaned back in his chair. "It was not my particular area of expertise—Hemphill might know more—but I was fairly *au courant.* Cloning a human being was—is—certainly possible theoretically. However, I doubt that it actually took place. Mammalian cloning took place, but the techniques..."

He picked up a pencil and tapped it on the desk. His eyes took on a faraway look. He was happy. "You would have to get the eggs—a laparoscopy, of course, would do the trick. And Pergonal would help increase egg production. You could use a laser to enucleate the egg. Then, of course, you'd have to get the donor nucleus. *In vitro* fertilization, I suppose. Then use the Sendai virus for cell fusion, perhaps, or do it manually with micropipettes, if you're skillful enough. Of course, you'd have to synchronize the cell division—"

"Well, you certainly sound like an expert to me, sir," I said, having heard enough.

He smiled condescendingly. "Just general knowledge. But you see my point. If human cloning wasn't done, it was because there was little scientific benefit from doing it, or no funding for it, or because someone thought it was immoral. Not because it couldn't be done."

"Yes, I see. Fascinating."

"Nowadays, of course—" He gestured vaguely—toward the broken equipment in the reception area, I imagined—and his expression became glum. "Perhaps Professor Cornwall is better off if—oh, well."

He fell silent. How had he survived? By luck, probably, if you wanted to call it luck. In the old days, he undoubtedly had a nice little academic life somewhere, with his frogs and his viruses. And then: *Welcome to the new world, Professor Costigan.* No more lasers, no more micropipettes, no more white shirts.

I stood up. "I want to thank you for your time, Professor Costigan. You've been a great help."

"Not at all, not at all. Happy to be of service."

We shook hands, and I headed for the door.

"Of course," Professor Costigan said, "Cornwall could be in England."

I turned around. "England?" I inquired.

"Well, yes."

I came back. "What makes you say that?"

"Well, you know, the British might have taken him, back when they were, uh, in charge, as it were."

"They took American scientists?"

"I believe so. I don't know how many, or what happened to them all. Things were very confused back then, of course."

"Why did they take them?"

"I suppose it was an opportunity on both sides," Costigan said. "It also happened with the Germans after World War Two, I believe. The British get the scientists, and the scientists get a place to carry on their work."

"Did the British ask you to go?"

He looked uncomfortable. Not the most tactful question I could have asked. "I was not in the immediate area at the time so, no, I wasn't asked. As I say, things were confused, and no one seems to know how many they took. Perhaps none of it is true. There are all sorts of rumors about what happened back then."

"Would Hemphill know?"

He grimaced. "Yes, I imagine Hemphill would know. Perhaps you should ask him."

Costigan stared at me a little belligerently. In England they had micropipettes. And he hadn't been asked. I wanted to apologize, but it wouldn't have done any good. Besides, I was too eager to go visit George Hemphill. "Thanks again, Professor. I've learned a lot."

This time he said nothing in return; he simply stared down at the frayed cuffs of his shirt as I left his office.

I raced through the corridors and out to my bicycle. No time to think about Costigan's problems; we all have problems. I flipped the old guard another penny, and I pedaled off to Cambridge.

CHAPTER 6

I picked up Mass. Ave. off Huntington and took it straight across the Charles into Cambridge. The bridge wasn't safe, but it was no more dangerous than any of the others, and I had to get across the river somehow. You take your chances. The only traffic I encountered was a guy in a horse-drawn wagon—probably from the communal farm over on the old Harvard athletic fields. He tipped his hat to me, but made sure I saw his shotgun.

I slowed down as I passed MIT. A couple of mangy dogs barked at me from the steps of a gutted building. I fingered my Smith and Wesson, but they were evidently too sick to give chase. Cornwall had probably climbed those steps. Maybe he was better off dead, as Professor Costigan had implied—bulldozed into some pit with all the other nameless corpses. That was the only way he could escape the pain of looking at those steps, and remembering.

On the other hand, Professor Hemphill probably passed those steps every time he came into Boston. And Bobby Gallagher had his memories of MIT too, evidently. The two of them managed to keep on living; why not Cornwall? Everyone said it was easier to have been born afterward, to have been spared all the memories—that was why the kids at Northeastern looked so happy, I suppose. But people carried on in any case. It must be in the genes or something.

I pedaled through Cambridge.

Once upon a time the suburbs were the safe place to live, I am told—insulated from the dangers of city life and the rigors of country life. Times have changed. If you live in the country, you live behind barbed wire, like Mr. Fitch; or, at least, you can see strangers coming and prepare your defenses, if you think you need them. In the city, you have the rudiments of civilization once more—police and fire departments, neighbors who will look out for your property, businesses with security guards to protect themselves and you. But the suburbs are too built up to allow you the kind of protection Mr. Fitch has, and too spread out to allow you the kind of protection the folks in Louisburg Square have. They are a no-man's-land, inhabited only by the brave and the stupid.

And, of course, the sentimental, who are a little of both. It was hardly surprising that someone like Professor Hemphill would live in suburban Cambridge—he probably lived in the same house he had always lived in, and couldn't bear the thought of moving. The only surprise was that he was still alive. Of course, it was surprising that any of us were still alive.

I kept my hand on my gun as I looked for his house. His street had once been beautiful, I am sure. Now a couple of the houses were rubble. One had a side caved in; it looked as if it had been kicked by some enormous foot. Number 360 was a brick Colonial with shutters that had long ago lost their paint. It was surrounded, of course, by barbed wire.

I got off my bicycle and went up to the front gate, which was, of course, locked. I gave a shout. "Hullo! Professor Hemphill!"

A dog started barking. After a few moments a gun came poking out through a crack in the front door. All very straightforward and predictable, like a conversation about the weather. I raised my hands. "Hi, there," I called out. "Nice to see you. My name is Walter Sands. Professor Costigan at Northeastern gave me your name and address. He said you might be able to tell me something about a man named Robert Cornwall."

The door opened wide. A bald-headed man in a blue turtleneck sweater came out, leading the obligatory Doberman on a leash. Neither looked pleased to see me. I smiled my most endearing smile. Eventually the man came to the gate and unlocked it. I waited for him to jerk the dog to a sitting position, and then I entered. "You can't be too careful nowadays," I said.

"Come inside," Professor Hemphill replied.

I followed him and the dog inside. Hemphill was short, and looked shorter because he slouched as he walked, as if he had a bad back, or maybe felt the weight of the world. His skin was the translucent kind that always seems ready to blush, and his features were the thin, nervous kind that always seems ready to twitch. He looked as if he hadn't shaved in a couple of days, and hadn't smiled in several years.

His house was lovely; he had guarded it well. The hall was dominated by a large grandfather clock, ticking away as solemnly as it must have thirty years ago. The stairway's oak banister and newel post looked freshly polished. The gilt on the mirror sparkled; the parquet floor gleamed.

Hemphill led me into a sitting room; more parquet, a Queen Anne sofa, somewhat faded, and a small marble fireplace from the days when they hadn't really needed fires. I stopped in front of the painting hung above the mantel. "Sargent," I said.

"Very good," Hemphill replied. "It's my wife's grandmother. How in the world do you know about Sargent?"

"A friend of mine named Bobby Gallagher deals in stuff like this. He'd pay you a lot for it."

"Not for sale," Hemphill said curtly. "Now please hand me your gun."

I did as I was told, and I sat down on the sofa when Hemphill gestured to it. He sat in an armchair by the fireplace, leaving both our weapons on a sidetable next to the chair. His hands were trembling a little. He didn't seem to be the type to thrive in this kind of world; but here he was, and I was sure if I tried to get my gun back, either he or his dog would manage to kill me.

"Robert Cornwall, Mr. Sands. Why do you want to know about him?"

"I met his son in the service," I said, repeating my lie. "He never knew his father, and he asked me to find out what happened to him."

Hemphill stared at me then, until I began to think his social skills had gone to hell out here in the suburbs. "I knew Robert Cornwall," he said. "I believe he's dead."

His tone was quiet and final, and my heart sank. This was not what Dr. Winfield wanted to hear. I felt obliged to press on with the interview, however. "You say you believe he's dead. Do you know for sure?"

Hemphill blushed. "Why do you ask that? Do you think I'd lie to you?"

"Not at all. Maybe you just assume he's dead, which I suppose is a good assumption. But did you see him die? Can you tell me anything about the circumstances of his death?"

"Well, I mean, he's not around here. What else could have happened to him?"

"He could have gone to England," I suggested.

Hemphill stared at me some more. "No, that's not possible," he said finally.

"Why? I was told the British took scientists back with them. Didn't that happen?"

"Yes. Certainly. In fact, they asked me to go."

"And you turned them down? Why?"

Hemphill shrugged. "I wanted to stay here. My—my wife was missing, and I had some hopes of finding her."

"But Cornwall could've gone, right? Do you know for sure that he didn't?"

"We don't live in total scientific isolation here, Mr. Sands," he pointed out. "We still receive the journals that are put out in England and other places that have more resources than we do. If the British took Cornwall, he would be doing science over there, and we would know about it. We certainly know about a lot of other American scientists in Britain. I haven't seen anything by him, so I assume he wasn't taken. You can have Costigan show you the back issues of *Nature* and the like at Northeastern, if you don't believe me."

"I believe you," I said. But something was out of focus; somehow I wasn't getting the picture I had hoped this man could provide me. "Tell me about Cornwall," I said. "How well did you know him?"

Hemphill's stare slowly turned into the misty far-off look of someone remembering the old days. I had seen that look often enough in my life: on Bobby Gallagher's face, on the faces of toothless old women dying in alleyways, on the faces of hard-boiled army officers. On my father's face. Hemphill's hands were still shaking.

The look disappeared finally, to be replaced by the mask of civilization. What Hemphill gave me when he spoke was an edited, emotionless summary. He could have been lecturing on invertebrate anatomy, or reciting an obituary.

"Cornwall and I were both assistant professors in the biology department at MIT," he said. "We collaborated on a couple of projects, and we saw each other socially as well. He was a superb scientist, I believe, and he was certainly aware of his talent. He received his Ph.D. from the University of Chicago. And, Mr. Sands, he was not married. He had no children."

"Ah." The Sandman's first mistake. I couldn't believe my stupidity. There was nothing to do but plunge ahead, however. "Did Cornwall work on cloning?"

Hemphill nodded.

"Cloning of mammals?"

"Yes."

"Cloning of human beings?"

Hemphill shrugged. "Clone one mammal, you can clone them all."

I couldn't think of a reason not to tell him the truth.

"Professor, my friend doesn't really think he's Cornwall's son—he thinks he's Cornwall's clone."

Hemphill shook his head. "No, that's not possible."

"Why? Why couldn't Cornwall have made a clone of himself and impregnated a woman with it?"

"It's not that easy." Hemphill shifted in his chair. Like Costigan, he was preparing to lecture. "Cloning a mammal is one thing; cloning an *adult* mammal is something else altogether. The success of the procedure declines precipitously with the age of the donor nucleus—and I'm talking days from the moment of fertilization, not years. We studied this at MIT. It probably has something to do with changes in the DNA due to cell differentiation. Cornwall couldn't have cloned himself, even if he knew how to clone a human being. He was too old, Mr. Sands."

"My friend is a dead ringer for Cornwall," I said. "Maybe Cornwall solved this problem with cloning adults and didn't tell you."

Hemphill shook his head. "Cornwall was not the kind to hide his scientific achievements. And that would've been a considerable achievement."

"So then, what is my friend?"

"I don't know, Mr. Sands. A human being, like all the rest of us. Perhaps Cornwall had an affair with a grad student and she became pregnant. I wouldn't put it past him."

I wasn't getting very far with cloning. I decided to change the subject. "Can you think of a reason why someone would want to murder my friend?"

Hemphill stared at me. "Murder?" he repeated.

"Two days ago, near Northeastern, after he tried to find out something about Cornwall."

Hemphill blushed. "What are you suggesting—that there's some deep dark secret about all of this?"

"I'm really not suggesting anything, Professor Hemphill. I'm just trying to learn what there is to be learned."

"I can't think that there's anything at all to be learned, Mr. Sands. It was a long time ago, and anything that happened back then is as irrelevant as the stock certificates I probably still have waiting for me in some safe-deposit box downtown. Why doesn't your friend just go on with his life?"

"I don't know," I said honestly. "It seems to matter to him."

Hemphill was silent for a moment; then he arose and walked over to the barred window. The dog stirred himself and growled, just to make sure I didn't get any ideas about going for my gun. Hemphill stared out at the barbed wire surrounding his home. "Cornwall couldn't have cared less about politics. He thought that this war wouldn't affect him—that he would go on with his work, somehow, because his work was important, and the world would have to realize that. I remember the last time I saw him—after the war, when everyone was beginning to realize that it may have been a tiny war, but things would never be the same again, things were going to be unimaginably worse for an unimaginably long time. And—and he found out I wasn't going to go to England, I was going to stay here and wait. And he laughed at me. 'George,' he said. 'You only have the one life. Don't waste it.'"

"It sounds as though he would've gone to England, then, if he'd had half a chance. Are you sure he's dead, Professor?"

Hemphill stared out the window, his gaze misty. "Yes, he's dead, Mr. Sands. And all that was a long time ago. Now I think you'd better leave."

"But I'd really like to—"

He turned abruptly to me, and the dog got to its feet, drooling as it waited for the command to attack.

I stood up. "Well, thanks for your time, Professor. Sorry if I dredged up unhappy memories."

Hemphill laughed. "I only have the one life, Mr. Sands. I don't intend to waste it on unhappy memories." He handed me my gun. "I'll see you to the door."

I pocketed it. "Much obliged," I said.

When I pedaled off, the dog barked after me until I was out of sight.

CHAPTER 7

I sat on a bench at Downtown Crossing and brooded. Hemphill had seemed awfully sure that Cornwall was dead. And that meant my client was not going to be happy.

I didn't have any positive proof—no death certificate, no gravestone—but that kind of proof didn't exist anymore. Hemphill's emphatic statement was the most you could expect. I had done my job quickly and well. Case closed.

Now what? Go to the Ritz and make my report? I couldn't face that just yet. Go back to my office and wait for the Sandman's second case? That seemed like an even worse idea. So I sat and watched the people go in and out of the Salvage Market. After a while I got hungry, so I bought a hunk of cheese and a hard roll from an old vendor, and I chewed while I brooded.

Then Jesus Christ came by, lugging his seven-foot wooden cross. I waved, and he stopped by my bench. A little boy in a tattered jacket was with him. The boy looked at me nervously. Jesus gave him a little push, and he offered me a yellow scrap of paper. I took it.

A message had been scrawled in pencil on the scrap. It took me a moment to make it out.

The End Is At Hand.

I smiled at the boy and put the paper into my pocket.

"This is total bullshit, you know," I said to Jesus.

"I pray for you daily, Walter," he said.

"Thanks for nothing." I noticed the boy staring at the remains of my roll and cheese. I gave them to him. He looked up at Jesus, who nodded. The boy started eating hungrily. "Why don't you sit down?" I asked. "That goddamn cross looks heavy."

"Of course it's heavy," Jesus said. "The sins of the world." He sat down, laying the cross next to my bicycle, and he hoisted the boy onto his lap.

I looked at him and shook my head. His name hadn't always been Jesus Christ. It had once been Jimmy Parducci, and he had been reasonably normal and unreasonably happy. He had a wife and a baby and a good job killing rats for the government, and what more could you ask for out of life? Then his wife contracted one of our peculiarly gruesome modern diseases, and all that changed.

When she died, he got religion. He had a vision or something, in which God told him that the last time had been just a warning, and if we didn't straighten out soon, He was *really* gonna give us what for. So Jimmy changed his name and took up the cross and wandered through the city, warning us to repent before it was too late. In my argumentative youth I had tried to point out to him that I—and most people—wouldn't be too thrilled with God, if what happened back then was His idea of a warning. But there is no arguing with revealed truth. Jimmy continued to spread the word, and his baby was growing up into a shy but obedient disciple, and I suppose there were worse ways for them to be spending their lives—except that the boy always looked cold and hungry and a little more frightened than he should have been, and if I were God Jimmy would have had to answer to Me for that.

"Are you living a good life, Walter?" Jesus asked me.

"Within reason," I said.

"I've heard that you are now a private investigator."

"True," I said.

"I've read about private investigators," he continued. "They live very immoral lives."

"Not true. They represent justice in its purest form."

"Oh, Walter," he said softly. "Repent, for the hour is nigh."

I shrugged. "I'd like to," I said, "but I've got this blond secretary with the hots for me back at the office and, well, you know how it is."

He shook his head. "Oh, Walter," he repeated.

I reached out and tousled the boy's hair. He stared at me and continued to chew solemnly. It was time to move on. "See you around," I said. I stepped over the cross and picked up my bike.

"I'll pray for you," Jesus called out. I ignored him.

After some hesitation, I decided to go to City Hall. It was in Government Center, just a short jaunt from Downtown Crossing; I locked my bike in a rack outside the strangely shaped building and went inside.

There was a large, brightly lit Christmas tree standing in front of the broken escalators. That seemed to say something profound about our government, but I didn't stop to figure it out. I hiked up an escalator for a couple of flights, then followed the signs to the Water and Sewer Department. I stopped in front of an office midway down a dimly lit corridor. The nameplate next to it said:

Charles T. Moseby
Asst. Director

The door was open. Inside, a dwarf was sitting at a desk littered with papers.

"Excuse me," I said. "It has come to my attention that there are citizens of this Commonwealth carrying concealed weapons on their persons. To whom should I report this outrageously illegal behavior?"

Stretch looked up and grinned. "Hello, Walter. You're under arrest." He was wearing a tie, his shirtsleeves were rolled up, and there was a pencil stuck behind his ear. Your typical dwarf bureaucrat.

He motioned for me to come in. "So what really brings you to the seat of power?" he asked.

I sat down opposite him. The room was surprisingly warm. I wondered how he could stand coming home to our frigid town house every night. "I'm here on business, actually," I said.

"If it's Bobby's business, Walter, I'm afraid I—"

"No, no. My own. Remember—my first case?"

"Oh, right. The search for the long-lost…whatever."

"Precisely." I hesitated. I didn't really see how this was going to achieve anything, but what did I have to lose? "I've been checking around, Stretch, and it seems that there's a possibility the guy I'm looking for got scooped by the British back when they were here maintaining law and order. They evidently felt obliged to kidnap some of our leading scientists."

Stretch nodded. "I think I heard about that. But what's it got to do with the Water and Sewer Department?"

"Absolutely nothing—except that it seems possible that somewhere in the reaches of our sainted government's archives there might be a list of who got taken. Or maybe there's some foreign service type who remembers, or who can find out. We're such good buddies with the British now, they'd probably be happy to tell us. So I thought I'd come to see my own good buddy Stretch, who knows all sorts of people in the government and maybe could help me out."

Stretch pondered. "It's a tall order," he said.

"Then you're just the man for the job."

He glared at me. "Is that a size joke?"

I smiled. "My, we're sensitive today, aren't we?"

"Anyone who lives with Linc has a right to be sensitive."

It was Linc who had started calling him Stretch. "All right, I apologize," I said. "So what do you say?"

"I guess I can look into it," he said. "If any information does exist, though, it's probably down in Atlanta, so it might take me a while to get a hold of it."

"Anything you can do, Stretch. I realize it's a long shot."

Stretch sized me up. "My services come at a price, Walter."

"Name it."

"You listen to a lecture."

I groaned. "Anything, Stretch, but not that."

"Shall I give it to you now, or do you want to wait until we get home?"

"Please, Stretch, I've suffered enough for one lifetime."

"I know, Walter. We all have. But you've got to get out of this dream world you're living in. You've got to accept the world as it is, and yourself as *you* are."

Except for his sensitivity about size jokes, Stretch didn't seem to let being a dwarf bother him. But it wasn't my fault he was so well adjusted. "You've got me wrong, Stretch," I replied. "I do accept the world as it is. I just think it's ready for a private eye."

"Oh, come on, Walter. You're just playing at it because you don't know what else to do with yourself. The country needs people like you—you're tough, and you're smart, and you're good. We can't afford to let you waste your life pretending it's 1937. Frankly, I'd rather see you working for Bobby Gallagher. At least what he does is *real.*"

"People have to go it alone in this world—even more so than in the old days," I said. "That's where a private eye can do a lot of good: he can help them when no one else will."

"Oh, bullshit." Stretch is never vulgar. He was very upset with me. And I remembered the way I had talked to Jesus Christ. Did Stretch think I was as useless as Jesus? It wasn't fair, but how could I argue with him? And then he struck a low blow. "Look, if my opinion doesn't matter, what about Gwen? She loves you, Walter."

"What about her? She's never said she disapproves."

"You know Gwen. She doesn't have to."

"Well, if she loves me, then she should accept the way I want to live my life."

Stretch shook his head sadly. "I guess I don't know how to convince you. Maybe you'll just have to get it out of your system. Maybe failing on this case will do the trick—they don't fail in those books you read."

"I haven't failed yet."

"If you're looking for my help, you can't be doing very well."

I glared at him. "Is the lecture over?"

"The lecture's over," Stretch said softly.

I stood up. "I'll see you later, then. I've got private eye work to do."

"Okay, Walter. I'll see what I can do to help. Honest I will. No hard feelings?"

"Ah, you're too short to be angry at for very long."

Stretch grinned. "That's more like it."

I walked out of his office.

CHAPTER 8

Dr. Winfield was eating supper in his room when I arrived to make my report. There was a half-consumed steak and a bottle of wine on a tray next to his bed. The smell of the steak and the heat in the room made me feel a little light-headed. I took my parka off and sat in an armchair by the window.

"Glass of wine?" Winfield asked. "The vintages are starting to improve again out in California."

I shook my head. I noticed that most of the wine was already gone. Winfield's eyes were a little glazed. "Anyone try to kill you today?" I asked.

"Didn't give 'em an opportunity. Just stayed in here and let you do all the work." He lay back on the bed and picked up his glass. "So what did you find out?"

I took a breath. "The evidence seems to suggest that Robert Cornwall is dead," I said. And I told him what I had discovered from Hemphill.

Winfield's gaze drifted past me as I spoke. I couldn't tell if it was because he was drunk, or because he didn't think me interesting enough to look at. At any rate, my report sounded pretty meager; if I were the client, I would not have been impressed.

"This guy Hemphill—he didn't actually *see* Cornwall

die, right?" Winfield demanded when I had finished.

"He didn't say he had seen Cornwall die, but he seemed awfully sure of it."

"But the only evidence he gave was that Cornwall wasn't publishing in these scientific journals, right?"

"Yeah, that's right, I guess."

Winfield finished his wine and sat up. "He's guessing. If he really knew, why wouldn't he give you more details?"

"I don't know. If he was guessing, why wouldn't he say so?"

Winfield waved away my objection. He put down his glass. He picked it back up again. He rose from the bed, swaying a bit. "Cornwall is in England," he said. "It's so obvious, really, when you think about it."

It wasn't obvious to me. "But if he's in England, why—"

"Why hasn't anyone heard of him? Think, Sands. Remember my theory that the government was making him work on a secret cloning project? It was full of holes, obviously. I admit it. But what if he's been working for the *British*? They have the resources—of course he'd go, if they asked him to. He has to continue his work."

This idea was no better than his previous one. "But what would he be doing for them?" I asked.

"Clones. Clones of military leaders, of politicians, of scientific geniuses. Of course, they'd keep it all secret."

"But Hemphill doesn't think Cornwall could clone adults, and he knows more about the subject than either of us."

"He doesn't know everything. The article I showed you yesterday—didn't you read it? Cornwall was working on a way around the problem. Obviously, he succeeded. And that's why I'm here, and he's in England."

"But England's government is as antiscience as our own. They're no more likely than we are to be running a secret cloning project."

Winfield shook his head. "Hatton has only been in power there—what, nine, ten years? Cornwall would have gone to England over twenty years ago. The project would have been in full swing by the time the antiscience people took over. Maybe they just let it continue—maybe they had *themselves* cloned. It wouldn't be the first time a government's public posture didn't coincide with the way things really were."

"Well, if Cornwall is working in England, who is trying to kill you?"

That made him pause for a moment. "Maybe they have spies over here," he said uncertainly. "Or maybe you're right, it was just a coincidence. It doesn't really matter, does it?"

I had no idea if it mattered. The whole thing seemed like some sort of alcoholic fantasy. All I had managed to do was find someone who was sure that Cornwall was dead, and here my client was imagining some bizarre conspiracy with the British government. It was absurd.

Winfield sat back down on the edge of the bed. He stared in annoyance at the empty wine bottle. "The thing for me to do," he said slowly, "is to go over there and find him."

I chuckled. It was a joke, right? Winfield did not chuckle. "Trips to England are a lot more expensive than trips to Boston," I pointed out. "I don't think even a doctor could afford one."

Winfield gave me a what-do-you-know-about-it glance. "That's the least of my worries."

"So what else is worrying you?" I asked.

He clasped his hands and brought them up to his face. He appeared to be making an effort to sober up. "Going to England would be a serious step," he said. "It would involve burning a lot of bridges. That's all right. I'm willing to do it. I *want* to do it. But I need more information." He looked over at me. "I recognize a certain…credulity on my part, Mr. Sands. I want Cornwall to be alive. I want him to be special. All right, I'm rational, I can fight against that. So you have to bring me concrete evidence that Cornwall went to England. I don't need proof that he's still alive, just that he went there at some point. I give you three days to find me the proof. If you don't get it to me by then, I'm going home."

Three days? The deadline seemed as absurd to me as the search itself. "I'll do what I can," I said. "But I should tell you that if the evidence exists, it might take more than three days to find it. I've already talked to my contact in the government, and he's going to search for information about who the British took; but what we're looking for might be in some file in Atlanta, or in the back of someone's desk drawer, and there's no telling how long it'll be before we get our hands on it."

"But you see, Sands, I *have* to go back to Florida in three days. If I don't get back, people start asking questions, they look into things…my bridges would be burned."

I didn't follow that, and I wasn't sure I wanted to. "If finding Cornwall is this important to you, why not go to Florida and come back when you get more vacation time, or whatever?"

"Three days," he repeated. "Then I return to the leukemia and the melanoma and the polio and the birth defects, and I leave all this behind. Understood?"

I shrugged. If the case was a pipe dream, it didn't really matter what kind of deadline he gave me. Private eyes don't get to choose their cases—at least, not private eyes at my level of experience. As long as I got paid, I wasn't going to argue. "You want me to report in daily?"

"No, just when you have something."

I stood up and put my coat on. "I figure I worked six hours at two dollars an hour. Plus expenses—parking and lunch—I figure you owe me twelve dollars and sixteen cents."

Winfield looked at me as if I had just asked him for a new Cadillac. "You've got a nerve, Sands," he said. "I offer you something like this, and you still want your crumby two dollars an hour?"

I was puzzled and a little angry. "Something like what? You're offering me three more days of work trying to find some evidence that probably doesn't exist. We had an agreement: if I did an acceptable job today—"

"Sands, you've got a chance to go to England, goddammit. England—where life is halfway normal, where there's heat and food and television and good-looking women. Don't screw it up by pissing me off."

I sat back down. "Have I missed something here?" I asked slowly. "When was it established that I was going to England?"

Winfield waved his hand irritably. "Well, of course I'll need a bodyguard. And you seem reasonably bright—I might have you, I don't know, track down clues or something. Listen: you know, if you go over there, you don't have to come back. Theoretically you have to leave when your visa runs out, but they can't deport you if they can't find you, right? Meanwhile you find some nice British girl to marry or you figure out who to bribe, and you're all set. But the main thing is to get over there, right? This is the chance of a lifetime, Sands. Just get me the evidence."

Perhaps the heat and the smell of the steak were making me hallucinate. England? Me? I was familiar with both objects, but the combination of them seemed utterly ludicrous. *Me. In England.* Where was the catch?

It was obvious. Winfield was just getting more work out of me without having to pay for it. And besides, the proof he wanted simply didn't exist. I had talked to Hemphill; I knew he wasn't guessing about Cornwall's death.

But still, there was a chance—wasn't there? And the chance was obviously worth three days of my life. *In England. Me.* "Okay," I said. "I'll see what I can do."

Winfield smiled. "Good man," he said. "Three days. Bring me proof."

"Coming right up," I said. But I didn't have the faintest idea how I was going to find it.

CHAPTER 9

"So how's the case?" Linc asked at supper.

"I made a little progress. The guy I'm looking for is probably dead, but he may conceivably be in England."

"Well, that narrows it down. Is your client satisfied?"

"He's keeping me on the case, so I guess he's satisfied."

"I'm helping Walter find out about the England angle," Stretch announced. "Gonna check out all the scientists the British took back with them while they were here."

Gwen looked at me. "What happens if he's in England?" she asked.

"Oh, I dunno," I said. "It's almost certain that he's dead, anyway." I concentrated on my stew.

After supper we all went into the parlor and listened while Gwen played the piano. Linc huddled in a blanket on the couch. Stretch tried to sing along with a Beatles' song. He was almost as bad as Ground Zero. I sat in an armchair next to the piano and watched Gwen's eyes studying the ragged sheet music, her fingers moving gingerly over the keys. We went to bed early.

"Are you happy?" she asked as we lay in the darkness.

"Sure," I said. "It felt good to be on the job. I didn't screw up very much, and my client seemed pleased."

"I'm glad," she said, and she snuggled into the crook of my shoulder.

I waited until she was asleep, and then trekked upstairs. But my room didn't give me the satisfaction I needed. Tonight I was too restless, too excited, and the shadows were too dim. After a while I took a book from the shelf. I stared at it, then went back downstairs, put my parka on, and walked out into the night.

Used to be that going outside in the city at night was an open invitation to get yourself murdered. Things are better nowadays, but still I was on my guard as I walked the few blocks to School Street. I stopped in front of a small store. The sign over the door said:

Art's Filthy Bookstore

It had never been clear to me whether the adjective applied to the store or its merchandise; I had a feeling it was deliberately ambiguous. There was a light shining inside. I pounded on the door.

After a few moments there was movement. A slot at eye level in the door opened and Art peered out into the darkness. "Who is it?" he demanded.

I took out the badge that Mickey had given me and held it up in front of the slot. "Vice Squad," I said. "Open up. This is a raid."

Art cackled delightedly and started undoing the locks. In a minute or so the door opened and I stepped inside. "Nothing objectionable here, Officer," Art said. "Look for yourself."

I looked. Art probably had the largest collection of pornography in the commonwealth—maybe on the entire East Coast. His store was crammed from floor to ceiling with old *Penthouses* and *Playboys* and *Hustlers,* with *Fanny Hill* and *The Story of O* and *The Delta of Venus* and *Emmanuelle,* with hundreds of novels by Anonymous about Victorian gentlemen and their willing maids, with thousands of novels that told the steamy inside stories of the sexual hijinks of Hollywood stars, of the international jet set, of the glamorous people in the high-powered worlds of advertising, finance, fashion, publishing…crammed with anything that might feed people's fevered imaginations about the old days, that might tantalize and delight and exhaust them with visions of pleasures they could never possibly share.

Jesus Christ did not approve of Art.

Art didn't approve of himself, really, but a guy's gotta make a living, and this was what people wanted in a bookstore. So he gave them their cheap thrills, and he saved his affection for the occasional discriminating customer. Like me.

He was a little man, with bright eyes, long white hair, and a beard that hadn't been trimmed in twenty-two years. He looked the way Santa Claus might look, if Santa Claus were forced to subsist on our modern diet.

"You're absolutely right," I said, picking up a dog-eared copy of *Greta, She-Wolf of the Nazis*. Greta glared at me from the cover, whip held menacingly in one hand. She was bursting out of her too-tight storm trooper uniform. "Just good, wholesome literature here. I must have been misinformed." I handed him the book I had brought. "Here's a present for you."

Art nodded with satisfaction as he examined it. "Brin. *The Postman*. Hardcover, 1985. Very good condition—better than the one I have. Postwar Oregon, right?"

"Right. Bobby Gallagher and I carted off an old lady's library the other day, and this was in it. He let me keep the book—no one else would want it."

"This is excellent, Walter. Thank you. Let's go add it to the collection."

We went through the store, past a "No Admittance" sign, and into a storage area. It, too, was piled high with books, but there was also a cot, and a sink, and several locked cabinets. Art opened one and placed the book reverently inside, next to a softcover and another hardcover edition of the same novel.

"Are there any you don't have?" I asked.

Art shook his head. "Who knows? You wouldn't believe how many books got published in the old days. There were a lot of people writing back then."

I stared at the books—row after row. I had only bothered to read a few of them. It always seemed like such a waste. *On the Beach. Alas, Babylon. A Canticle for Leibowitz. Fiskadoro.* "It looks like they were all writing about the same thing," I murmured.

"There were a lot more *She-Wolves of the Nazis* than post-holocaust novels," Art pointed out.

"You're the expert." I watched Art lock up the cabinet. "You know, this is a very weird hobby," I said.

Art smiled. "You think so? Perhaps that's because you're so young, You don't feel the need to connect. This is my way of connecting."

"They also wrote books about useful stuff, like how to make glass, and how to treat typhus."

"But I'm not a useful person. Did you ever think that some of these writers are still alive—looking at the world as it is, and comparing it to the world they had imagined? I wonder how they feel about it."

"Probably they think: geez, it coulda been worse."

"True. But it's harder living in a world than it is imagining one. Now, you didn't come here just to give me a present. What can I do for you, Walter?"

"Books on England."

"Ah, England. What about *Riddley Walker?*"

"Real books," I said. "About the real England."

Art laughed at the distinction. "But those books aren't any more useful than *Riddley Walker.* What about something on how to make glass?"

"I may be going to England," I said. I told him my story.

He was suitably impressed. "Imagine that," he murmured. "Imagine that." He wandered over to a few stacks of books in the corner and started wading through them. "Not much call, you know, anymore. People want fantasy about the past, not reality." He came out with a picture book and an old travel guide. "Best I can do, I'm afraid."

"They'll be fine. The place has probably changed a lot anyway."

Art shrugged. "Not as much as this place has." He sat down on the edge of his cot. There was a wood stove in the room, but it wasn't giving off much heat. Art didn't seem to mind. "England," he said dreamily. "Do you ever think, Walter, about how much we owe certain people who will undoubtedly remain anonymous forever? People say history is determined by great economic and social forces, that individuals don't make a difference. But I can't believe that. Someone gives an order, or refuses to carry out an order, or carries it out badly, and England is spared. Someone holds back at the last second, and the bombs aren't dropped that should've been dropped, and we're here, alive, swapping books and chatting by the light of an oil lamp. And maybe those people are still alive, like those old writers. I wonder what they're thinking about. Do they think they did the right thing? Are they proud of themselves? Or do they think that, at the most important moment of their lives, they fouled up, and they'll never have a chance to atone for their mistake?"

"I think," I said, "that maybe people don't think as much as you think they do."

Art cackled. "But what else do they have to do nowadays? There's no TV."

"They read dirty books."

"Ah, you're a cynic, my friend."

"Gee, I wonder how that happened."

Art shook his head. "I hope I had nothing to do with it." He paused. "You know," he said, "if you don't get to go, Walter, you might consider going into business with me."

"Selling dirty books? There's barely enough—"

"Not selling them, Walter. Writing them." Art's eyes glittered. "I don't have the imagination, but I'm sure you could do it. Imagine if I had new novels to sell my clientele—new dreams to dream. I've got a friend at the

Globe who says they might be willing to rent out their printing press, and—"

"Um, I don't think so, Art. Maybe, if this England thing falls through, you know—"

Art smiled and raised a hand to stop me. "Just a thought. Anyway, enjoy your books. And enjoy England, if you get to go. Shakespeare, Dickens, Browning: 'Oh, to be in England…' And Matthew Arnold. Remember 'Dover Beach'? 'The cliffs of England stand,/ Glimmering and vast, out in the tranquil bay.' So much to see. I envy you."

I remembered the poem. "This all feels like a dream," I said.

"There's nothing wrong with dreaming," Art replied.

I wasn't so sure. I always felt a little woolly-minded after visiting Art. His bookstore was like a drug that made me want to live the way he did, accomplishing nothing, just pondering unanswerable questions as time drifted by. In its own way, that was as sinful as reading the filthy books that Art sold—at least, I'm sure that's what Stretch would say. And Stretch, in his own way, spoke the truth.

Still, a little dreaming was okay, it seemed to me. I felt no compunctions, therefore, about returning to my chilly library and reading the books Art had given me I studied the pictures and memorized the text and imagined myself in England: warm, well fed, happy. It was a good dream, as dreams went, because it was, at least conceivably, attainable. It kept me happy until sleep, and another dawn, arrived.

Bobby Gallagher's headquarters were across the Fort Point Channel in South Boston, on a dismal street of endless warehouses. The police knew enough to stay away from that street. I pedaled over there the next morning.

A twelve-year-old black kid was squatting in the snow next to the front door, a shotgun cradled in his arms. His name was Jason, but for some reason Bobby called him Doctor J, so that's what everyone else called him too.

"Hey, Doctor J," I said.

"Hey, Wally."

I got off my bike. "Is the man in?"

He nodded. "Doin' some business."

"Lemme go inside and wait for him, okay?"

"Sure thing." He got up and pounded a complex rhythm on the door. After a moment Mickey opened it and smiled a greeting.

"The bike okay here?" I asked Doctor J.

"It ain't goin' nowhere."

I went inside, and Doctor J resumed his guard duty in the snow.

Brutus started barking as soon as the door closed behind me. Fortunately, he was chained to the metal railing of the stairs leading up to Bobby's office, so he couldn't do any damage. Brutus was an extremely large German shepherd, and we didn't get along.

"Who's he talking to?" I asked Mickey, gesturing upstairs.

"Tax people, I think."

"Problems?"

Mickey shook his head. "They need computer parts."

"Ah."

Mickey went back to working on the van, which was parked in the middle of the warehouse floor. I watched him for a while and then got bored; engines have always baffled me. I wandered around the warehouse and stared at the stuff Bobby had accumulated: television sets, lawn mowers, microwave ovens, pinball machines. They were just for show, of course. Anyone who broke in was welcome to steal a lawn mower. The good stuff was upstairs, in a room your casual thief was not likely to be able to enter; that room held the computer parts, the jewelry, the guns, the ammunition. Bobby preferred to deal in your smaller, more portable items. He knew what he was doing.

Eventually the upstairs door opened and Bobby came out, followed by two nervous-looking men in gray overcoats. Each was carrying a shopping bag. Brutus wagged his tail as they went past; he was a very stupid dog. They hurried outside, with Bobby thanking them effusively and inviting them to do business again anytime. When he came back inside, he was grinning. "R. Gallagher, Inc., Suppliers to Government and Industry. Impressed, Wally?"

"Are they gonna come back and audit you, now that their computers work?"

"Hell, no. I also bribe them. A totally separate transaction. What's up?"

"Can we talk?"

"Sure. Come to the inner sanctum."

We went upstairs. Brutus growled at me as I passed.

The inner sanctum was decorated in faded fake-wood paneling, stained ceiling tiles, and orange shag carpeting. Very sophisticated. A photograph of John F. Kennedy was displayed prominently above the sagging couch. Scattered elsewhere on the walls were photographs of Bobby's mother, the 1984 world champion Boston Celtics, and Bobby himself, in younger days, just as fat but with more hair, shaking hands with some forgotten politician. There was a 1986 calendar with a photograph of a mostly naked woman luxuriating on a mound of tires. There was a plaque that said "Erin Go Bragh" and another that said "Schlitz— Breakfast of Champions." And behind the gray metal desk there was a crucifix.

Bobby sat down beneath the crucifix. I sat on the couch. "So how's the case coming, Mr. Private Eye?" Bobby asked. "Any car chases yet? Any beautiful but mysterious broads wanna go to bed with you?"

"Not so far. I could maybe use your help, Bobby."

"Sure. Waddaya need?"

"I need to find out the names of the scientists that the British took from around here when they were occupying New England."

Bobby looked at me the way Winfield had when I asked to be paid. "Why, uh, do you think I'd know that, Wally? I was pretty busy staying alive back then. Didn't keep very close tabs on everything the British were up to."

"Of course. I'm not asking *you*, Bobby. I'm just wondering if you can help me come up with a way to find out. See, my client thinks this guy Robert Cornwall may have been scooped by the British—apparently they took some of our scientists while they were here. My client is even willing to go to England to track Cornwall down—and he'll take me with him—but we need some evidence that Cornwall was one of the ones taken. He's given me three days."

"How the hell can he afford to go to England?"

"I don't know. But he says he can, and I believe him."

"And you get to go with him?"

"That's what he said, Bobby."

"Jesus. So waddaya want me to do?"

"Well, you've got a lot of contacts in the government. I thought maybe you could ask around, see if anybody knows what happened back then. Ideally, I could use something in writing—a list, you know, or something like that."

"What about Stretch?"

"I asked him, too, but I'm not sure how much he'll help. I'm worried that he thinks it'll be for my own good if he doesn't find out anything. If I screw up my first case, maybe I'll come to my senses."

"Will you?" Bobby asked.

"Not planning to," I said.

"You know, that offer about working for me still stands."

"Yeah, well, my refusal still stands, too, I guess."

Bobby gazed at President Kennedy, or maybe the Celtics. He seemed to have that faraway look I had seen on Hemphill's face the day before—although, with Bobby's bad eyesight, it was tough to be sure. "Such a strange world, Wally," he murmured. "Who'd've thought we'd get a government that promised to ditch all its weapons and ban computers and get people making babies again? Jesus Christ, make love, not war. Who'd've thought a bright young guy with the world to conquer would pick the one most dead-end job around—except maybe for director of civil defense? Who'd've thought—well, a lot of things."

I was getting awfully tired of this. First Jesus Christ, then Stretch, and now Bobby. I stood up. "If you're not going to help me, Bobby, just say so and let me get on with—with my investigation."

"Now take it easy, Wally," Bobby said. "I'm just musing here. A guy's got a right to muse, don't he? Of course I'm gonna help you."

I sat down. "Thanks," I said.

Bobby smiled. "What are friends for?" But he still didn't look happy; the faraway look hadn't disappeared. "If you go to England, are you coming back?"

"Oh, I don't know, I haven't really—"

"Don't bullshit me, Wally. You've always wanted to get out, and this is your chance. Right?"

"Well, what of it?" I asked defensively.

"I just like to know what's going on, that's all. You sure you want to go live with those Limey bastards?"

"I could move to Ireland once I'm over there, if it'll make you happier. The trick is to get over there." I thought about it. "You know, with this connection you've got going with Fitch, you could probably afford to leave before very long too."

Bobby looked uncomfortable. "Yeah, well, I dunno, maybe I'm used to things around here."

"Shit, the inmates get used to the asylum." I went back to the original subject. This one was making me uncomfortable too. "Anyway, will you help me? I've got two days left to come up with something, and then my client is going home, so we've gotta act fast."

"Okay, Wally. I'll see what I can do."

"You're a good guy, Bobby."

"Ah, bullshit."

He went back to staring at President Kennedy, and I left the room. Brutus just missed my ankle as I went downstairs. Outside, Doctor J was still squatting in the snow, and my bicycle was untouched.

CHAPTER 10

It was my turn to cook supper: pea soup with hard biscuits. I bought the biscuits, but I had to make the soup. I'm no chef. Linc sat at the kitchen table and watched me stirring the disgusting stuff. Every day he seemed to look a little paler, a little more feverish. I wished I could send him off somewhere away from the cold and the slush and the ceaseless struggle—to Florida, to California, even to England. But that wasn't the way life was; and anyway, it was too late.

He started whistling one of the Beatles' songs Gwen had played: "Yesterday, all my troubles seemed so far away…"

He was not a bad whistler. "The Sandman is upset," he said when he had finished.

"The Sandman wishes his soup were thicker," I said.

Linc whistled a few more notes. "The Sandman apparently doesn't want to bare his soul, even to his good buddy Linc," he observed.

"He wishes his soup were thicker and his case were solved," I said, baring my soul. "The Sandman spent a good part of the day at his office, staring at the walls. He wishes he could think of some way to solve the case besides asking his friends for help. He wishes he knew what his life was all about."

Linc slid down in his chair and scratched at his beard. "I thought," he said, "that private eyes had self-confidence coming out their ears. Nothing bothers them; they're always in control."

I stirred. "The Sandman perhaps wonders if he's really a private eye."

"The Sandman can be whatever he wants to be."

"Yes, indeed. Maybe that's why the Sandman is upset." I stirred and stirred. Eventually Linc started whistling again.

Later, while we all ate the watery soup, I quizzed Stretch. "Have you come up with anything yet?"

"Well, no, not really, Walter. I've got a call in to a guy I know in Atlanta, but he hasn't got back to me. I've checked around with some people locally, but they don't know anything."

"Don't they even remember the British taking people?"

"Sure, vaguely. But as for names…" He shrugged.

"Well, keep trying. Maybe Bobby'll have better luck."

Stretch was miffed. "You've got Bobby looking too?"

"Why not? He knows people. He owes me a favor. People owe him favors."

"If what you want exists, I'll be able to find it," Stretch said defensively.

"Great. Maybe Bobby'll find it too."

"You know," Linc said, "if you got one case, you're bound to get another. It's just a matter of time."

"Yeah. This is the one I've got, though, and this is the one I want to solve."

"I thought," Gwen said, "that you were pretty sure you had solved it—that this fellow was dead."

"But I don't have any proof. And my client would prefer it, obviously, if the guy was still alive."

"But what you're after is the truth, isn't it?" she asked.

I shrugged and looked at Linc's bowl. "Eat your soup," I said to him. "You need it."

"You didn't stir it enough," he replied.

* * *

I think I should explain how I met Gwen.

It was during the Frenzy, that awful time when we all teetered on the brink of barbarism, and some fell in. The youth camp where I had been living had pretty much fallen apart, so I wandered back to the city with a kid named Miguel. We lived in the North End and spent our days scrounging for food—fishing on the waterfront, trapping pigeons, stealing whenever we had the chance. Nights, we stayed inside. The barbarians came out at night, and we had no desire to meet up with them. Miguel found a guitar and taught himself to play. I read books. There have been worse times in my life.

One day we split up as usual to scour the city for food. I returned at dusk; Miguel didn't. I never saw him again.

What happened to him? Who knows? People come and go, and life continues. I lived by myself, lonely and afraid—emotions I was all too familiar with.

The Frenzy got worse, and even daytime wasn't safe. I was walking along Atlantic Avenue one sunny afternoon carrying a fishing rod and a bucket with one lousy bluefish in it, when the biggest man I had ever seen came out from behind one of the girders supporting the Central Artery. He had a bushy black beard and a scar on his forehead that extended from temple to temple. He was pointing a submachine gun at me.

I thought the submachine gun was a bit much.

"Gimme," he said.

I gave him the bucket.

"Gimme," he repeated.

I gave him the rod.

He looked me over and apparently decided there was nothing else worth taking, including my life. He stomped off.

I took out my gun and aimed it at him. Then I put it away. Even when I was fifteen I didn't kill people.

That's when I decided to leave the city. I could understand the guy taking my fish, but not the rod too. Stealing a person's food is sometimes necessary; stealing a person's means of getting food is barbaric. It was time to find someplace less barbaric.

I packed up a few belongings and left the North End. I had vague dreams of heading south, where I had heard there was still civilization. Mostly, though, I just wanted to move on, to be somewhere else besides Boston. I made it to the next town over: Brookline.

I have mentioned the danger of the suburbs. If you are streetwise (and I am that, if nothing else), and you are caught in a suburb at dusk, you find a house that looks empty, and you hole up for the night. That's what I did.

I looked for one with no smoke coming out the chimney, no vegetables planted in the yard, no barbed wire or guns or barking dogs. The house I chose was a fancy Colonial with a two-car garage attached to it. There was an in-ground pool in the backyard half filled with rotting leaves. A rusted wheelbarrow lay face down in the high weeds. The place was dark and quiet and most of the windows had been broken. It looked okay.

I climbed into the house through one of the broken windows and searched it from top to bottom. It had been pretty well picked clean over the years, but I saw no evidence of recent inhabitants. There was a thick layer of dust over everything; the plumbing didn't work; no one answered my friendly shouts. So I settled in.

A bed in one of the rooms was still made. I took off the dusty spread, sat down, and ate some of the food I had brought: leftover fish, an apple, a stale biscuit. I found a few *Ladies' Home Journals* in the corner of a closet and read them contentedly until there was no more light. Then I got under the covers and tried to sleep.

Back then, I still hadn't gotten used to my peculiar brand of insomnia.

It must have been a couple of hours later that I began to think that I was not alone. Clearly a hallucination. No one could have been quiet enough to come into the room without my noticing. But I became convinced that someone was there in the dark, watching me, judging me, getting ready to do what people generally do to intruders.

Finally, I couldn't stand it. I inched my hand across the bed toward my jacket, where my gun lay waiting; meanwhile I strained to hear someone breathing, a floorboard creak, clothing rustle.

My hand made it to the edge of the jacket before I felt cold metal against my head.

"Don't move or I'll blow your fucking brains out," Gwen said.

Not very convincingly, I'm afraid. A certain tone is required for sentences like that, and Gwen had not mastered it. Nevertheless, I thought it prudent not to move.

Then an astonishing light burst into my eyes, and for a split second I thought: the bitch did it—she blew my brains out.

Reason prevailed, however. I blinked, and my pupils did what they were supposed to do, and I saw a flashlight shining, not very steadily, in my direction. I hadn't seen a working flashlight in years.

"You're a kid," Gwen said.

I tried to make out something of the figure holding the flashlight. The figure wasn't very large. "So are you," I said.

"But I've got a gun."

"True. Listen, I didn't know anyone was here. I'll be happy to leave."

The gun stayed pressed against my head. *Jesus,* I thought, *gimme a break.*

Finally, the gun moved away. The flashlight's beam dropped to the floor. There was a strange, low noise, and the figure slumped onto the bed.

Gwen started crying her eyes out.

I was young; I wasn't sure of the etiquette in situations like this. I waited until the bawling had subsided somewhat, and then I said, "You want an apple?"

And that's how I met Gwen. In fact, she didn't want my apple, although she was touched by the offer—touched enough to share her secret with me. After we had both calmed down a bit, she took me to the basement and showed me where she lived. Hidden behind a workbench, which cleverly rolled away when you pushed an inconspicuous little lever, was a fully equipped, mint-condition, top-of-the-line fallout shelter, stocked with a portable generator and canned goods and medicine and a radio and a dosimeter and all the other neat stuff that was supposed to help you survive a nuclear war.

The family who built the thing was probably camping next to a Minuteman silo when the bombs fell.

Gwen had found the shelter by accident, while doing exactly what I had done: checking out the house to make sure it was empty. Having first pinched herself to make sure she wasn't dreaming, she then did what anyone would have done: she moved in, and she kept quiet.

Paradise, huh? For a while. But it's a dull sort of life, hoarding your good fortune. If you're starving, all you want is food. If you have more than enough food, all you want is someone to share it with. Gwen was scared of everyone, but she needed a friend.

I was happy to be her friend.

We opened up a can of pineapple slices and talked. I had never eaten pineapple before; I was a little scared that I'd be poisoned, but I wasn't scared enough to resist the temptation. The pineapple was delicious.

Gwen told me her story. It wasn't that different from mine, I suppose. She, too, had been orphaned, had wandered from youth camp to youth camp, had begged in the city and scrounged in the country, had somehow managed to survive until she stumbled into paradise. But her story *was* different, because it was her life she was talking about, in that shy, laconic way of hers. And even then, even that first night, her life seemed special.

I told her my story, too, and to my ears it sounded exceedingly dull and commonplace. So we started talking about other things—about everything, about God and California and television, about the old days and these days and the days to come, and we ate lima beans and beef stew and tunafish until we couldn't eat or talk anymore.

Then she asked me—shyly, laconically: "Wanna dance?"

There was a cassette tape player among the many treasures in the shelter. She loaded a tape (the Beatles, I found out later), started it, and held out her arms to me. There wasn't much room for dancing, but we didn't need much. We swayed to the music, we felt the warm reality of our bodies locked together, and we were happy—utterly happy, for the first time in our difficult young lives.

"If I fell in love with you,
would you promise to be true
and help me understand..."

And when the dancing was over, the kissing started, and before long we were making awkward love on the floor. "Are you a virgin?" she asked me.

"No," I said. It was the first time I lied to her. And I suppose she knew, because Gwen knows everything, but she didn't say anything. Our life together had begun.

We probably set some records for lovemaking over the next few months, if anyone had bothered to count. We were too young and stupid to worry about pregnancy; anyway, it would've been a waste of time, as a doctor subsequently informed Gwen. And anyway, it wouldn't have made any difference. We both had a lifetime of need waiting to be satisfied, and we just couldn't tear ourselves apart.

During our occasional rest periods, I taught Gwen how to write.

We stayed there through the winter, rationing the lima beans and the pineapple slices, burying our garbage at night in the swimming pool, going once in a while on forays to a nearby library that had not yet been sacked. We didn't speak to another human being for seven months. By spring we were both a lot older and healthier and better educated, and we knew it was time to move on. We took the medicine and the flashlight and a few other irreplaceable items from the shelter and headed back into Boston. A passerby on Beacon Street told us the latest news: troops had come up from Atlanta and were setting things right downtown. The Frenzy was over; people were starting to live lives that might pass for normal in this abnormal world.

Gwen and I held hands and smiled at each other in the warm April sun. What more could life offer us?

Next stop, Louisburg Square.

And here we still were. But time changes everything, doesn't it? Decisions have to be made, dreams have to be dreamt. I couldn't stay in paradise forever, and Louisburg Square was hardly paradise. Was it?

We lay in bed together, awake.

"I ran into Cindy Tappen at Northeastern yesterday," I said.

"How is she doing?"

"Great. She loves it. She says I ought to go to school too."

Silence.

"I was thinking maybe she's right," I said.

"What would you study?" Gwen asked.

"I dunno. Something useful. Agriculture. Creative writing."

Silence. I had said all I could force myself to say. "Is this because your case is going badly?" Gwen asked finally.

"No, not at all. A person just has to—to plan for the future. Maybe I could be a private eye in my spare time."

"It's not exactly a spare-time job," Gwen observed. Silence. She moved away from me and stared up into the darkness. "Going to school would kill you," she said.

"That's being rather melodramatic, I think."

"Maybe, but private eyes are melodramatic." She paused. "And you're a private eye, I think."

I smiled. That was the nicest thing Gwen had ever said to me. "So what are we going to do about this, Gwen?"

"I don't know, Walter. But it's very important that you solve this case."

"I think you're right." Silence. "Gwen, did you ever get the feeling you were born in the wrong century?"

"Walter, everyone in the world has that feeling."

"True." We both stared into the darkness. I turned to her. "Gwen, would you like to make love?"

She turned to me. "Yes," she said.

We were no longer setting records, but we did all right.

CHAPTER 11

It snowed the next day. I spent the morning in my office, trying—and failing—to figure out what else I could do. My three days were half gone, and I didn't have any ideas.

After I had visited Bobby, I had gone back to Northeastern and poked around some more, hoping to find another professor who knew something about Cornwall. No luck. Then I went to the Registry over on Nashua Street, just to satisfy myself that Winfield hadn't missed some reference to Cornwall in their records. No luck. I considered going back to Government Center and trying on my own to find records of the scientists taken by the British. But our government didn't work that way. If you didn't know someone, you didn't get anywhere.

So I sat and watched the snow and felt my dream slip away with the passing minutes.

Maybe it was all for the best. No matter what Gwen said, she really wouldn't *mind* if I went to school. But that was ridiculous. She was right: I was a private eye.

And besides, I wanted to go to England.

Finally, I started reading a book—the only solace I could think of. And that meant I didn't see the van appear out of the snow and come to a halt outside my building.

I did, however, hear the clomping of feet on the stairs,

and I was at my door in time to open it for my visitor.

"Jesus fucking Christ, can't you get any lights on the stairs?" Bobby complained. "I couldn't see a damn thing."

"Hi," I said. "You can't see a damn thing anyway."

He wiped the snow off his coat. "I really do think the weather is worse nowadays," he muttered. He peered around at the bare dirty walls, the yellowed linoleum floor. "So this is your office. Very stylish. Bet it impresses the shit out of your clients. Sorry—client."

"My Renoirs are out being reframed," I said. "Have a seat."

He sat. "Even if you don't have electricity, at least you could get a phone. Save Mickey driving in a goddamn snowstorm."

"Can't afford one. Besides, they don't work for shit. So, Bobby, what brings you and Mickey out in a goddamn snowstorm?"

He looked around some more. "Don't suppose you have any Scotch, do you?"

I shook my head. Did my finely tuned senses detect some uneasiness?

"Don't see how you can be a private eye and not drink," he grumbled. "So how's your case comin'?"

"Okay."

Bobby glanced at the book lying open on my desk. "Working hard, I see."

I didn't bother to reply. I figured he would come to the point in his own good time.

"The thing is," he said, "I think maybe you're making a mistake about wanting to go to England. I mean, not just England—forget about the Brits—but anywhere. I mean, things are getting better around here, right? At least compared to a few years ago. And you've got all your friends—Gwen and Linc and Stretch—he's kind of a jerk, but I suppose he's okay. And you and me, right? We go back a long way too."

"Friends help friends out," I observed.

Bobby nodded. "That's what they do, I guess," he said softly. "You're a lucky man, Wally."

I didn't say anything.

"I talked to a guy this morning," he went on after a brief silence. "He works for the Feds—he's one of the guys overseeing the locals, making sure they enforce all those wonderful edicts comin' out of Atlanta. Anyway, he's corrupt as hell, and we maintain a very close, meaningful relationship, if you know what I mean. His boss, on the other hand, is a turd. He thinks he has a sacred duty to get those laws obeyed—he's sorta like Stretch, you know? Taller, though.

"Anyway, I brought up your case with my friend. And he says he thinks—he thinks, mind you—that he saw a folder in his boss's file cabinet one time, and it was filled with documents about the British occupation, or whatever you wanna call it. He thinks he can get his hands on that folder."

"But he doesn't know if—"

"He doesn't *know* anything, Wally. But he figures if what you're lookin' for is anywhere, it's in that folder."

"When can he get ahold of it?"

"Tomorrow, maybe the day after."

"It has to be tomorrow," I said. "My time's up tomorrow."

"All right, all right. I'll talk to him, see if I can set something up for tomorrow."

I let it sink in for a few moments. "This is really fantastic, Bobby," I said finally. "I don't know how I can ever repay you."

"I don't know either, Wally." Bobby stood up. "I'll talk to this guy in the morning and try to set it up, then I'll let you know what's goin' on."

"Great. I'll be here. If there's anything—"

"Just don't spread it around that I'm bribing this guy, all right? The last thing he needs is for Stretch or someone to turn him in."

"Of course. Thanks, Bobby. This is really—"

"Yeah, yeah. I know." He looked around once more. "So what are you gonna do with your fuckin' Renoirs if you go to England?"

"I'll give 'em to you, of course. I bet Mr. Fitch would like them."

"That's really generous of you, Wally."

"That's what friends are for," I said.

Bobby grinned. "I'll be in touch."

He turned and left my office. I stood by the window and watched as he walked out and climbed into the van next to Mickey. When they had disappeared, ghostlike, into the snow, I sat back down at my desk. My book suddenly didn't seem interesting anymore. I tossed it aside, leaned back in my chair, and thought until it was time to go home.

"Bobby may have found what I need," I said at supper. "I'll know for sure tomorrow."

"How did he find it?" Stretch demanded. "Who did he get it from?"

"I'm sworn to secrecy. But it sounds promising."

"I'd be careful about Bobby's friends, Walter. They're not to be trusted."

"Do we have a little jealousy here?" Linc wondered.

"I just don't want Walter to be misled," Stretch said.

"Why would anyone want to mislead Walter?" Gwen asked.

"I don't know. I just think he ought to be careful, that's all."

"Of course I'm going to be careful, Stretch," I said. "But it's pretty straightforward: I need proof that'll satisfy my client. If he doesn't accept my proof, it doesn't matter what I think."

"And if he accepts it, you've solved the case," Gwen said.

"More or less. I mean, I don't actually have this guy Cornwall to show my client."

"But that's out of the question, if he's in England," Gwen pointed out.

"Well, right." I looked down at my stew.

"This is exciting," Linc said.

"It certainly is," Gwen agreed.

I agreed too, but somehow no one seemed very excited. Linc left the table a few moments later and went up to bed. The rest of us finished our meal in silence.

CHAPTER 12

A nother day at the office—another day of waiting, helplessly, for events to take their course.

A private eye shouldn't be helpless; a private eye should be in control of events. That was what attracted me to the business in the first place: I had spent my life feeling like a leaf in a hurricane, powerless in the wake of the ultimate power, the power that had transformed everything. Here was a chance to change. The events I would control might be trivial, but only if individual lives are to be considered trivial—a subject open to debate, I suppose, but one on which I have my own opinion.

The thing was, at this point I didn't really care. This had gotten a lot more serious than simply determining my self-image as a private eye. My entire future was at stake, and that made for a certain tension in my soul as the morning dragged on.

I tried to be rational, to keep my perspective. There were plenty of ways in which things would not work out: the mysterious file might not exist, or might not contain the proof I needed; Winfield could be lying about having the money, or about taking me along. The odds, really, were absurdly against me.

But there was a chance. And that made rationality very, very difficult.

Early in the afternoon there were the customary footsteps on the stairs and knock on the door. "Come in," I said.

Doctor J entered, sans shotgun. "Hey, Wally, how you doin'?"

"Okay, I guess. You got a message for me?"

He nodded. "The boss says: Charles Fingold, Room 304, JFK Building, two-thirty. Got it, Wally?"

I repeated it to him.

"You got it."

"Did he say anything else?"

Doctor J smiled. "He says fo' you to get a phone. I say so too."

"Well, both of you can go to hell."

Doctor J's smile widened into a grin, "He says good luck. I say so too."

I grinned back. "That's more like it. Thanks."

He gave a little wave, and then he left.

The JFK Federal Building is across Government Center from City Hall. I was there on time.

A soldier searched me at the door and took my gun away. A bribe would be required to get it back. Irritating, but that's life. Except for holdouts like Linc, people had gotten used to the government, and more or less accepted it. There had been too much chaos; we were willing to pay a few bribes in return for a little normality. When the soldier let me pass, I walked quickly up to the third floor.

Charles Fingold had a secretary—a good-looking redhead. A private eye should flirt with a good-looking secretary, but things were too serious for that. She told me to have a seat, and I obeyed. I waited while she went into her boss's office to tell him I was here.

The Feds treated themselves well, I noticed. The building was nicely heated and in good repair. Plenty of electricity too: the fluorescent lights all worked, the secretary's computer hummed agreeably. All the buildings were like this in England, I imagined.

The secretary came out of the office and motioned for me to enter. She smiled alluringly as I walked past. I managed a gulp.

"Shut the door," Fingold said.

I obeyed.

"Sit down."

I sat.

"If anyone asks, you were here for a job interview. We're looking for a few good locals. Understood?"

"Understood."

Fingold had a Southern accent, not unlike Winfield's. He was about fifty and military-looking, with short, iron-gray hair and gray eyes to match, a stiff white shirt, and a trim physique. But there was also something about him that looked—well, bribable. His jaw was a little slack and his eyes were a little dull, as if they had seen too much to care a great deal. The eyes looked at me warily. "I owe your friend a favor," he said, "but this isn't the kind of favor I feel comfortable performing."

"I don't understand," I replied. "Isn't this just some old document you're providing me? It isn't like, oh, letting people smuggle in computer parts."

"You're right," Fingold replied. "You don't understand. Look, the British are our allies now, and the government is pretty sensitive about what they did when they were here. The British insist they were just trying to help out, and people around here seem to think they were trying to take New England over while it was too weak to resist. Frankly, the United States government doesn't really care what happened back then. We just don't want old wounds reopened."

"All right. But you don't have to worry. I'm just trying to find a guy's father—I'm not writing an exposé for the *Globe.*"

Fingold shrugged. "Look, basically it doesn't matter to me what you do with the stuff, as long as it doesn't get traced back to me, and I don't have to take care of the consequences. Okay?"

"My lips are sealed," I said. "Now, can I see what you've got?"

Fingold stared at me, and then opened the top drawer of his desk. He took out several creased sheets of paper. "I think this is what you're looking for," he said. "Your friend says you've got a photographic memory. Says you know everything you read—Shakespeare, whatever—by heart. What if I were to just show these sheets to you and let you memorize them?"

"May I see them?" Fingold slid them across the desk.

Three typewritten sheets, rather smudged, stapled in the upper left corner. No letterhead, just a typed return address. The top sheet was a letter from Mr. J. T. Carstairs of the Ministry of Science in His Majesty's Government. It was addressed to Mr. Frederick Wheeler of the Department of State and was dated seven years ago. I wondered for a brief moment how it had gotten from Atlanta to Boston, to this office, into my hands. But that didn't matter. Here it was, and my heart thumped as I read it.

Dear Mr. Wheeler:

Your recent enquiry has been forwarded to my office. In response, I have enclosed a list of those scientists whom our American Relief Expedition accommodated with air transportation to England. I have been informed by the leaders of the A.R.E. that no scientist was taken against his or her will, and that emigration was offered solely as a means of protecting these valuable men and women, who were at such risk in the postwar environment.

Let me assure you that the scientists were well taken care of while they were in our hands. After landing at Heathrow, they were housed temporarily in dormitories at the University of London while they made arrangements to carry on their work in Great Britain. In no instance was anyone forced to take a particular job as a prerequisite for emigration, and in no instance was anyone who wanted to leave Great Britain forced to stay. We have no specific knowledge of the current whereabouts of these scientists, but it is my understanding that several may in fact have subsequently returned to the United States. If you request, I will look into this matter. It is our sincere hope that we be able to clear up any and all misunderstandings arising from the work of the A.R.E. If you have any further questions concerning this matter, please do not hesitate to bring them to my attention.

Yours most sincerely,

J. T. Carstairs

Interesting letter, but not half as interesting as the list attached to it. I turned the page.

T. J. Anderson

P. F. Bamberger

R. R. Bernstein

X. Boyce

L. A. Carrington

T. Cerpinski

R. M. Cornwall...

...and on. Maybe seventy-five names, double-spaced, two columns, finishing up on the third sheet. I didn't look at the rest of the names.

Once upon a time I shared a bottle of vodka with an old man in a cold basement while some hungry rats looked on. Maybe the man wasn't so old, but he looked as if he had suffered far too much and only wanted to forget. I was very young and got very drunk. I do not know how successful the old man was, but I forgot: for a brief while, my only reality was the spinning, buzzing euphoria inside my brain. Such a wonderful reality.

But it ended soon enough, with a headache and an upset stomach, and I was back there in that basement with the rats and the wretched, dying man. The old, implacable reality had returned, the only reality I had ever known, and I resolved never to have another drink. It was too awful to escape for a while, and then have to go back again.

When I laid the sheets of paper down, I felt as if Fingold had given me a never-ending bottle of vodka. I looked up at him and gestured at the sheets. "Could I borrow these for a while? I promise to bring them right back."

Fingold shook his head. "Absolutely not." He passed me a pad of yellow paper. "Why don't you copy down the information you want?"

"I'm afraid that won't do. I need proof for my client. Hell, I could just make up a list out of my head and show it to him. Why should he believe me? He'll want to see the originals."

Fingold took the sheets from the desk. I stared at them: the pardon snatched from the condemned man. I tried smiling my most winning smile. "Listen," I said. "This is pretty important to me. Isn't there some way—"

He waved me silent and stood up. "Come with me," he said, looking disgusted.

I went with him. We left his office, walked down the corridor, and turned into a small alcove. It contained a waist-high boxlike gray machine.

"The damn thing never works," Fingold said, "but I guess it's worth a try."

He pulled up the lid on the machine and placed the top sheet face-down on a piece of glass inside. He pressed a button. There was a flash of light and the hum of movement inside. After a few seconds the machine disgorged a piece of paper—the thing looked to me like a gray monster sticking out its white tongue at the world. "Son of a gun," Fingold said. He picked up the piece of paper and gave it to me.

Xerox. I saw the word on the side of the machine—a word from the world I had never experienced. A strange, wonderful word. I managed to restrain myself from yelping with delight. "This will do," I said. "Can you make Xeroxes of the rest?"

"Say a prayer."

I did. He did. I folded the Xeroxes and put them in my pocket. "Thank you very much," I said to Fingold.

"Don't mention it," he replied. "I mean that. Just tell your friend I did my part."

"I'll be happy to."

I held out my hand. Fingold shook it—somewhat reluctantly, I thought—and then headed back to his office.

I walked down to the lobby and cheerfully bought back my gun from the soldier. Then I hurried off to the Ritz, thinking of other wonderful words from the old days, words that till now had been as foreign to my experience as hieroglyphics: *Coke, Jacuzzi, parking meter, Big Mac.*

Words that might now be more than a congeries of letters on a page, a faded photograph in a moldy magazine. Words that Dr. Winfield might now bring to life for me through some magic I dared not imagine.

I had come through for him. Would he come through for me?

CHAPTER 13

D r. Winfield was shitfaced.

He looked as if he hadn't left his room since the last time I had been there. He was barefoot and unshaven, and the white shirt he wore was wrinkled and stained. He had graduated from wine to whiskey: a half-empty bottle stood on the night table by his bed. He did not inspire confidence.

"Mr. Sands, your deadline has arrived," he said mock-dramatically when he opened the door. "Want a drink?"

"No, thanks."

He staggered to the bed and sprawled face-down on it. I was afraid he had passed out. "You want to see what I've got?" I asked.

He said something unintelligible to the bedspread. I waited, and eventually he half turned over and waved. I put the sheets into his hand and sat down. He managed to turn himself completely over, groaned, squinted at the pages for a few moments, and then tossed them aside.

The gesture did not inspire optimism. I waited for a further response, but Winfield merely closed his eyes and folded his hands corpselike on his chest. "Um, Dr. Winfield?" I murmured.

He opened a bloodshot eye. "Yeah?"

"Just making sure you're still alive." Damned if I was going to beg for his reaction.

"Still alive," he muttered. He opened both eyes and gestured at the sheets. "Interesting, huh?"

"I thought so."

"Have a hard time getting the information?"

"Not especially," I had to admit.

"No one tried to kill you?"

"Not that I noticed."

"Still, it's real. He's over there. Doing something amazing."

It wasn't clear to me that we had any proof he was doing something amazing, but then, it was becoming apparent that Winfield didn't need any proof. Like me, he had a dream—a dream of his clone, his creator—and the dream was all that mattered.

"So what do we do now?" I asked.

"Find him, of course."

"The evidence is sufficient? You want to go to England?"

Winfield reached over and poured himself a drink. "Who cares about the evidence?" he said. "I was gonna go anyway. Don't wanna go back to Florida. Work day and night—for what? Keep people alive so they can feel more pain, and then they die anyway. They all die. Shit." He gulped down the whiskey.

He didn't care about the evidence. Swell. "Are you taking me?" I asked.

"You want to come?"

"Yes."

"Then sure. Come on along. I could use the company."

"Okay."

Winfield poured himself another drink. Now what? Everything was going as I had dreamed it would, so why didn't it seem real?

"When do we leave?" I asked.

Winfield gestured dismissively. "Anytime."

"Do you have the money for our tickets?"

He looked at me as if I were an annoying fly, and he was trying to decide whether to answer me or swat me. Finally he stumbled to his feet and went over to the closet. He rooted around inside it for a few moments, and then came out holding a large peanut butter jar filled with white powder. He set it down next to the whiskey bottle on the night table and flopped back onto the bed. "Our tickets," he said.

"What is it?" I asked, not sure I wanted to know.

"It's the best hospital-approved morphine a doctor can steal. Know anyone in the market?"

I stared at it. Then I stared at Winfield. This wasn't in my dream. But private eyes don't get to choose their clients; and people who want to go to England had better not be very choosy about the source of their funds. So what should I do?

I closed my eyes. There was no choice. Patients in Florida were screaming in pain, but I had had my share of pain too. "Yeah," I said. "I guess I know someone who's in the market. Can I use your phone?"

Bobby was sure to be impressed.

Bobby was impressed enough to send Mickey in the van for us right away. Winfield was not inclined to go, but I suppose he realized he couldn't stay in that hotel room forever—and he wasn't going to let me take off by myself with his peanut butter jar. He cradled it in his lap as we made our way through the snow to South Boston.

The two of us confused Brutus as we climbed the stairs to Bobby's office: he wanted to wag his tail at Winfield, he wanted to maul me. The best he could do was to growl indecisively as we went by. That was all right with me.

Bobby greeted Winfield effusively. "So nice of you to come, sir. I'm sure we'll have no trouble with our little transaction. Tell me, what do you think of our fair city?"

Winfield made a face. "The weather sucks."

"Oh, well, it's not like it used to be, but it's still quite, er, invigorating, wouldn't you say, Mr. Sands?"

"Um—"

"That's right. Incidentally, Mr. Sands here is quite possibly the best private investigator in the city."

"Prob'ly the only one," Winfield muttered.

"Well, you know, I hadn't thought of that. Now let's take a look at this white stuff here, shall we?"

There wasn't much haggling. Winfield seemed bored by the whole business, and Bobby, friend that he was, obviously didn't want to ruin the deal and keep me from going to England. The only problem was that he didn't have enough cash available to handle the deal by himself—and Winfield wasn't interested in computer parts. "Gotta bring in a partner on this one," Bobby said when the price was agreed upon. "Would you excuse me while I attempt to make a phone call?"

Winfield and I went outside. Winfield still clutched the peanut butter jar. The ride over seemed to have sobered him up a little, but not enough to carry on a coherent conversation with me. He shut his eyes and leaned back against the wall. "England," he muttered.

Bobby came out a couple of minutes later. "All set, gentlemen. My partner is as interested as I am. Will tomorrow at three be convenient?"

"Sure, sure," Winfield replied.

"Wonderful." We all went back inside and sat down. Bobby opened a desk drawer and took out a bottle of Scotch and a couple of greasy glasses. "Shall we have a drink to conclude the negotiations?"

Winfield perked up. "Sounds good to me."

Bobby poured a couple of ounces into each glass and passed one to Winfield. Bobby held his up in the air for a toast. "To friendship," he said.

"To England," Winfield said.

Bobby forced a smile and downed the Scotch. He shook his head. "They don't make this stuff like they used to," he complained.

Winfield finished off his drink. "It does the job, right?"

"That's certainly true. Care for another?"

"Don't mind if I do."

That was my cue to leave. I stood up. "I guess you people don't need me anymore."

Winfield looked at me, bleary-eyed. "You're goin' to England, Sands. Don't you wanna celebrate?"

"I guess not."

"Mr. Sands is the best non-drinking private investigator in the city," Bobby said. "You want Mickey to drive you home, Mr. Sands?"

"Nah. The weather's so invigorating, I think I'll walk."

"Come get me tomorrow," Winfield ordered.

"Yes, boss." I gave the two celebrants a wave, then walked off toward Louisburg Square, alone.

CHAPTER 14

I took my time—savoring my success, but mostly dreading the moment when I would have to tell my little family about it. That wasn't going to be easy.

I wandered through the city, steeling myself for the task. But maybe wandering wasn't a good idea. Wandering brought memories, and memories always confuse things.

Gwen and I had already moved in when we found the cardboard sign, which had fallen off the door and lay facedown amid rotting leaves on the front steps. "Property of Charles T. Moseby," it said in rain-streaked letters. "He Will Return." Well, property rights were somewhat illusory back then (still are, really); if Charles T. Moseby wasn't there, it wasn't really his. Gwen was frightened, imagining some stealthy creature pressing a gun to her temple in the middle of the night, but I was inclined to stay. People were always leaving places and planning to come back; they never did. And I liked the town house, liked the statue of Christopher Columbus outside, liked the cartons of books in the attic. We stayed.

Mr. Moseby returned several months later. It was a beautiful early fall evening, and we were sitting on the steps, enjoying the last of the good weather. He walked to the foot of the steps and stared at us. "This is my home," he said forcefully, like a bureaucrat sure of his rules. "You'll have to leave."

We stared back. It was hard not to. He was wearing a filthy brown pinstriped suit, a white shirt, and a paisley tie. He carried a battered, bulging briefcase. He fit my image of a traveling salesman—except that there were no traveling salesmen in our world.

And he looked like he was about nine years old.

There were enough dwarfs around, of course, that his size didn't shock us. It was hard to know what to make of the suit and tie, though. "Could we maybe talk about this?" I asked.

"There's nothing to talk about. You're trespassing."

"The laws nowadays are a bit vague on the subject of trespassing," I pointed out.

"There is a moral law. The moral law hasn't changed."

"You look hot and tired," Gwen said. "Would you like a glass of cider and something to eat?"

That stopped him. When you're thirsty, cider is a more interesting subject than the moral law. "Well, I *have* been traveling all day," he said. "Yes, I guess I would like some cider. But then you'll have to leave."

"Let's go inside."

He came in, and he drank some cider and ate some cornbread, and we talked.

Mr. Moseby had been on the road. (Hell, let's call him Stretch. The nickname came later, but it's hard to think of him any other way.) Like me, he had left the city during the Frenzy, but he had made it a lot further than Brookline. And most definitely unlike me, he had a purpose in his travels beyond that of simply getting away.

Stretch wanted to find out for himself if America could survive. Was there anything left in this country to give him hope—anything to strive for, to become a part of? He needed to know. So he traveled, in his silly old suit, trying to discover where things worked and where they didn't, where there was hope and where there was despair and where there was frenzy. People fed and sheltered him, and people ignored him, and people tried to kill him. People pitied him as a victim of the bomb and shunned him as if his condition were contagious. And out of it all he found what he was looking for. And then, as promised, he returned.

Most people, I think, find what they are looking for. Of course, it is far easier to find despair nowadays, but for someone like Stretch it was not impossible to find hope; for someone like Stretch, every mushroom cloud has a silver lining. The future did not lie with people like Mr. Fitch, barricading themselves on their farms, isolated, inbred, self-sufficient—or, if it did lie there, it was not a future Stretch was interested in. No, the future lay in people helping each other out, in rebuilding what needed to be rebuilt before chaos totally overtook us, in creating out of the ashes something stronger, purer, and saner than what had come before. It lay in cities, where people were forced to cooperate, to govern themselves, to be civilized. Stretch had found cities that worked. And that's what he wanted to be a part of.

It was hard not to laugh at Stretch; it was impossible not to admire him. His past was no different from Gwen's or my own—full of death and loneliness and terror. But Stretch had come out of his past determined, not just to survive, but to improve the world. And even if that goal was ludicrous, no one could fault him for trying to achieve it.

Just as the moral law cannot substitute for peach cider, however, high ideals are not an adequate replacement for human companionship. Stretch, it turned out, was as lonely as he was thirsty. After a few hours of conversation around the kitchen table, he agreed to drop all trespassing charges, and Gwen and I agreed that Louisburg Square was big enough for the three of us.

And so we became a family, although we could never really agree about who adopted whom. Gwen got a job as a messenger for the reborn *Globe* and dreamed of becoming a reporter, Stretch started his climb to the top of the water and sewer biz, and I—well, I did this and that, while I waited for inspiration to strike. There was always money coming in (and money suddenly had value once again), there was always food and fuel and companionship. And eventually our family grew.

The new arrival came in a not atypical way: he tried to kill one of us. To be fair, Linc denied that he would have killed Gwen, but such after-the-fact denials are suspect. The fact is, he scared Gwen just as much as Gwen scared me when she put the gun to my head that night in Brookline, and we owe it to her that things ended up as well as they did.

She was riding her bicycle along the Esplanade late one afternoon, delivering something for the *Globe*. The Esplanade was not her safest route—residual barbarians (there will always be some) liked to lurk in the bushes that lined the bicycle path. But the path was straight and smooth, the view of the Charles was beautiful, and she knew how to take care of herself, so she thought it was okay to risk it.

In fact she was right, because the attack, when it came, was not all that dangerous. A wild man jumped out of the bushes, brandishing a knife. He lunged, she swerved, he missed, she accelerated. End of attack; another day in the life.

When Gwen had put a little distance between herself and the attacker, she stopped and turned around. He was still coming toward her, still waving the knife. She could have shot him, I suppose, but, like me, she wasn't the shooting kind. Instead she just watched, and he saw her watching, and then he stopped, too, and then he fell in a heap to the ground.

This is where the story gets strange. Instead of pedaling off, satisfied that he wouldn't bother her, Gwen headed back to the fallen mugger. He was unconscious. She took the knife out of his unresisting hand and tossed it into the Charles. She checked his breathing: still alive. She raced home and brought us to where he was and made us bring him back.

Why? Gwen never gave a satisfactory answer. She acknowledged that it was stupid, the mugger could have been feigning his collapse, there could have been other muggers waiting to grab her. But still she did it. There was something in his eyes, she said, when we pressed her about it. But, damn it, I don't think she could have even seen his eyes in the fading afternoon light on the Esplanade. Best not to waste too much time thinking about such matters, I suppose. She did it, and that's that.

Linc was in bad shape: feverish, malnourished, delirious. Was he worth the effort of trying to save? Everyone I know has been forced to make that sort of decision; this one seemed easier than most. Stretch and I tried to persuade Gwen to get rid of him. But Gwen refused: something in his eyes. She cared for him; he got better; he stayed.

Linc was older than the rest of us: he remembered Saturday morning cartoons, riding in a shopping cart through the supermarket, the smell of chocolate chip cookies fresh from the oven. He was always vague about what happened to him afterward. Sometimes he claimed amnesia, but no one took his claim very seriously. If he didn't want to remember, or didn't want to talk about what he remembered, that was understandable; that was all right with us. What mattered was the present. And in the present, he was no longer a barbarian. He worked hard, when he had the strength, he was devoted to Gwen, and his sharp tongue made life more interesting without making it nasty. We were glad to have him.

And that's our family. Others have drifted in for a week, a month, a season, before drifting on to other families, other lives; but we have stayed together.

I drifted away, of course, when duty called and it was time to serve my country. But I came back. I came back, to tears and hugs, and the silent satisfaction of Gwen lying contentedly in my arms once more.

I came back, and that's why I was finding it difficult to go home from Bobby's.

Eventually I got tired of wandering, though. It was dark and cold and I was hungry. Time to quit stalling; there were things to be done. I turned my steps toward Louisburg Square.

Stretch, damn him, had picked that night to put up Christmas decorations. He was strewing pine boughs when I entered. Linc was on the couch in the parlor, stringing popcorn and cranberries; in the corner, a large tree leaned in its stand. Gwen was playing "Silent Night" on the piano. She stopped when she saw me.

"Ho ho ho," I said. "Have all you kiddies been good this year?"

"Yes, Santa," Linc said. "Will you please put some coal in my stocking for Christmas?"

"No, I'm sorry, little boy, according to my list you've been very naughty—you haven't been finishing the wonderful food people cook for you. You're getting an electric train instead of coal." I kissed Gwen on the forehead. "Sorry I'm late."

She smiled. "How did everything go today?"

"Terrific."

"What happened with the information Bobby was supposed to get for you?" Stretch asked.

"He got it," I said. I went into the kitchen. Stew. I slopped some into a bowl and returned to the parlor.

"Well, what happened?" Linc demanded.

I ate a mouthful of stew. "There is a list of scientists who went to England," I said. "The name my client was looking for is on the list."

"That's great. So your client is gonna go over there and track him down?"

I nodded. I ate another mouthful. The time had come. "It looks like I'm gonna go with him," I said.

Silence. "How?" Stretch asked finally.

"My client has sources of wealth I'm not at liberty to reveal."

"Why is he taking you?" Linc asked.

I shrugged. "I guess he likes my work."

"Gee, that's terrific," Stretch said. "England. Imagine that. The stories you'll be able to tell us." He paused and stared at me, suddenly unsure of himself. "Walter, you're coming back, right?"

I looked into Stretch's guileless eyes, and I realized I could no more tell him the truth than I could keep myself from going to England. "I'm a private eye, Stretch," I said, "and this is my case. When this case is over, I come back and get another case. That's the way the job works." I looked down at my stew and spooned some down my throat. I had never been more interested in stew.

Gwen stood up. "Congratulations, Walter. This is very exciting. I wonder if you'd excuse me, though? I'm not feeling well, and I think I'd like to go up to bed."

"Oh, sure, sure. I'll be up—"

"Take your time, Walter. Good night all."

She left the room. No one said anything. I stared at my stew. "Finish it," Linc said finally. "It's good for you."

I set the bowl down. "So who wants to help me straighten this Christmas tree?" I asked.

We decorated for a while, but the mood wasn't right without Gwen, and eventually Stretch drifted off to bed too. That left Linc and me in the chilly parlor. He set the string of cranberries and popcorn down and leaned back on the couch, pulling his blanket around his shoulders. "Waste of food," he muttered. "I don't know how Stretch talks me into it every year."

"Beneath that crusty exterior, Linc—"

"Get fucked." He thought for a moment, and then smiled. "England, huh?"

I nodded. "England."

"Congratulations." He thought for another moment. "So which is it, Walter: are you a liar, or a fool?"

I should have known it would come. "Um, perhaps you could be a tad more specific."

"Oh, that's not necessary, is it? You don't have to answer, Walter. But listen: I hope you're a liar and not a fool. I hope you're not thinking: I'll come back, be with my friends, help Stretch rebuild the country."

"Why?" I managed to ask.

He lifted himself up on an elbow and stared at me. His eyes were on fire. "Walter, maybe you don't even know yourself which you are. You try to act so sure of yourself, but you're not, you're improvising, like all of us. Walter, listen to me. You've only got one life. Don't waste it if you don't have to. Mine's been wasted, but I like to think it was due to circumstances beyond my control. I know I'm dying, but you're dying, too, everyone is dying. All that matters is what you do before you take that last breath. You've got some control now. Don't screw it up. Get out of here and do something exciting, do something important. Enjoy yourself. Live well. Understand, Walter?"

He fell back, exhausted. His pale skin was beaded with sweat, despite the chill of the room. His eyes still stared at me, but the fire was gone.

After a while, you can almost smell the approach of death—the cells one by one giving up the battle, surrendering to chaos and nullity. You never quite get used to it.

"Okay, Linc," I murmured. "Can I help you up to bed?"

He flopped a hand in assent. I went over and lifted him from the couch. He put his arm around my shoulders and we walked slowly upstairs together. He let go when we reached the door to his bedroom. "Get out," he whispered, and then he disappeared into the darkness.

Gwen was still awake. I got into bed next to her, and she wordlessly moved into the crook of my shoulder. We lay like that for a long time, both awake, both silent.

"What are you thinking?" I asked after a while. I never asked her that.

Gwen shifted in my arms. "I'm thinking: maybe in England you'll be able to sleep."

"Fat chance."

She kissed my cheek. "Someday sleep will come easy," she murmured.

She waited.

"And dreams will come true," I managed to say.

"Someday."

She turned over then, and soon she was snoring softly.

CHAPTER 15

A nd then the dream started marching resolutely toward reality.

Bobby's business partner arrived promptly the next day, accompanied by two thugs and a third, somewhat less thuglike individual. I recognized the thugs. One had a yellowing bruise on his chin from where I had clubbed him; the other's face was covered with cuts from the windshield I had shot out. They didn't look happy to see me.

"Mr. O'Malley, meet Dr. Winfield and Mr. Sands," Bobby said.

O'Malley was tall and sandy-haired and missing a couple of teeth. He was wearing a cashmere topcoat, starched white shirt, and a silk tie. I thought he looked a bit silly, but Winfield seemed impressed. O'Malley glared at me. "Get rid of the punk," he growled.

Bobby nodded to me. "Mr. Sands, would you and Mr. O'Malley's associates like to step outside?"

"Wait a minute," O'Malley said. "This one here stays." He grabbed the arm of the less thuglike one. "He's a chemist. Gonna test the stuff. Think I'm stupid, Gallagher?"

Bobby smiled. "What a great idea. I wish I'd thought of it. Of course he stays."

"Wait a minute", Winfield protested in turn. "Sands is my bodyguard. I need some protection here."

"Mr. Sands will be right outside the door," Bobby said. "And believe me, he can handle everyone in this room. He's the toughest private eye in the city."

Winfield didn't look happy, but he let me go. Bobby shut the door behind me and the thugs.

The two of them kept their hands in their pockets, fingering their guns. I smiled at them. "Terrible weather we've been having lately, don't you agree?"

They fingered their guns.

I tried again. "People say it's worse now than in the old days. What do you think?"

Maybe they didn't think—or couldn't think. I sat down at the top of the stairs and kept quiet. They watched me warily, and didn't take their hands out of their pockets.

It wasn't long before the door opened and O'Malley came out, accompanied by his chemist. O'Malley was carrying a brown paper bag; I could discern the outline of a peanut butter jar inside. "Let's go," he said to the thugs. He headed for the top of the stairs. "Outa my way, punk," he barked at me.

I smiled and got up. "Merry Christmas," I called out as they clomped past me down the stairs. I was sure Brutus would lick their hands.

Bobby was standing in the doorway to his office. I shook my head at him. "First the tax people, now O'Malley. How much lower are you gonna sink, Gallagher?"

He grinned. "Business is business, Wally."

I followed him back inside. Winfield was sitting beneath the crucifix, counting his money. He glanced up at me when he had finished, and he looked almost happy. "What's next?" he asked.

Stretch had been reluctant to help when I brought it up at supper. "There are procedures to be followed," he explained. "You can't just march in there and throw money around."

"Yes you can, Stretch," I said. "Trust me about this. We just need an introduction."

"Well, I don't know—"

"Stretch, can you do it?" Gwen demanded.

"Well, I suppose. But—"

"Then do it."

Gwen almost never gave orders. When she did, no one disobeyed her.

Next day, Stretch had a word with the people in the Passport Office while Winfield and I waited in the lobby. He came out after a few minutes, his faith in government a little shaken. "They'll do it," he said through clenched teeth. "Ten new dollars for each of you. The only thing you have to do is sign a form saying you're coming back. They don't fool around with that requirement."

"Oh, well, we'll sign any forms they give us," Winfield said cheerfully. "Won't we, Sands?"

"Have you got the money?" I asked.

He had the money.

Mickey drove us out to get the tickets. "Place used to be crowded," he remarked as we traveled along the deserted road to the airport.

"How did they stand it—traffic jams and all that?" I wondered.

Mickey shrugged. "Guess you get used to it."

"I guess."

No one was at the ticket counter when Winfield and I arrived. I had a brief, awful feeling that I had it all wrong—that the flights to England were just one of those crazy rumors you half believe because it makes life a little more interesting. Somewhere in Colorado there's a race of mutant super-geniuses who are plotting to take over the world. Aliens saw our little smoke signals twenty-two years ago and have landed in Washington. The government is going to reintroduce professional baseball in the spring. Things like that.

Well, I just had to hope my feeling was mistaken. "Hullo," I called out.

There was a shuffling sound in the back room behind the counter, and a gray-haired woman poked her head out. "Yes?" she demanded.

"Two tickets for England, please," I said. "Next flight."

The woman came out, ostentatiously aiming a snub-nosed revolver at us. She was wearing a threadbare red blazer with little wings on the breast pocket. There was a long scar on the side of her neck that a white kerchief didn't quite cover. She had an exophthalmic stare that made her look perpetually surprised and slightly crazy.

"England," she said noncommittally. She didn't put the gun down.

"We understand there's a flight leaving on Thursday."

"Thursday?" She seemed to consider this surprising piece of information. Then an idea came to her. "Passports. Can't go anywhere without passports."

We showed her our passports. She seemed vaguely disappointed. She put the gun down and started shuffling through papers. Finally she seemed to find what she was looking for. "Ah," she said. "Thursday. Booked solid. Sorry." She picked up the gun and turned to leave.

"Excuse me," I said. I nudged Winfield. He put a five-dollar bill on the counter.

The woman turned back. She stared at the bill in astonishment. "Thursday," she repeated. Her vocabulary seemed rather limited. She shuffled some more. "Smoking or nonsmoking?" she inquired.

"Jesus Christ," Winfield exploded. "Why don't you just give us the fucking tickets? I can pay for the damn things, if that's what you're worried about."

The woman simply blinked at Winfield.

"Nonsmoking," I said.

She glanced down at a paper. "Ah," she exclaimed. "I have two cancellations in nonsmoking."

"We'll take them," I said.

She immediately grabbed the five-dollar bill and started filling out the tickets. It took a while; they seemed to be very complicated tickets. Finally, Winfield handed her enormous amounts of money, and she handed him the tickets, and the transaction was complete.

"Thanks a lot," I said.

She smiled a toothless smile. "Have a nice flight," she replied. Then she picked up her revolver and disappeared.

Good-byes.

Art was selling a nervous teenage boy a yellowed copy of *Alien Sex Vampires* ("Blood Wasn't All They Sucked!"). "Excellent choice," Art murmured. The boy hurried out, and I told Art my news.

"England!" he said, and he embraced me. "You'll stay there permanently, of course?"

"Well, I don't know."

He chuckled, and then his eyes brightened. "You know what you should do?" he said. "Write a novel. About us— the people back in Boston. Not right away, of course, but someday. Powerful emotions recollected in tranquility. I'm sure they still publish novels over there."

"Oh, I don't think I can—"

"Of course you can. You've read enough of them. Wouldn't that be something? To be a character in a novel. Do it, Walter. For us. Make us immortal."

Little enough to ask, I suppose. "Okay, Art," I said. "Immortality. You got it."

He cackled. "Thanks, Walter. England! Now be sure to send me a postcard from Stratford-on-Avon and—and Wimpole Street."

I grinned. "Sure thing, Art. Immortality and postcards." We embraced again, and I left his shop.

"And Dover Beach!" he called out after me as I walked through the slush on School Street.

* * *

Cindy Tappen was sitting in the cafeteria at Northeastern. I told her.

She was suitably impressed. "You're a private eye? And you're going to England? Walter, that's so—so sexy."

I shrugged my most casual, sophisticated shrug. "It's a job."

She leaned closer, put her hand on my thigh. "When you come back, Walter, why don't we get together, have a shot at making that baby you were talking about the other day—okay?" Then, like Stretch, she thought it through. "But wait a minute. *Are* you coming back, Walter?"

"If I wasn't before, I sure am now," I said. I squeezed her hand.

Cindy grinned. "I can hardly wait."

On the way out, I saw Professor Hemphill slouching along one of the cinderblock corridors. I hadn't planned on saying good-bye to him, but fate had thrown him in my way. "Professor," I called out.

As before, he didn't look pleased to see me. "Yes?"

"I just thought I'd tell you," I said. "You seemed so certain that Robert Cornwall was dead. But I found some evidence that he did in fact go to England."

He blushed. "Are you saying I'm a liar?"

Touchy fellow. "Not at all. I'm just telling you what I found out." I told him about the letter.

He seemed unimpressed. "Have you considered that your evidence might be fabricated?"

Well, no, I hadn't. "Why would anyone fabricate evidence?"

"I don't know. Why would I lie?"

I shrugged. "I don't know." It looked like I wasn't going to get anywhere with him. "Well, listen, we're going over there to find him, and if we do I'll let you know what really happened, okay?"

That seemed to give him pause. "You're going to England?"

"Right. Me and my client—the one who thinks he's Cornwall's clone."

"Your letter doesn't say if Cornwall is still alive, does it?"

I shook my head. "It just says he went there. Maybe he's dead. Maybe he's hanging around, waiting for visitors."

Hemphill looked puzzled. And then he got that misty, faraway look I had seen before. Too many memories, I figured. A friend he thought was dead might still be alive. Maybe he didn't have that many friends still alive. Eventually he shook it off and came back to the present. "Well, this is certainly interesting news," he said, in a tone of dismissal. "Please let me know what you find out."

"I'll be happy to."

And I left him there, an old man in a dreary hallway, struggling to escape from the past.

Stretch was full of practicalities. "You should put up a sign in your office window saying you're coming back."

"Fat lot of good a sign did *you*."

"Well, we can check the place for you," I reminded him.

"All right. I'll put up a sign."

"How much money are you going to take?"

"Oh, I don't know." I had been planning to take every cent I had, but suddenly that didn't seem like a good idea. "I guess I'll let my client take care of me. I'll be back soon enough. You can look after my money."

"Well, all right. The exchange rate makes it practically worthless over there, anyway. Now, what about clothing?"

"Stretch," Gwen said. "He's a big boy now."

"Bigger than Stretch, anyway," Linc said.

I stared at my stew.

"I'm going away, Ground Zero. Know any good-bye songs?"

The old man's hands moved over the accordion keys. "Good-bye thongth," he mused, and then it came to him. "Beatleth. *Magical Mythtery Tour.*" He played a couple of chords, and then started to sing.

You thay good-bye, and I thay hello, hello, hello.

I don't know why you thay good-bye I thay hello.

(Hello good-bye hello good-bye.)

I don't know why you thay good-bye I thay hello.

This was not the most meaningful Beatles' song I had ever heard. I tossed a penny into his hat. "Thanks, Ground Zero."

"Good-bye," he said.

"Hello," I said.

The last night. A last supper to remember: ham, boiled potatoes, cornbread, beans…it was embarrassing. Bobby came for the last dessert—walking over from South Boston with Doctor J, since Mickey was fixing up the van for the drive to the airport in the morning. He arrived, red-cheeked and runny-nosed from the cold, carrying a bottle of Scotch. "See if you can find some more of these over there, will you, Wally?" he said as he opened the bottle. "I'm running low."

"I'll keep an eye out."

Linc and Stretch joined Bobby in drinking the Scotch. Everyone ate Gwen's apple pie. Linc made a toast. "To the Sandman. May his fame spread to every jealous husband and worried parent and good-looking blonde in distress. May his fees be exorbitant and his risks trifling. May he live life to the fullest and die in bed."

"To the Sandman," everyone cried.

I stared at my pie. No one said being a private eye was easy.

When the apple pie was gone, we moved to the parlor. Gwen sat on the piano bench; I sat next to the Christmas tree (still not quite straight); and Bobby, Linc, and Stretch plunked themselves down on the couch with the bottle of Scotch. The Scotch made them rather maudlin, and they started reminiscing about all the good times they had had in their lives. Strange, the pockets of happiness and humor they could find to talk about. I suppose even the inhabitants of hell have their little memories of the place to cherish.

They noticed after a while that I wasn't talking. "Wassa matter, Walter?" Stretch demanded. He wasn't used to Scotch. "Dincha ever njoy yourself here?"

"Come on, Wally," Bobby said. "What's your favorite memory?"

I didn't like this game. I thought for a moment. "I suppose," I said, "that it was the first time I ate pineapple slices."

"God, tha's the dullest thing I ever heard," Stretch mumbled.

Linc laughed. Bobby shook his head.

"Why don't we sing carols?" Gwen suggested. She turned around on the piano bench and started playing "God Rest Ye Merry, Gentlemen." That seemed to put an end to the memories. After a few carols Linc went to bed and Stretch passed out. Bobby finished off the Scotch, then Doctor J led him, drunk and dim-sighted, out into the night. The party was over.

Gwen and I carried Stretch upstairs; he wasn't much to carry. We tucked him in, then went into our room and silently got into bed ourselves.

"We've been through a lot together, haven't we, Gwen?" I whispered into the darkness.

"A lot."

"Saying good-bye isn't easy."

"Then don't say it, Walter. You'll be back."

I teetered on the brink of confession, and then retreated, a coward at heart. "It doesn't seem fair that I get to go and you don't."

Gwen allowed herself a sigh. "Whoever said life was fair?" she asked. "You're doing what you have to do. Don't feel guilty, Walter. Life's too short. Whatever you do, don't feel guilty."

Fat chance. But when Gwen gave an order, you had to obey. "Okay," I said.

"Now, tell me, where are you going to visit while you're over there?"

"Oh, I haven't really thought about it. Art gave me a list of literary sights: Stratford-on-Avon, Dover Beach…."

Gwen considered. "Dover Beach. Isn't that where ignorant armies clash by night?"

"Well, um, sort of."

"Well, you should think about all the wonderful places you're going to see, and don't worry about good-byes. Okay?"

"Okay."

We kissed, and she turned away. Before long she was asleep—or maybe just pretending to be asleep. Then I realized that we hadn't gone through our nightly ritual— that we would never go through it again. And that was almost enough to make me forget all about my dream. "Gwen?" I whispered.

No reply. I wanted to shake her, to make her wake up and say the words we had said to each other for so long. But I didn't. If Gwen had wanted to say them, she would have said them. Gwen knew what she was doing; Gwen knew everything. I hugged her from behind, feeling her thin body beneath the flannel nightgown, smelling the soapy cleanness of her skin, remembering. *Ah, love, let us be...* It was too much. I got out of bed.

Too restless to read, I walked downstairs, found my coat, and went out into the night. It was cold and clear. I crunched over to the statue of Columbus. "I guess I should say good-bye to you too," I said. "You understand, right? 'There lies the port; the vessel puffs her sail; / There gloom the dark, broad seas.' Another one of those English poets. The guy wasn't talking about you, but the point is clear, right? 'Tis not too late to seek a newer world,' right? You know it, everyone knows it."

If the statue knew, it wasn't saying. I stood staring at it for a while, hands jammed into my pockets, waiting for inspiration. Then I felt a crumpled piece of paper, waiting to inspire. I took it out and read it by starlight.

The End Is At Hand

Swell. I closed my eyes and fought off the memories while I whirled through space in the midst of those silent stars. Was it the whirling or the memories that made me dizzy, that made me clutch at Columbus to keep from falling into the snow?

Hard to say. After a while I returned the paper to my pocket and walked back home. I sat next to the Christmas tree and stared out the window until it was light, and Mickey arrived in the van to drive Winfield and me to the airport.

CHAPTER 16

H ello good-bye hello good-bye.
We were in the air. We were flying. It was real.

I was terrified; I was ecstatic; I was numb. I had lived so long amid technology's detritus that it was astonishing to be able to sit back and let technology help me, let it set me free. I was certain it would let me down—we would crash into the Atlantic, we would explode in midair, we would sputter to a stop and have to turn back. But none of these things happened. The engines hummed peaceably; the clouds rushed past us, heading dopily in the wrong direction; the flight could not have been more normal. I was the one who wasn't normal.

Winfield was hung over and didn't say much. That was all right with me. There were about a dozen other passengers. They all looked vaguely official, and they all seemed to know each other. They ignored us, except for a suspicious glance or two, so I had little to do but dream and fret until, after endless hours, the plane landed, and we were in England.

England. *This fortress built by Nature for herself/Against infection and the hand of war.* "It doesn't seem possible," I murmured.

Winfield shrugged. "Boston was what didn't seem possible."

I walked groggily across the tarmac and into the terminal, trying not to gawk. It was twilight. There were electric lights everywhere. Music was playing. We got on an escalator that worked and found our baggage whirling around on a conveyor belt. Then we went to Customs.

It took a while. The agent was extremely interested in us. He studied our passports, counted up Winfield's cash to make sure we wouldn't be a burden on society, and asked us the purpose of our visit.

"I'm looking for my father," Winfield said, and he gave a vague summary of his story.

The agent nodded sympathetically. That was as good a reason for coming to England as any. "Have to search your bags, however, I'm afraid."

Nothing to be done. He found the Smith and Wesson in my underwear. He took it away. "Not in England, sir," he said.

I had a feeling that a bribe was not in order. Everything was all right, though, because finally he let us pass, and we had arrived—officially, legally, undeniably. Winfield changed his new dollars for pounds at a booth in the terminal, and then we walked outside; the terminal doors graciously slid open for us when we reached them. "Isn't it amazing?" I said.

"I need a drink," Winfield said.

We took the Tube from Heathrow. The train was clean and fast and not very crowded—a far cry from what Gwen was used to in Boston, where one old car made the trip through the subway, a solitary piece left on the underground gameboard, and you prayed it wouldn't break down before it reached your stop.

There were advertisements above the windows—glossy colored photos of beautiful people smoking cigarettes and drinking beer. I stared at the ads hungrily, but Winfield didn't seem to notice them. Maybe, I thought, he was comparing himself to Cornwall, who had probably arrived in style at Heathrow with the other scientists and been treated as an honored guest while the government figured out how to use his talents. And here Winfield was— accustomed to being king of the hill, with prestige and money and shiny new shoes—now an anonymous traveler with nowhere to stay and little to spend. The money that rented him a suite at the Ritz back home would scarcely buy him a good dinner in London. Maybe he was finally realizing what he had gotten himself in for by coming here.

Or maybe he was still hung over.

"Where should we get off?" he wondered after a while.

I studied the transit map across from us. "How about Piccadilly Circus?" I said, for want of a better suggestion.

Winfield shrugged. "All right."

When the train reached our stop, we had a tough job just getting out of the station. But finally we found the right escalator and the right stairway and the right door, and we made our way out into the London night.

We stood for a moment while our senses adjusted to the neon and the traffic and the noise and the sheer number of people bustling past. So many people. I had a vision of them all living their lives at the same time I was living mine—getting drunk and going to work and falling in love and making babies—and the vision made me realize how small my world had been. To live in that world was to live half-blind, like Bobby groping through the night. Now my eyes were being opened, and it was scary, because in my world all that had mattered was staying alive. Here other things could matter. Here I could matter.

In the center of the Circus was a statue. Eros, I remembered from Art's guidebook. Teenagers were standing and sitting all around it, not doing much of anything, apparently content just to be in the middle of the excitement. I felt the same way.

"I'm freezing," Winfield said. "Let's go."

I reluctantly followed. We tramped around for a long time, looking for a place where we could afford to stay. It quickly became clear that hotel prices were out of our league. "We could look for a rooming house or something," I suggested.

"We'll find a place," Winfield insisted. I think his pride would have been destroyed if he couldn't stay in a hotel.

As we searched, and my senses became adjusted, I began to notice that England, too, was not what it once was. I knew that intellectually, of course: no place had totally escaped the consequences of the war. But now I could see it for myself. There were lots of cars by American standards, for example, but they were mostly ancient, and the few new ones were tiny three-wheelers that looked like tricycles for adults. There was neon, but there wasn't the explosion of it that you saw in old photographs. And Piccadilly had its share of boarded-up stores and broken windows. Still, I wasn't disappointed: the place was wounded, but alive. Definitely alive.

Near Russell Square we finally found a dingy hotel that Winfield could, barely, afford. The night clerk was an Indian who looked at us over half-spectacles and seemed faintly amused by what he saw. "We do not get many Americans anymore," he said.

"I'm not surprised," Winfield growled. He had to pay two nights in advance. There were no porters to be seen, and no elevator, so we lugged our bags up the dimly lit stairs to the second floor.

Our room was full of stains: water stains on the walls and ceiling, grease stains on the purple scatter rug, stains I didn't want to think about on the faded bedspreads. Louisburg Square it wasn't.

But it was warm, and the electric lights worked, and so did the radio, and the faucets in the bathroom gave you as much hot water as you wanted. I have lived in far worse places.

Winfield threw down his bags and washed his face. "Let's go get a drink," he said.

I was more interested in taking a bath, but he was paying for everything, so I felt obliged to tag along. When we reached the lobby, the Indian clerk looked up at us and smiled. "Are the accommodations satisfactory?" he asked in his staccato accent. I felt a little out of my depth. Was he making fun of us?

"They'll do," Winfield said. "Where's the nearest pub?"

The clerk gave us directions. We followed them, and found ourselves in a dark, warm, womblike place that was empty except for a stout barmaid and a couple of old men at the bar who looked like they were part of the furniture. There was a fake blue Christmas tree by the door, frosted with plastic snow and dotted with red lights that blinked on and off. Winfield advanced purposefully to the bar.

"What can I get you gentlemen?" the barmaid asked. She was fiftyish, with dyed blond hair and naturally rosy cheeks.

"Whiskey," Winfield said. "A double. On the rocks."

"Ooh, an American," she gushed. "Don't get many Americans anymore. And you, sir?"

The old men had stopped muttering at each other and were staring at us out of the corners of their eyes. Life had suddenly gotten interesting for them. "Uh, do you have any apple juice?" I inquired.

The barmaid looked puzzled for a moment, as if trying to decipher my accent. Then she seemed to decide she had heard correctly. "Oh, we wouldn't have none of that, sir."

I thought hard, and came up with a magic word from the old days. "How about a Coke, then?"

She nodded vigorously, like a mother pleased with the progress of her dim-witted son. "Very good, sir." She poured the drinks, Winfield paid her, and we took them to a table.

Winfield downed half of his in a swallow; he closed his eyes and looked much happier. I took a sip of mine and almost choked on the bubbles. Carbonation—another new experience. I can't say I liked it. I started hiccuping.

Winfield glared at me. "Hold your breath," he said.

I held it.

After a while he got bored watching me turn the color of the Christmas tree. He swallowed some more of his drink. "Now, what's our plan?" he asked.

I exhaled. Plan? "What plan?"

He glared some more. "Why are we here, idiot? Our plan to find Cornwall."

"Ah." My case. I had a job to do. It had sort of slipped my mind. I thought for a moment, then got up and went over to the barmaid. "Excuse me," I said. "Would you know where I could find some sort of directory that lists people's telephone numbers?"

"What, let her love?" the barmaid asked.

I didn't quite get that. I hiccuped. "Excuse me?"

"What letter, luv?"

"Oh. Um, C."

She rummaged around behind the bar and finally pulled out a large volume. "Here you go."

I took it. "Now, is this for all of England or—"

"Lord, it's just London, you know, and the front part of the alphabet at that. They've got other ones for different places. Don't they have 'em in America now?"

"Not in my part of America, anyway."

"How do you get along without 'em?"

"You get used to it. *Hic.*" I took the directory back to the table and opened it. "Well, there are more than a dozen Cornwalls here," I said, "but no Robert Cornwall. Maybe he doesn't have a phone, or maybe he doesn't live in London—or maybe he's dead. I suppose we could call up these people here and see if they've heard of him."

"Are you crazy?" Winfield said.

"Why? What's the problem?"

"In case you've forgotten, Sands, someone tried to kill me because I'm looking for Cornwall. Now maybe that person knows I'm here and maybe not, but I don't want to start calling around and letting the world find out I've arrived. Besides, do you really think the government would let his name be listed in the goddamn phone book?"

"I don't know. Depends on whether your hypothesis is correct."

"Let's assume that it is, shall we? Now, why can't we snoop around that Ministry of Science where the letter was from and see if we can find out something there?"

It was clear our partnership was not going to be a smooth one. "I'm a private eye, not James Bond," I said. "Breaking into a government office and trying to steal some secret file or whatever that we don't know even exists is a sure way to get us both thrown in jail. Look, maybe the first thing to do is go to the library and do some research. We might find an obituary right off the bat—or maybe someone has done an exposé of secret government projects, and Cornwall is mentioned. His name must have cropped up somewhere in the past twenty-two years. It's dull work, but no one will shoot us or arrest us."

Winfield swallowed the rest of his drink, "You found a secret file in Boston," he pointed out.

"I had friends in Boston. The only person I know here is you."

He didn't seem happy, but he also didn't seem inclined to argue with me. "Who's James Bond?" he asked finally.

I hiccuped.

Winfield had another drink while I held my breath. When we finally left, the old men looked sorry to see us go. The barmaid wished us a happy Christmas.

We returned to the hotel, and I got to take my bath. It wasn't a Jacuzzi, but it felt wonderful. It even cured my hiccups. When I went back into the bedroom, Winfield was asleep. I felt so relaxed that I thought I might be able to sleep, too. No luck. I lay in bed, listening to the sounds of the traffic—traffic!—and Winfield's snores, and I realized that the new world hadn't changed my old habits.

Gwen had thought it might. Ah, well. What were they doing in Boston? Thinking of me, probably—maybe wondering if I was thinking of them. I tried to figure out the time difference. It was after supper there. They would be in the parlor together—reading, knitting, maybe playing cards. Living their lives as I was living mine.

When, after endless hours, dawn came and I finally dozed off, I dreamed of them—dreamed that they were in England with me, and we were all climbing that statue in Piccadilly. First one to the top gets a glass of Coke! But none of us could quite make it: Stretch was too short, Linc too sick, Bobby too blind, Gwen too tired. And me? What was wrong with me? I was afraid, I think—afraid of the height, afraid of the hiccups. The prize remained out of my grasp, and finally I slid down the cold metal body of the deity and joined my friends on the ground. "It's all right," they said to me, and they held me tight in the middle of the traffic and the neon lights.

But then I awoke, and there was just Winfield and bright sunlight and the squealing brakes of buses. My friends were thousands of miles away, and I had a job to do.

CHAPTER 17

No friends now, just me and my brain. And Winfield, of course. Time to forget all the distractions and show him, and myself, what I was capable of.

I figured we should start at the top, so we went to the British Museum, which was near our hotel. It was hard not to be distracted there. I wasn't used to museums that weren't ruins; I wasn't used to a past that was preserved for its own sake, not salvaged to buy today's supper. I was tempted to wander off and see some of what had been preserved, but managed to resist. We found our way to the Reading Room. The people there immediately pointed us off to their newspaper division, in northwest London. We hiked to King's Cross and took the Tube.

The librarians at Colindale were intrigued by our story of the search for a long-lost father, so they gave us passes and explained how to do the research. "We don't get many Americans anymore," they remarked. The refrain was starting to bore me. Finally, we sat down at our computer terminals and set to work.

More distractions. I read through old periodicals, searching for references to Cornwall. But my gaze kept slipping away to articles about the things I had lived through. Was this how it had really been? Was this what it had really meant?

Such useless distractions—not simply because they weren't part of my job. Private eye or not, I didn't need to know what it had really meant. It was enough that it had happened; everything else was trivial and pointless.

I tried to concentrate on Cornwall, but I couldn't find any mention of him. I came across references to other scientists in Mr. J. T. Carstairs's list, but Cornwall remained elusive. Winfield's luck was no better. By the time the Reading Room closed I was hungry and my head ached and we had made no progress.

Winfield was not happy. We sat in a tea shop and had sandwiches while he fumed. "This is a waste of time," he said. "We've got to come up with a different approach."

"But we haven't exhausted the possibilities of this one yet," I pointed out.

"It's boring. He's here—somewhere in this country—and we're just sitting around reading old newspapers."

"Well, what do you suggest, then?"

He bit into his sandwich and didn't reply. When he had finished eating, he threw his money on the table and stomped out.

I followed, faithful retainer that I was. I wasn't particularly happy about the current arrangement, however. The trouble was, he had all the money, and that meant there wasn't much I could do except hang around with him. The prospect of spending the evening with Winfield in some pub was pretty depressing. I may have done stupider things than leaving all my money behind in Boston to convince people I was coming back, but at the moment I couldn't think of one.

"Listen," I said as we took the Tube back to the hotel. "This is crazy, me having to tag along with you everywhere. Why don't you give me a per diem, and that way I can get my own meals and stuff and not bother you?"

Winfield stared at me.

"Most private eyes get a per diem, you know," I said, a little desperately. "I'm not asking for pay, just meal money."

He considered, then took out his wallet and handed me a five-pound note. "That's for everything until tomorrow night," he said. "I don't care if you spend the night at the hotel or not, but you better be ready to get back to work tomorrow, or I'll find you the same way I'm going to find Cornwall."

I pocketed the money. It was a fortune in America, almost a joke here. "Don't worry," I said. "I'm not going far on this."

We stared at each other for a moment, then Winfield turned away. He got off at Leicester Square, looking for a pub. I got off at Charing Cross, looking for bookstores. Art's guide was right again. When I came up from the station, I was in the midst of more bookstores than I had ever seen in my life. I went into the nearest one.

It had new books. I opened one reverently, feeling the spine crack a little, smelling the fresh inky smell. Art would have been in heaven here. *Think of all those writers,* I could hear him say, *even as we speak, staring at their blank sheets of paper, imagining the words we will one day read.* I smiled.

I had to buy a new book. I couldn't afford a hardcover, so I studied the paperbacks. There were no private-eye stories, but I found a mystery complete with an inspector from Scotland Yard and a corpse in the vicarage. I bought it and a postcard. Then I stood by the door and wrote a cheery message to America.

Dear All,

Arrived safely in the Promised Land. Drank Coke, took a hot bath, bought a book. Haven't cracked the case yet, but making progress. I'll keep you posted. Miss everyone already.

Walter

P.S. We're at the Guilford Hotel, Russell Square, if you want to write.

I stuck the card into my pocket until I could find a stamp, and I walked out into the London night.

I wandered through the city. Wandering didn't cost any money, and was excellent entertainment—better, certainly, than sitting in some pub watching Winfield get drunk. I wandered down to Trafalgar Square, over to the Thames, along the Strand, through Covent Garden, feeling as though a lifetime of reading was finally coming alive for me, and a lifetime of desire was finally being satisfied. This was it. I had done it.

I stood outside a movie theater for a long time, fingering my remaining money. It had been a mistake buying the book, I thought. I had read books before; I had never been to a movie.

But then I remembered that, with a little luck, I was here to stay. There would be other days, there would be more money. Eventually I would do everything I wanted.

My hand moved from the money to the postcard. *Miss everyone already.* I turned away from the theater. Maybe it was time to take another bath. I returned to the hotel.

The desk clerk had stamps. I bought one and mailed the postcard, then went upstairs to our room. Winfield hadn't returned. I read my book while I bathed.

It wasn't a very good book. Were people not writing as well as in the old days? Maybe. Or maybe the problem was that the author was trying to make believe it was still the old days, and hadn't got it quite right. People had accused me of not getting the old days quite right, too, I realized. But there was a difference. Wasn't there?

The book was almost finished, and I was extremely wrinkled, by the time Winfield staggered into the room. I got out of the tub and dried myself. Winfield was spread out on his bed when I came out of the bathroom, towel wrapped around my skinny frame. He looked at me, and apparently didn't like what he saw.

"This world sucks," he said, by way of opening the conversation. "Sands, do you realize how sick we are? Leukemia, melanoma, liver cancer, typhus, genetic defects, cataracts. Chrissake, even the healthy people are a mess by the old standards."

"I'm sorry to hear that," I said. I put on a pair of underpants and sat down.

Winfield pushed himself up on his bed. "Sands, can you imagine how—how *frustrating* it is to be a genius in times like these?"

"It must be torture for you," I murmured sympathetically. He glanced at me, searching for sarcasm, and then evidently decided any sarcasm from me wasn't worth worrying about. He suddenly smiled. "But you know what makes it better? Knowing that I have a clone. Maybe his life, here, is better than mine."

"But Cornwall isn't you," I pointed out, "even if he is your clone. He didn't grow up in postwar Florida, and you didn't teach at MIT."

Winfield waved his hand, dismissing his life. "Trivial. All that matters is those strands of DNA, spiraling around and around, spinning out our destiny. And that DNA is the same for Cornwall and me. When we find him, you'll see. There'll be a meeting of the minds, Sands, so intense, so complete, that it will leave you awestruck."

"I can hardly wait," I said.

Winfield shut his eyes. "Tomorrow, Sands. Tomorrow we make progress."

"Yes, boss."

His head slumped to one side. The genius had passed out. I went back into the bathroom for my book and read on until I found out who done it.

Progress finally arrived late the next afternoon. Winfield motioned me over to his carrel and pointed to the terminal. On the screen was an article from a ten-year-old London *Times:*

MINISTER QUESTIONED ON BROMFORD EXPERIMENTS

The Ministry of Science was accused in the Commons of "grotesque improprieties" in experiments taking place at a government research establishment near Bromford. **Mr**

Charles Allenby, *Minister of State for Science, responded that, while the exact nature of the Bromford research was classified, he could assure the Commons that there were no improprieties.*

Mr Edward Hounslow *(Warpington, Lab) asked if children were involved in these experiments.*

Mr Allenby *said that he was unaware of the details of the research.*

Mr Hounslow: *Is it not true that women have been hired to bear children that are not their own?*

Mr Allenby: *I cannot say one way or the other. I can say that the research at Bromford is vital to our national security.*

Mr Hounslow: *Are these children aware that they are vital to our national security? This is but one more example of the moral bankruptcy of the policies of the ruling party. Have they not evidence enough of the evils unrestrained science can wreak upon the world?*

Mr Allenby: *I can assure you that nothing untoward has taken place at Bromford.*

End of story. "Well, that sounds interesting," I said. "Let's see if there's a follow-up." There was nothing for a week, and then a brief article:

ALLENBY   ANNOUNCES   CLOSING   OF BROMFORD CENTER

Mr Charles Allenby, Minister of State for Science, yesterday announced the cessation of research programs being carried out at the government's Bromford Research Center. He denied that the decision was influenced by Labour MP Mr Edward Hounslow's charge that Bromford was the site of 'horrific genetic experiments.'

'Some of the experiments involved an attempt to improve the treatment of genetic mutations induced by radiation,' Mr Allenby said. 'Surely this is an appropriate goal of modern science. Unfortunately, budget reductions have made it impossible to carry forward these lines of research, and we have decided to shut down our Bromford establishment.' He stated that some staff would be made

redundant, and others would be transferred to the Ministry's Uxbridge center.

When asked for details of the Bromford experiments, Mr Allenby declined comment, citing national security.

Mr Hounslow, the Labour MP from Warpington whose questions on the floor of the Commons brought the Bromford establishment to the public's attention, charged that the Minister's decision was a blatant attempt to cover up evidence of wrongdoing at Bromford. While applauding the decision to end the experiments, Mr Hounslow warned that he would continue to press for complete disclosure of what took place in them. 'I have not finished with this issue yet,' the MP stated.

If Mr. Hounslow hadn't finished with the issue, the London *Times* apparently had, as well as every other newspaper and periodical we checked. We scoured the next few months' worth of issues, but there wasn't a word about Bromford.

"A conspiracy of silence?" I asked provocatively. Winfield looked at me as if I were finally catching on. We had made no further progress by the time the library closed, but the two articles were enough to get Winfield excited.

"We've got to find out more," he said on our way back to the hotel.

"Any objections to calling this guy Hounslow?" I asked. "He's not likely to be the one who's trying to kill you."

"I suppose it's worth a try," he replied. I borrowed the phone book for the letter 'H' from the desk clerk when we reached the hotel. No Hounslow. "Would you have the book for Warpington?" I asked the clerk.

He smiled a knowing smile. "We have no such book," he said. "You might call directory inquiries, however."

"Oh. How do you do that?"

He did it for us, and then passed the receiver to me. The person at the other end of the line gave me the number with hardly any delay. It all seemed vaguely miraculous. I thanked the clerk, and Winfield and I went up to our room to make the call.

Winfield was in a state by this time. "You wanna call?" I asked him.

He picked up the phone, but his hand was shaking as he tried to dial. "You do it," he said. "But don't screw it up."

"Yes, boss." I dialed the number. Clicks and screeches. That was more familiar. I hung up and tried again. A distant, rhythmic buzzing, and then success. "Yes?" a scratchy old man's voice said.

"Mr. Hounslow?"

"That is correct."

"The Member of Parliament?"

"The former MP, yes. To whom am I speaking, please?"

"My name is Walter Sands, sir. I'm a reporter from the United States, and I'm investigating what happened to American scientists who came to England after the war."

"Reporter? I didn't think they had much of that going on anymore."

"Oh, you'd be surprised, sir. At any rate, my research indicates that one of these scientists—a Professor Robert Cornwall—may have been involved in research taking place at the government's Bromford Center before it closed. Apparently you had some knowledge of what went on there, and I was hoping you might recall something about this man Cornwall."

"Oh, my word. Bromford. I certainly remember Bromford. But I'm afraid I never learned the names of any of the scientists there. Terribly sorry."

I shook my head at Winfield. He looked disgusted, and then motioned for me to press ahead. "Well, perhaps you could tell me what you know about Bromford, then. It might help me determine if Cornwall was there. My research indicates that you had a run-in with the government about Bromford ten years ago."

"Oh, yes, there was quite a row for a day or two. See no harm in talking about it now. I was one of the early ones, you see—antiscience, after the war. What good has science done us, after all? Just sheer luck we didn't end up like you chaps in America. At any rate, by the time the Bromford business came up, the movement was more than respectable—in fact, we had found our leader in Hatton and we were on our way to power. Well, it started when a woman came to see me—not well educated, you know, but articulate and quite trustworthy. And she told me what had happened to her at Bromford several years before. They put a baby into her that wasn't her own. They made her a—Oh, what's the term?"

"Surrogate mother?" I suggested. That perked Winfield up.

"Yes, that's it. They kept her there until she bore the child, then they took it away from her and said cheerio. She never saw the child—or the inside of Bromford—again. Totally disgusting."

"Why did she wait so long before telling anyone?"

"She had become a convert to our movement, you see, and she realized the evil of what had taken place—what was still taking place—at Bromford."

"Her child—the child she bore—was still there?"

"I don't know for sure, but *something* was still going on at Bromford. I simply couldn't find out what."

"The government simply closed the place when you started questioning them."

"Precisely."

"It sounded as if you wanted to make more of a fuss about it at the time, but nothing seemed to come of it. Why was that?"

"Two reasons, really. My witness suddenly disappeared—she emigrated to Australia, I later found out. Apparently she wasn't quite as strong a convert as I had hoped, and the government were able to buy her off. More important, Charles Hatton told me to drop the whole thing."

Hounslow sounded bitter. "Why would Hatton want you to drop it?" I asked. Across the room, Winfield looked quite interested by that question. "Wasn't it a good issue?"

"I thought so," Hounslow replied, still sounding bitter. "But Hatton was beginning to believe he could become Prime Minister, and he was becoming cautious. He was afraid the issue might turn against us. What if the government *were* curing babies of genetic defects at Bromford? We couldn't be against healthy babies. So I was forbidden to mention Bromford again. The strategy was correct, I'm sure, since we won the election. But I must say it continues to bother me. What happened to the child that woman bore? What really went on there? I don't know."

"But wait a minute. Couldn't you find out once you came to power?"

"It wasn't I who came to power," Hounslow said, and the bitterness was stronger now. "It was Hatton; I remained a backbencher. And Hatton, once he became Prime Minister, seemed more interested in staying in power than in uncovering old horrors. Forgive my cynicism. I'm an old man who has lived through a great deal."

"I understand. Would you know, sir, if anyone else might be able to give us information about this man Cornwall or what went on at Bromford?"

Hounslow paused to consider. "I'm sure the records are there somewhere at the Ministry of Science," he said finally. "Now whether the Ministry will let you look at them—I'm afraid I just can't say. It's all passed me by, you see. I prefer pottering about in my garden now to worrying about our government."

"I can understand that, sir. Thank you for your time. You've been extremely helpful."

"Happy to oblige. Glad to see you Americans getting back on your feet. It's been a long time."

"It certainly has."

I hung up, and summarized for Winfield what he hadn't been able to make out from my side of the conversation. He paced the small room, too excited to sit still. "It all fits, then," he said. "Cornwall was cloning at Bromford. Hounslow made a stink, and they had to shut Bromford down. But obviously Hatton liked what Cornwall was doing, and he probably had Cornwall start it up again somewhere when he became Prime Minister."

"That's quite a leap of reasoning," I said. "From what I've read of the Hatton government—"

"I don't care what you've read," Winfield said. "What you've read failed to take into account the fact that someone doesn't want me to find Cornwall. Jesus, the government would probably fall if this became public knowledge. Let's go to Bromford."

That seemed a bit sudden to me. "Even assuming that it was Cornwall there," I said, "—and I admit that's a pretty good assumption now—the trail's going to be pretty cold at Bromford."

"Well, what do you suggest, then? Shutting ourselves up in the goddamn library for another day?"

"Today was reasonably productive," I pointed out. "And we have a better idea of things to look for now."

"Then look for them yourself. I've got other things to do."

I shrugged. He could go back to America, for all I cared. "Fine with me," I said. "Can I have my per diem now?"

He tossed me five pounds, and then called down to the desk clerk to find out how to get to Bromford.

Winfield left on a train early the next morning. He was vague about exactly what he was going to do in Bromford, and I had no investigative tips for him. But it made him happy to be on the move, and it left me on my own for the day, so there was no reason to complain.

I was conscientious enough to go to the library and do my research, but without Winfield in the next carrel there was considerably less urgency to the task. I studied up on Bromford and Charles Hatton and the Ministry of Science, but I didn't find out anything exciting; my mind started to wander, and eventually my body followed.

I took the Tube back to Russell Square and revisited the British Museum. It's a big place; but then, there's a lot of history, a lot of the products of human genius, to cram into it. The place was actually rather depressing, in a way: all that history, all that genius, leading to this. And what was next? I looked at the Elgin Marbles, battered by war—saved to be, inevitably, destroyed in another war. They had escaped this one, but they wouldn't escape forever.

I came across a display on Shakespeare; it included a specimen of his signature on some contract. *We shall not see his like again.* I thought of Mr. Fitch, back in New Hampshire. Wouldn't this give him a thrill?

And that brought me back further, to my time in Washington, which I mostly spent shooting dogs and making sure the salvagers didn't shoot each other. One day I was with a sergeant who had seen me squirreling away books to read off-duty. He waved at a pile of rubble across the street from us. "Folger Library," he said. "Biggest collection of Shakespearean stuff in the world in the old days. Mighty impressive now, eh, Private?"

We poked around it for a while. If there was anything left, it wasn't going to be easy to find, and the government hadn't the time, the manpower, or the inclination to look for it. The country needed copper wire more than it needed rotting volumes about a long-dead writer. We walked away, and I shot a lot of dogs the next couple of days.

And now I wondered: if Shakespeare had been born twenty-two years ago, would his genius have flowered? Probably not. Like that other genius, Dr. Charles Winfield, he would have been frustrated; he would have spent too much time in pubs; maybe he, too, would have looked for some way out, even if it was only the dream of some other life that would—and would not—be his.

When I finally returned to the hotel, I was not as happy as I should have been. Here I was in the Promised Land, free, with a heated room and a bathtub awaiting me. But it wasn't enough, or why was I stomping through the British Museum, brooding about the vanity of human wishes?

It was Gwen's problem in the fallout shelter, of course. Get what you want, and you want a little more. This was my first case, damn it, and I wasn't making much progress. And that bothered me, even in the Promised Land.

There was no message from Winfield when I arrived at the hotel. The Indian desk clerk smiled apologetically. I bought a newspaper and went up to my room.

London newspapers were better printed than the *Globe,* but none of their reporters was as good as Gwen, it seemed to me. Anyway, I was more interested in the movie listings than in the news. The previous night, after everything had been settled about the trip to Bromford, Winfield and I had split up, as usual, and I had attended my first movie. I had been a little disappointed—it was a prewar comedy, and I didn't get the jokes. I had felt like a hick, straining to understand why everyone was laughing, and just not being able to figure it out. Maybe I could find something that was more to my taste, something that would chase away my depression.

Sure enough—a Humphrey Bogart festival was starting at Notting Hill Gate. Humphrey, patron saint of private eyes. Going to one of his movies would be like going to church. Maybe if I prayed to him at the theater he would help me crack the case.

Unfortunately, I didn't have enough money left to go—never mind eat supper. Where was Winfield? I needed my per diem.

He called while I was taking a bath. I sloshed back into the bedroom and answered. His voice was tinny and distant but unmistakable.

"How did it go?" I asked.

"I didn't find anything," he said. "Not a fucking thing." He wasn't happy. There were voices in the background, clinking glasses. At least he had found a pub.

"Are you still in Bromford?"

"Yeah. I missed the last goddamn train. I'll have to spend the night. No one here remembers anything—at least that's what they say. They're probably lying, of course. The research center is a goddamn old people's home now. Jesus, you'd think at least someone would remember if an American lived here once. We're rare enough. Did you find out anything?"

"Nothing to speak of," I said. "I think we're about done with the newspaper library."

Winfield was silent for a moment. It was not a pleasant silence. I dripped. Glasses clinked. "Goddamn it," Winfield said. "We've got to find him. I don't have enough money to fool around like this. Understand?"

"What do you want—"

"I don't give a shit. You're supposed to be the expert. That's why I brought you over here. So find him. Fast. I don't care if you have to break into the fucking Prime Minister's house. Understand?"

"Yes, boss."

"And you better be there when I get back tomorrow. Understand?"

I hung up, then got a towel and dried myself. I looked at the newspaper, lying open on the bed to the movie listings. *Saint Humphrey, pray for us.* Sam Spade probably would have told his client to shove it.

Not if it was his first case, maybe.

I got dressed and went down to the lobby. The desk clerk smiled his knowing smile. *Those Americans and their crazy problems,* it seemed to say. I tried to smile back. "Could I borrow the telephone directory for the letter 'C'?" I asked.

"Hello, I'm sorry to disturb you, but I'm a reporter from the United States, and I'm doing a story on an American scientist who I believe emigrated to England after the war. His name is Robert Cornwall. I wonder if you would be related to him?"

Cornwall, R. was very sorry, but she couldn't help me.

Cornwall, R. did not answer.

Cornwall, R. (or whoever answered Cornwall, R.'s phone) did not speak English, and our conversation got nowhere.

Cornwall, Arthur had a cousin named Robert, but no, he was from Bristol and had never been to America.

Cornwall, Beatrice thought I had a nerve calling up

perfect strangers, and she had a mind to report me to the authorities.

Cornwall, E. and Cornwall, Edgar did not answer.

Cornwall, George was surprised there were reporters in America, and wondered why they wanted to write a story about Robert Cornwall. No, he didn't know any Robert Cornwall, he was just curious.

Cornwall, Harold's wife was pretty sure he didn't have a relative named Robert, but he wasn't in right now, and could I call back later?

Cornwall, John's brother had died of radiation poisoning while with the American Relief Expedition, and he hoped we would all suffer the way his brother had suffered.

Cornwall, K. said why, yes, her father was Robert Cornwall, the American scientist. What was the story about?

Er, um. I stared at the listing in the directory. This was really happening, wasn't it? The voice was young and innocently curious. What was I supposed to say to Cornwall's daughter? "Well, the fact of the matter is, Ms. Cornwall, I'm not a reporter. I represent a man who is a relative of Professor Cornwall's from America. We've come to England to try and find him."

There was a pause. "What kind of relative?"

"Well, perhaps I should leave that to the relative himself to explain."

"Why did you say you were a reporter if you weren't?"

"Well, the relative wished, uh, to avoid having to explain the circumstances of his search to a lot of people."

"Are *you* this relative?"

"No, no. As I say, I'm his, um, uh, representative." I was turning in a stunning performance here. Sam Spade, eat your heart out. "Would it be possible to meet your father?"

A pause. "Well, maybe I should meet you people first. My father is rather a private person."

"Of course. I understand perfectly. Name the place and time, and we'll be there."

She gave me the address of a pub in Soho. "I have classes during the day. How about five-thirty tomorrow afternoon?"

"That would be perfect."

"How shall I recognize you?"

"Oh, I wouldn't worry about that, Ms. Cornwall. We'll be the two American-looking gentlemen. See you tomorrow."

I hung up and said a prayer of thanksgiving to Saint Humphrey. We had wasted a few days, but that was all right; the case was on the move. All I needed to complete my happiness was some money to buy food. You can't have everything, I suppose.

For a change, I couldn't wait until Winfield got back.

CHAPTER 18

It was quarter to six, and Winfield was drinking his third Scotch. "She's not coming," he said.

"Take it easy," I replied. "This is more important to you than it is to her."

He stared at his drink. "It could be a setup, you know. Maybe she works for the government, and—"

"Oh, give it a rest."

He glared at me, then twisted around and gazed at the other patrons of the pub. Maybe she had sneaked in through a back door. Maybe someone was getting ready to shoot him. He was a little nervous. I suppose I couldn't blame him.

He was at the bar ordering another drink when she came in. Her gaze swept the place as his had, pausing for a moment when she saw me and then moving on: I couldn't be the one. And then Winfield turned from the bar with his Scotch, and their eyes met.

An apple cleft in two is not more twin/Than these two creatures. Well, not exactly. But they knew. It wasn't hard to know.

She shared his jet-black hair and dark eyes. Her skin was paler, although flushed at the moment from the cold December air. The other features were identical: high cheekbones, long, narrow nose, firm jaw. Maybe not twins, but they were related; that much was clear.

For all the similarities, though, there was something, well, *nicer* about her face than Winfield's—a calmness in the eyes, lips more ready to smile than to frown. Maybe it was due to the environment—living a cozy, protected life in England rather than a struggling, deprived one in America.

Or maybe, it occurred to me as I watched her, the difference was in the eye of the beholder. Was it because those features belonged to a woman that they appeared so pleasant to me? She was stunningly attractive, and I wanted very much for her to be a better person than Winfield.

She went over to him and extended her hand. "Katherine Cornwall," she said.

Winfield was confused for a moment. His drink was in the way as he tried to respond. He set it down finally and shook hands. "Charles Winfield," he responded. "Very glad to meet you. Can I, uh, buy you a drink?"

"Half of bitter, Gil," she said to the bartender.

"Righto, Kath."

She smiled at Winfield while the bartender poured her the poisonous-looking liquid. "I take it that you are my mysterious relative?" she said.

"I believe so, yes."

"Well, it sounds as though I'm in for a fascinating story, then. Shall we sit?" Winfield paid for her beer, and led her over to where I was waiting like Patience on a monument. I stood up, and she smiled at me. I recalled the way Winfield's gaze had drifted past me when we met, not interested enough to meet my eyes. Katherine Cornwall's gaze was direct and friendly. "Are you the gentleman I spoke to last night?"

"That's right. Walter Sands, Ms. Cornwall."

"Please call me Kathy." She shook my hand. "Now who would like to tell me the story?" She took off her peacoat. She was wearing a green turtleneck sweater, faded jeans, and black boots. The sweater went well with her hair. She put her coat and shoulder bag on the banquette next to me. A tattered copy of *The Seagull* peeked out of the top of the bag. We all sat.

I looked at Winfield. This was his show now. He surprised me by telling the truth—except for the stuff about cloning. "My mother was a student of Cornwall's at MIT," he said, "but she moved to Florida just before the war. That's where I was born. I never knew my father, but my mother told me about him. When I could afford it, I decided to go looking for him. I found out that he had gone to England after the war, so here I am."

"You're my—what?—half-brother, then?"

"Something like that."

"How could you afford to come to England? Travel is so expensive nowadays."

"I'm a doctor. I do quite well, by American standards."

"You're awfully young to be a doctor."

Winfield tried to look humble. "Your father is a very brilliant man, Kathy. I share his genes."

Kathy smiled, "I wish I shared a few of those brilliance genes." She took a sip of her beer. "Father never mentioned that he had left a son behind in America," she noted.

"He probably didn't know. I was born after the war, you see. If he knew my mother was pregnant, I suppose he assumed that I had died. It would have been a reasonable assumption."

She nodded, and stared at him in open appraisal. It was hard to say how she was taking all this. I had a feeling she was tense, but barely a hint of that broke through her politeness. "You certainly look like my father," she said.

"So do you," Winfield replied.

"Then I expect we are brother and sister." She smiled again. "What shall we do about it?"

Winfield downed his Scotch. "Tell me about him, for starters," he said.

"All right." She thought for a moment, then reached into her bag and took out a wallet. She fumbled through it for a moment, and then found a photograph that she passed to

Winfield. "Here he is, perhaps ten years ago," she said. "Quite a resemblance, don't you think?"

Winfield nodded and passed it back. I caught a glimpse of it as Kathy put it away—a somewhat faded photo of a man in sunlight, squinting unhappily at the camera. It could have been Winfield, somewhat older, somewhat heavier. "Was he at Bromford when this was taken?" Winfield asked.

"Why, yes. What else do you know about him?"

He shook his head. "Almost nothing."

"Well, let me see if I can summarize, then. He married my mum just before he started at Bromford, and that's where I lived until I was about nine. Then he went to Oxford to teach, and we went along—for a while, anyway. Then my parents broke up, and Mum and I moved away. He gave up teaching a couple of years ago, but he still lives in Oxford."

"Do you see him much?"

"Once in a while."

"What kind of person is he?"

She stared at her beer glass. Sum up your father for us in fifty words or less. "He's very…private. I'm sorry, it's rather difficult—"

"I understand. Do you know anything about his work— what he was doing at Bromford, for example?"

She shook her head. "That's one of the things he's private about. Besides, I'm very stupid about science. I mean, I understand that his work has to do with biology and genetics and such, but I don't know the details."

"Why did he and your mother break up?"

She looked at Winfield. Had he pushed too hard? But she simply smiled wryly. "I expect she found him too private."

"I'd like to see him," Winfield said. "Is he too private for that?"

"I suppose not," she replied—a trifle slowly, I thought, as if weighing her answer as she spoke it. And then more quickly: "Shall we go together? My Christmas holiday starts tomorrow, and we could leave after my last class. I

can bring my gift and fulfill my daughterly duty. Would
that be all right?"

"That would be perfect." Winfield beamed. It was all
turning out as he had hoped. "Shall we have another round
to celebrate?"

Kathy finished her beer. "Thank you." Winfield went to
the bar to buy the drinks. She turned and looked at me a
little hesitantly, searching for something to say.

"So you want to become an actress," I said, helping her
out.

She smiled a perplexed smile. "How did you guess?"

"Simple enough. A young woman doesn't get her copy
of Chekhov that ragged unless she's learning a part. Nina, I
suppose?"

She looked down at her bag, then at me. Her smile
widened. "That's very perceptive. Have you read
Chekhov?"

"Just a little," I lied, figuring I had shown off enough.
Still, I felt mightily pleased with myself. "Does your father
approve of your choice of careers?"

The smile mostly faded. "I don't think he especially
cares, to tell you the truth."

"What about your mother?"

"Oh, she positively loathes the idea."

"It's not very pleasant to have your family oppose your
chosen profession," I remarked, from experience.

"What exactly is your profession, Mr. Sands?"

"Call me Walter. I help people like Dr. Winfield find
what they're looking for."

"That's an interesting profession, Walter. Does your
family support it?"

"Their opinions are mixed, to tell you the truth."

Winfield returned with Kathy's beer and his Scotch.
Nothing for me, thank you. And the talking resumed. As
before, it excluded me. I thought Winfield had performed
rather well up to that point, but once the visit with his
"father" had been arranged, he became more his usual
self—opinionated, condescending, obnoxious. He wanted

to impress his newfound relative, I think—to prove he wasn't a hick, despite his strange accent, to prove he deserved to be Cornwall's offspring, despite his strange background.

It was hard to tell how his relative responded to the performance. Kathy was perfectly polite, friendly, charming; but I had a sense that she was at least partially using her acting ability, that behind the façade of good manners she was judging him, and her judgment was not altogether favorable. Was that a flicker of distaste on her features as he arose to get yet another Scotch? Did her eyes glaze momentarily with boredom as he gave his expert opinion on the current political situation in Britain?

I wasn't quite sure, because I realized that my insights were not altogether to be trusted where she was concerned. I found myself rooting for her. I wanted her to be nice, and I wanted her to have some taste—especially when it came to men. If she was charmed by Winfield, then she would grievously disappoint me. I tried to steel myself for the disappointment.

After a few more drinks, Winfield suggested that they go out to eat. Kathy politely agreed, and suggested an Indian restaurant nearby. I tagged along. Winfield gave me a look that suggested my presence was unwelcome, but I ignored it. After all, he hadn't given me my per diem. At the restaurant, Winfield kept drinking and talking, Kathy kept listening, and I kept watching Kathy.

Winfield lurched off to the men's room at one point, and Kathy and I were left alone again. "Dr. Winfield certainly has a large capacity," she observed.

"This is a big day for him," I said, feeling unexpectedly loyal. "I think maybe he's overexcited."

"And tomorrow will be an even bigger day, I expect."

"Yes, it will."

She looked at me. "Will you be coming tomorrow, Walter?"

I had assumed I would, but the asking of the question put the answer in doubt. Was the case over? Was I free? At the moment I wasn't quite sure I wanted my freedom. "I guess it's up to Dr. Winfield," I said.

"It might be a good idea," she said.

I wasn't quite sure why, but I didn't want to disagree. "Yes, it might."

When the meal was over, Winfield proposed going back to the pub, but Kathy begged off. "I'm sorry, Charles, but I have early classes, and I have to do some preparation. Shall I meet you and Walter tomorrow? Three-thirty, let's say, at the ticket windows in Paddington Station."

"Soun's great," Winfield slurred. "Sure you won't—"

"Quite sure, Charles. It's been such an exciting evening, though. I'm really looking forward to tomorrow." She gave him a sisterly peck on the cheek, smiled quickly at me, and was gone.

Winfield glanced at me, then his gaze slid past, and he headed off in the direction of our hotel. I was headed in that direction myself, so I kept him company. "Beautiful girl, huh?" he said.

"Yes, indeed."

"Y'know, she's my daughter, sort of, if y'look at it the right way."

"You must be very proud."

He ignored me. "'Sbeen a long time coming. A long, long time." His dark eyes were moist. I felt a snowflake land on my cheek.

"What'll you do when you meet him?" I asked.

"He'll teach me," Winfield said. "We'll work together."

"Making more clones?"

"I'll carry on. He won't live forever. But he *will*—we both will. We'll make more lives for us to live, an' maybe one of them'll be amazing. Our genius, over and over and over. See?"

I saw. The snow fell slowly, as if hesitant to intrude on our conversation. "What is he doing at Oxford, do you think?" I asked. "Kathy said he was retired."

"I dunno. He's a very private man. I'm private too, y'know."

I wanted to point out to Winfield that the case didn't
make sense. If someone had tried to kill him in Boston for
asking about Cornwall, why was Cornwall apparently
retired and living a quiet life in Oxford? But Winfield was
too drunk to care about such things. I let it slide.

Winfield made it back to the hotel and passed out on his
bed as soon as we entered our room. I pulled off his shoes
and coat and left him there. Then I sat by the window and
watched the snow falling.

The traffic hissed by below; Winfield grunted and
snored. I had a long night ahead of me. I considered taking
my five pounds from Winfield's pocket and going out, but
somehow I lacked the energy.

I wondered again: was the case over? Looked like it.
Asked a couple of friends for help, made a few phone calls.
Simple. If there were things that didn't make sense, they
didn't particularly matter. Real life, I figured, was not as
tidy as fiction.

So why did I feel so strange? Was this how a private eye
feels after the last chapter, when he sits in his office and
realizes that those characters he's been dealing with are
gone forever from his life? Maybe.

And maybe my mood had nothing to do with the case.
Maybe it had to do with real life, pure and simple.

Maybe it had only to do with Kathy Cornwall.

She was prettier than any of the stained and dog-eared
pinups in Art's Filthy Bookstore. She was young and alive
and untouched by the chaos and disease that had permeated
my life. Imagine—studying to be an actress! She was a
dream I had never dreamed I would dream.

Ah, me. Life is certainly strange. There were Humphrey
Bogart movies playing at Notting Hill Gate, but I didn't go.
Instead I sat and watched the falling snow and, amid the
snoring and the guilt, I dreamed my dreams.

CHAPTER 19

Winfield didn't want me to come. "What's the point?" he asked. "What will you add?"

"I don't know," I said, "but Kathy seemed to think it was a good idea. Don't you remember?"

He shook his head vaguely. No reason he should. "All right, but you better start thinking about your future here. I probably won't need you after today."

"I'm saving up my money to run an ad," I said.

Kathy was waiting for us when we arrived at Paddington Station. She had on a tweed overcoat and skirt, and she was carrying a shopping bag that contained a gift-wrapped box. She looked tense, but she greeted us cheerily. "I've already bought the tickets," she said, "so let's just check our platform, shall we?"

We walked out into the concourse and watched the huge message board announce the arrivals and departures. Winfield looked like he needed a drink. "Did you tell your father we were coming?" he asked.

"Yes," Kathy replied. "I phoned him last night."

"How did he react?"

Kathy pondered for a moment. "That's difficult to say," she responded finally. "He's not the kind to display much emotion."

"Did he say anything about me? Did he talk about what happened back then?"

Kathy stared at him and shook her head. "I'm sure he'll be more forthcoming when you meet," she said.

"Sure. Makes sense." Winfield fell silent, dreaming about the moment that was about to arrive.

The silence became awkward after a while. "Shirt?" I asked Kathy, to break the ice.

She looked puzzled for a moment, then glanced at the shopping bag and smiled. "Good try, but not as good as yesterday. Dressing gown."

"Ah. Dressing gown. He'll love it."

"I hope you're right."

Our train was announced. We made our way to the platform and climbed aboard. The train was mostly deserted. We had a compartment to ourselves; Winfield and Kathy sat facing me. In a few minutes the train pulled out of the station.

Am I being sufficiently blasé about this? My first train ride—not quite as exciting as my first trip in an airplane, but good enough: the huge concourse, the muffled PA system, the conductor punching our tickets, the station giving way to rail yards flanked by grim flats and factories, giving way to bleak countryside…How often had I read about such a commonplace experience, in Dickens and Doyle and the rest of them? And now the experience was mine. It felt good.

I had plenty of opportunity to consider the experience, because no one was doing much talking. I tried to chat some more with Kathy; she was polite but preoccupied. And Winfield was in his own world, scarcely capable of saying anything to anyone, I think. So I stared out the window and thought about train rides, and wondered what was going to happen at the end of this one. It took us a little over an hour to reach Oxford.

"Now what?" Winfield asked as we made our way out of the station.

"Now we walk," Kathy said. "My father's house is about half a mile from here. It's in the wrong direction from the colleges, I'm afraid, so the route won't be particularly scenic."

Winfield shrugged; he wasn't interested in scenery. The three of us set out in silence.

Maybe it wasn't a good idea for me to be here, I thought as we walked. I felt like an outsider at some strange, private ritual. I didn't belong in this solemn procession over the icy sidewalks, past the quaint stone houses. And then I thought: why is it so solemn? Here we are, two days before Christmas, and a guy is about to meet his long-lost something-or-other. People should be a little happier. Shouldn't they? It wasn't my place to mention this, however. I was just along for the ride. I stuck my hands in my pockets and kept my mouth shut.

Finally Kathy pointed to a small house at the next corner. "That's it," she said.

We approached it like pilgrims heading for Canterbury. Would Winfield get down on his knees? It had a tidy little yard; smoke was rising from the chimney; there was sand on the walk.

"Wait!" Winfield said.

We waited. He stopped and closed his eyes and took a few deep breaths. Kathy looked at me, but I couldn't read her expression.

"Okay," he said.

Kathy led the way up the walk to the door. She rang the bell.

The door opened almost immediately. He must have been waiting for us—watching us come. "Hullo, Daddy," Kathy said. "Here is Dr. Winfield."

They stared at each other.

I felt as if I were observing an allegory of Time. The black hair turns gray and thin, the eyes require glasses, the firm skin wrinkles and sags. Same height, same build, same features. Were they the same person? I couldn't tell for sure; Time does too thorough a job. But the sight was enough to make me shudder and think of my own mortality, the dreaded future that would be as quick to arrive as the dreaded past had been slow to depart.

I looked at Kathy. Her eyes were fixed on her father. "Perhaps we should go in," she murmured after a few moments.

Professor Cornwall glanced at her, a little confused—perhaps a little frightened—and then he nodded. His gaze met mine for an instant and drifted past. I almost smiled, the experience was so familiar. Then he turned and led us into his home.

He brought us into a cozy library. Dark oak shelves were crammed with books. A coal fire burned in the small fireplace. A bottle of Scotch was open on the sideboard.

Cornwall and Winfield sat down opposite each other, Kathy and I remained standing. I studied Cornwall some more. He was wearing a tweed jacket and a faded gray sweater. He hadn't shaved very well. His clasped hands tensed and untensed in his lap as if he were squeezing an invisible ball. I had a strong suspicion that he needed a drink.

"Well," he said, and the word sounded bewildered on his lips. It sounded like a plea for help. He looked at Winfield; he looked at Kathy.

"Well," Kathy said.

The dialogue was hardly Shakespearean so far. Winfield managed to get out a full sentence. "You know me," he said—quietly, confidently.

Cornwall looked at Kathy; he looked at the bottle of Scotch.

"Dr. Winfield is your son," Kathy said.

Cornwall looked at his hands, squeezing, squeezing. "He's not my son," the old man whispered.

Kathy looked at Winfield, who took the statement in stride. "That's right, I'm not."

I noticed that she was still holding her shopping bag. Happy Christmas, everyone. "Then who are you?" she asked.

Winfield put on his condescending expression. "I'm not his son, you see. I'm his clone. The product of a complicated biological procedure that he developed back in America. I'm genetically identical to your father, Kathy. We're twins, born forty-some years apart."

Kathy processed that little piece of information, and then turned back to her father. "Is this true, Daddy?"

Tangled, leafless branches of an elm tree scratched against the bay window at the far side of the library. The fire hissed, a floorboard creaked, Cornwall squeezed. And I thought: does Winfield see what I am seeing—a weak, confused old man, a man who has not come through life well? Doesn't this scare him? Or is his dream too real, his ego too strong? The silence lengthened, until finally Kathy repeated her question. "Is this true, Daddy?"

Cornwall shook his head. "No, it is not true," he whispered.

"No?" Winfield repeated. "What do you mean, 'No'?" His voice was surprisingly calm, as if a trivial mistake had been made. Easily fixed. Try again.

Cornwall stared at his hands, unable to meet Winfield's gaze. "Cloning of adults is impossible at the moment," he muttered. "I looked into it at MIT, but there were…procedural difficulties. I was never successful."

"But you're mistaken, can't you see?" Winfield said, finally becoming excited. "You successfully implanted the embryo in my—my mother. Alicia Winfield. She volunteered for the experiment. Then she left Cambridge, the war happened. But the experiment worked. Can't you see? Can't you look at me and see?"

Cornwall raised his eyes slowly, but the effort was too much, and he dropped his gaze back to his hands. "I'm afraid you're the one who's mistaken," he said, and his voice was a little stronger. "You're not related to me—you're not my son, not my clone. Perhaps there is a resemblance that led you to hypothesize…something. But it never happened. Nothing ever happened."

"But—but it did," Winfield persisted. "You just have to look at me to know that it did."

Cornwall spread his hands, as if to say: *See? Nothing there.*

Winfield turned to Kathy, and his voice was getting desperate now. "You can see the resemblance, can't you? Anyone can see the resemblance." And he gestured at me, as if to prove his case.

"There's a resemblance," Kathy said softly, "but I don't know you. I know my father, and I believe him."

"He must be mistaken—or he's lying."

"Why would my father lie?" Kathy asked.

"I don't know. I—" Winfield's gaze returned to Cornwall, and he fell silent for a moment. I felt an unexpected twinge of sympathy for him. He must have rehearsed this scene so often, and now it was happening, and it had gone wildly wrong; the dream had turned into a nightmare. He must have started feeling sorry for himself at the same time, because when he spoke again it was in a low, pleading tone to Cornwall, who sat, shoulders hunched, eyes downcast, as he listened. "Look," Winfield said, "I don't know what you're thinking, I don't know what's going on. I only know that this is my life. I've given up everything to come here and find you. I've got to know who—what—I am, and you're the only one who can tell me. It's all right if I'm a clone—I *want* to be a clone. But just tell me the truth."

Cornwall seemed to shrink back in his chair. He looked at Kathy for help, but Kathy was silent. "I'm sorry if this is disappointing to you," the old man said finally to Winfield. "I don't want to hurt you, but this is the truth: you will have to find out who you are on your own. I can't tell you."

Winfield shook his head. He leaned forward and stretched out his hand to Cornwall. "It's my life," he whispered. "It's my only life. Can't you see?"

Cornwall shrank farther back into his chair and ignored the hand extended to him. And for some reason I thought of Professor Hemphill, back in Cambridge, and what

Cornwall had said to him once upon a time: *You only have the one life. Don't waste it.* Linc had given me the same good advice. Had Winfield wasted his life? It was beginning to look that way.

"It's my life!" Winfield screamed. And he leaped upon Cornwall, grabbing the lapels of his jacket and shaking. "It's my life, it's my life," he kept repeating, his voice hoarse and desperate.

The allegory of Time had become jumbled and weird. Since when did Youth attack Age? Since when did—

"Walter!" Kathy was calling to me. "For God's sake!"

Private eyes are men of action. I jumped on top of Winfield and pulled him off the old man. We tumbled to the floor, and I managed to pin him beneath me. Winfield struggled for a moment, and then lay quiet in my grasp. Eventually I let him go and stood up. He stayed there on the floor, his eyes closed, gasping for breath.

Cornwall got shakily to his feet. He went over and stood looking into the fire.

Kathy joined her father by the fire. She put a hand tentatively on his back. "Are you all right, Daddy?" she asked.

"I'm fine," he murmured. He didn't turn to look at his daughter.

Winfield slowly got up from the floor. His eyes blazed at me, a convenient focus for his anger, but then he turned away. I was too unimportant. He spoke to Cornwall's back. "All right," he said. "I can't force the truth out of you. But I'll tell you one thing: I'm not going to rest until I find out the truth, one way or another. And that means you're not going to rest either. I've got nowhere else to go and nothing else to do, so you'd better prepare yourself. Understand?"

No one replied. Winfield spun around and left the room, elbowing me aside as he strode past. The outer door slammed, and then there was silence.

Boy, that was one swell reunion, I thought. *Glad I came.* And now what was I supposed to do? Rush after my boss? I had a feeling I wouldn't be very welcome. On the other hand, I sure didn't belong here. I straightened Cornwall's chair, which had moved in the ruckus, and retreated to a corner of the room, hoping someone would give me an order.

"I'm sorry, Daddy," Kathy murmured.

"It's all right. No matter." His voice was distant, tired. He went over to the sideboard and poured himself a large drink. Then he noticed me. "Who are you?" he demanded.

"He's a friend of Winfield's," Kathy explained. "I mentioned him on the phone last night."

"Oh." Cornwall swallowed most of his Scotch. That seemed to give him some strength. "I think you'd better go," he said to me.

He was right. "I'm sorry we bothered you," I said. "Doctor Winfield was very sure about—about everything."

Cornwall stared at his Scotch and didn't reply. I turned and left the library.

Kathy caught up with me at the front door. "What will you do?" she asked me.

"Go back to London, I guess. Thanks for the round-trip ticket."

"I'm sorry about this," she said.

"Why should you be apologizing?" I asked, a little puzzled. "Winfield and I were the ones—"

"Yes. But I should have known—I should have understood my father better. Oh, never mind. I expect I'm rather confused."

"That's okay." She looked lovely in the dim light of the vestibule. I sighed. "See you around, Kathy."

"Yes. See you around."

I walked out of Professor Cornwall's house.

It was dark. It was cold. I hadn't paid much attention to our route from the railway station, and I was afraid I would become lost. What was I doing here?

This wasn't the way cases are supposed to end—in anger and confusion, with the private eye groping through the night in a strange city. There must have been some clue I had overlooked, some spectacular deduction I could make to explain everything. Cornwall was hiding something. But what? Winfield had been mistaken. But it didn't *look* as if he had been mistaken. The government was to blame. The aliens who had landed in Washington were to blame. There was a massive conspiracy: everyone was to blame. What did I know?

Maybe that's the way things were, in real life: confusing, messy. I had had enough of real life.

I found the railway station eventually, and learned that I had just missed the train for London. Real life again.

Maybe Winfield had been on that train; if so, it was just as well I had missed it. But I had a feeling Winfield was more likely to have found a pub than the railway station. He probably needed a drink as much as Cornwall, and I doubted he could wait till London to get it.

I sat on the platform and waited for the next train. People came and went. A wizened mutant with one eye pushed a broom desultorily along the floor. Two professorial-looking men were arguing about Arthur Schopenhauer, or maybe it was Arnold Schonberg. The PA squawked incomprehensibly. A fat old lady with a shopping bag kept nodding her head and muttering to some invisible companion.

I hadn't felt this lonely in years.

What was I doing here? Why was I sitting in this cold, crumby place? There were cold, crumby places in Boston where I could be sitting. And in Boston I would not be sitting alone.

The train was late, of course. I sat and sat, and I felt my feet freeze and tears tug at my eyes. This was not the way the dream was supposed to turn out. Something had to—

"Walter!"

It was Kathy, calling to me from beyond the entrance to the platform. She was wild-eyed and breathless.

I went over to the gate. The old black ticket taker gazed at us with vague curiosity. "Um, hi," I said cleverly.

"Oh, Walter," she gasped, "I think something terrible is happening."

One terrible thing sprang immediately to mind. "Did Winfield come back?"

"No—I'm not sure. Probably. There was a phone call, and my father—I've never seen him like this. He told me to get out. I argued with him, but he wouldn't listen. I had to leave. And—and—I didn't know what to do. I'm so scared. So I came here, hoping maybe—"

She started to cry. Tearful beauty asks for help. That's what the job is all about. "Let's go," I said.

We took a cab—my first cab ride. Kathy leaned forward in the back seat, her hands covering her face, trembling. I laid a hand awkwardly on her arm. "It'll be all right," I said. "I have a feeling Winfield's bark is worse than his bite. He probably just wanted to argue some more." I wasn't at all sure I had that feeling, but it seemed like a good thing to say. It didn't have much effect, however.

We heard the sirens before we reached the house. Kathy stiffened. The cab slowed down. We turned a corner, and I saw the flames.

"Seems to be a bit of a problem there, mate," the cabdriver said.

Kathy did not look up.

CHAPTER 20

I leaped out of the cab. The firemen were already starting to do their work. There was a small knot of onlookers. Neither Cornwall nor Winfield was among them. I rushed up to a bobby who was standing next to a firetruck. "Did they find anyone inside there?" I asked.

"I don't know that they've looked yet, sir," the bobby replied. "Still rather hot, I expect."

I thought for a moment. "Listen," I said. "I know something about this fire, and I think it might be arson. The person who set the fire is probably trying to get out of town. Can you take me to the railway station?"

The bobby gave me a stern look. "What is it that you know, sir?"

"There was a—a dispute earlier. Two people were quite upset. I was here, but I left. That girl in the cab back there—it's her father's house. She can tell you what happened too."

"Let's go and have a talk with her then, shall we?"

The bobby led the way back to the cab. Kathy was still sitting in the back seat, her hands covering her face. The driver was standing next to the cab, probably trying to figure out how to ask for his fare.

"Kathy," I said gently, "we've got to try and find

Winfield. Can you tell this officer what happened?"

She looked up.

"Please try to help, miss," the bobby said. Tearful beauty gazes at policeman. It was easy to see he was more prepared to believe her than me.

She told him the story—quickly, numbly.

The bobby nodded when she had finished. "Very well," he said. "I'll just report back, and then we can go." He strode off to his car.

"Do you want to come with us or stay?" I asked her. "They still haven't—you know—"

"I think I'd like to stay," she said.

"All right. I'll be back as soon as I can."

Kathy attempted a smile, and then her gaze moved, for the first time, to the burning house.

I joined the bobby at his little three-wheel police car. "All right, then," he said. "Hop in."

I hopped in, and we sped off to the railway station.

At the station, we rushed upstairs and over to the old black ticket taker. The platform behind him was empty. He looked nervously at the two of us. "Did you notice a man get on the train to London just now?" I asked. "Tall, black-haired, about my age?"

"No, sir," the ticket taker whispered. His eyes went down to his tickets.

"Are you sure?"

"Yes, sir."

"Any other trains leave in the past few minutes?"

"No, sir."

I don't think he enjoyed being interrogated. I rushed around the station then, looking on the other platforms, in the tea shop, the news shop, the men's room. The bobby kept pace with me, looking stern. No sign of Winfield. "Is there any other way out of the city?" I asked the bobby finally.

"Coach station," he suggested.

"Can we give it a try?"

"Righto."

We raced through the city streets to the coach station. The woman at the ticket window seemed pleased to see us: a little excitement for her evening. "We're looking for someone," I said. "Did you sell a ticket a short while ago to a tall, black-haired man, about my age, American accent?"

She shook her head. "No, dear, I'm sorry, no one like that's been here." She thought for a moment, trying to be helpful. "I did sell a ticket to an older man with an American accent—don't see many Americans nowadays. Seemed in a bit of a hurry."

An older man? That stopped me cold. What was going on? "Could you describe him?" I asked.

"Oh, he was tallish—gray hair—rather distinguished, actually. And, let's see, tweed jacket, gray sweater—he was carrying his overcoat. He was quite out of breath."

"Where was he going?"

"He booked a single to London."

"Has the bus—er, coach—left?"

"Oh, I'm afraid so. Gone twenty minutes." The woman leaned forward. "Did he commit a crime?" she asked conspiratorially.

I shrugged. "Beats me." I turned to the policeman. "Can we follow that coach?" I asked.

"We could, sir, but we'd never catch it. Besides, that doesn't sound like the man we're looking for, does it?"

"No, I guess it doesn't." I searched my mind for a spectacular deduction. Couldn't find any. "Any other way out of town?" I asked.

"One could have a car, of course," the bobby replied. "Or one could hitchhike. People tend to pick up hitchhikers around here. Lots of students, you know."

"Of course." I couldn't think of anything else to do. "Well, I guess we can go back. Sorry, um, you know—"

"Quite all right, sir."

We got back in the car, and the bobby radioed the station, telling them what he was up to.

"Archie," a polite voice responded, "Miss Cornwall is

here with us at the moment. I wonder if Mr. Sands would mind coming in himself?"

Archie looked at me. I shrugged my assent. I didn't have anything else on my engagement calendar. We drove to the station.

It was a dismal-looking low modern building. Inside, it was quiet, except for a drunk somewhere who was singing "Good King Wenceslas." Archie conferred with the officer at the desk, and then escorted me to a glassed-in office. He rapped sharply on the door.

"Come," a voice responded.

Archie opened the door. Behind a cluttered desk sat a young man with a neat mustache and a florid face. On the other side of the desk was Kathy, sipping a cup of tea. "Ah, Mr. Sands. My name is Inspector Grimby. Sit down, please. Would you like some tea?"

I shook my head and sat next to Kathy. Archie departed. *Inspector Grimby.* I liked that. I smiled at Kathy. She looked tired and distraught. "Your father's alive," I said.

Inspector Grimby raised an eyebrow. "How do you know?" he inquired.

"He bought a bus ticket for London. Archie and I talked to the woman who sold it to him. No sign of Winfield, though. He wasn't inside the house, by any chance?"

Grimby shook his head. "Luckily, no one appears to have been inside the house."

"But it was arson, wasn't it?"

Grimby's expression became a little cold. I braced myself for: *I'll be the one to ask the questions, if you don't mind.* He let me down—maybe he hadn't read enough novels. "The official verdict will have to await further investigation, of course," he intoned, "but the fire brigade informs me there was distinct evidence of petrol having been spread about the living room." He leaned back in his chair and rubbed an index finger alongside his mustache. "This business of your father leaving town adds an interesting new element to the case," he said to Kathy. "Why do you think he did that, Miss Cornwall?"

"I don't know," she said. "Maybe he was afraid."

"But from what you have told me so far, it appeared as if he were preparing for a confrontation with this man Winfield."

"Maybe he changed his mind and decided to run away," she offered. "Winfield came back, found the place empty, became enraged, and burned it."

Not a bad theory. Grimby considered it. "Any reason why your father would go to London?" he asked.

Kathy shook her head. "Not that I know of. Maybe it was the first coach available."

"But why wouldn't he simply come to us if he was afraid? We are certainly capable of protecting our citizens."

"I don't know. I expect he just didn't—didn't want to involve the police in it."

"Well, he has certainly failed in that respect. We consider arson to be quite a serious offense."

Kathy nodded solemnly. This guy was doing a good job in his role, even if he didn't know all the lines. He turned his attention to me. "Now, Mr. Sands, what is all this mumbo-jumbo about long-lost clones and such?"

"Um, well, a clone is a genetically identical—"

"Yes, yes, Miss Cornwall was kind enough to explain the concept. But you didn't seriously expect anyone to believe this fellow Winfield was Professor Cornwall's clone, did you?"

"Well, it seemed at least plausible to me."

"Yes, plausible enough to extract some money from Professor Cornwall—or so you hoped."

Now *there* was a lousy theory. Where to begin demolishing it? "It cost Winfield a great deal of money to come over here," I pointed out. "It hardly makes much sense for him to do that in order to put the squeeze on a retired professor."

Grimby smiled condescendingly. "Criminals are not often sensible, Mr. Sands. And, Mr. Sands, I am not unaware of your role in all of this. You may well be considered an accomplice to Winfield's deception."

Swell. "I'm eager to cooperate in any way I can. Ask Miss Cornwall."

"He's been very helpful," Kathy said quickly. "I really think there was no deception. Winfield genuinely seemed to believe—well, that he was what he said."

"We'll find that out when we find Winfield, won't we?" Grimby responded haughtily. "If you're so eager to cooperate, Mr. Sands, maybe you have a photograph of your friend that you can lend us for our investigation."

I shrugged. "Sorry."

"Wait," Kathy said. She took her wallet out of her handbag and produced the photograph she had shown Winfield and me in the pub. "That's a rather old snap of my father, but it looks remarkably like Doctor Winfield. Don't you agree, Mr. Sands?"

I nodded. Grimby picked the photo up and stared at it dubiously. "Well, we'll use it then, for want of anything better."

"You might also try looking in at the Guilford Hotel, Russell Square," I suggested. "That's where Winfield and I have been staying in London."

Grimby made a note. "Will you be going back there tonight?" he asked.

Hadn't thought about it. The loneliness of the railway station stabbed me again. "I'm not quite sure at the moment. Listen, I think you should also check on that, uh, coach Cornwall is on. He might be able to clear everything up for you."

Grimby glared at me. I guess I hadn't endeared myself to him. "I shall take care of this case, thank you. Please keep me informed as to your whereabouts. And, Miss Cornwall, where can I reach you?"

Kathy gave her London address. "I think I'll stay here tonight, though, and speak to you again in the morning, if I may."

"Of course. In fact, I would appreciate that." Grimby stood up. "Thank you for your time, Miss Cornwall, and allow me to express my sympathy on this unfortunate occurrence."

"Thank you, Inspector."

Grimby nodded icily to me. I nodded icily back. Private eyes never get along with guys like him. I followed Kathy out of his office.

The drunk was singing "Silent Night." Archie was having a cup of tea, and he nodded politely to us. A lot of eyes followed Kathy as we walked out of the station.

"I'm sorry," I said when we were outside. "I didn't mean for any of this to happen."

"Of course you didn't," Kathy replied.

"I mean, I knew Winfield was a bit—well, self-centered, and not the nicest guy in the world, but I didn't think he'd do something like this."

Kathy closed her eyes and leaned back against the wall of the station. A tear leaked out of her eyes and coursed down her cheek. I stifled an urge to wipe it away. "I wonder where they are," she murmured.

"I don't know, but I wouldn't worry. The police will find them. Grimby is a little pompous, but I'm sure he's efficient."

"Yes, I expect you're right." Kathy opened her eyes and looked at me. "And what are you going to do, Walter?"

"I guess I'll go back to London, if there's a train."

She nodded. *All is calm, all is bright,* the distant, drunken voice sang. Our breath hung in clouds in the cold night air. "I wonder if you'd consider staying in Oxford tonight," she murmured. "I'm a little scared of Winfield, and—and I expect I could use some help sorting things out in the morning. This has all been very—very—"

"I understand." Tearful beauty asks private eye to protect her. What more could I want? There was just one problem. "The thing is, Kathy, I can't afford to stay in Oxford. I've got this return ticket to London and maybe three pounds, and that's it. Working for Winfield hasn't exactly made me wealthy."

"Then you can think of it as working for me, Walter. I can't make you wealthy either, but at least I can afford a hotel room for you."

I thought for a moment. Was there a question of ethics here? I wasn't sure I was supposed to ditch my client in mid-case. On the other hand, Winfield hadn't given me my per diem; I could probably consider myself dismissed. I needed a job, and I liked Kathy very much. It was one of the easier decisions I had ever made. "You talked me into it," I said.

Kathy smiled a dazzling smile. "Thank you, Walter."

I smiled back. "Happy to oblige."

CHAPTER 21

W̲e ate supper in a dreadful fish and chips place; Kathy paid. She didn't say much during the meal. I wanted to discuss the case—find out what she really thought about the cloning business, find out more about her father and his strange behavior, find out why she had decided to trust me in spite of my relationship with Winfield. But she was disinclined to talk, and I had sense enough not to press her. There would be better times than this to have a chat.

After the meal we went to a hotel and checked in. The desk clerk appeared somewhat bemused by us: young couple, no luggage, asking for separate rooms. But of course he was too British to say anything. I didn't say anything either. Kathy and I stood outside her door for a moment. "I'm sorry I'm so—so confused," she said. "I feel as if I'm in a nightmare."

"It's perfectly understandable. You'll be better in the morning."

"Yes. I'll have to see about the house, I suppose. And I really should ring my mother and let her know. Oh, dear."

"In the morning," I repeated.

"Right." She smiled. "Well, thank you, Walter."

"Good night, Kathy."

"Good night."

We stood there one awkward moment too long, and then she disappeared inside her room.

I went next door to my own room. It was bland but warm. I sat on the edge of the bed and listened for sounds of Kathy. There was running water for a few minutes, the squeal of coat hangers being shifted, then nothing.

I lay back on the bed. *What was I doing here?* And, more important, how was I going to make it through the endless hours to sunrise? *Someday sleep will come easy.* Not tonight, not here. I thought of Gwen in bed, warm and familiar—and alone—and that thought seemed to make everything intolerable. I decided to take a walk. I left the room, tiptoed past Kathy's door, and went down to the lobby.

The desk clerk looked surprised to see me, but didn't say anything. I strolled out of the hotel into the ancient Oxford streets.

I tried haphazardly looking for Winfield—entering pubs I happened to pass and searching for his familiar face. No luck. I hadn't expected any. I gave up after a while and simply walked, looking at the looming, history-heavy buildings of the colleges and struggling not to feel like Jude the Obscure. Ah, the cruel fate that kept me from being a student here. Ah, to have the money and the leisure to learn all I wanted to learn.

It was bogus self-pity, anyway. I had learned all I needed to learn. If I had wanted to learn more, Northeastern would gladly have taught me. Northeastern was somewhat lacking in tradition, compared to Oxford, but tradition wasn't much help nowadays.

Ah, Northeastern. I thought of Professor Hemphill slouching along its cinder-block corridors. I thought of Cindy Tappen in her tight jeans and legwarmers. Ah, Boston.

I couldn't seem to help feeling sorry for myself. Private eyes are supposed to be loners, not lonely, I told myself. But then, if I were a real private eye, I would be in the sack with Kathy instead of wandering around in the cold and the dark thinking about education. So what did that say about me? I wasn't sure I wanted to know the answer.

It had been a long day.

When I finally returned to the hotel, the desk clerk was nodding off to sleep. I went up to my room and lay open-eyed on my bed till dawn.

I read the local newspaper while waiting for Kathy the next morning. There was an article about the fire. Kathy's name was mentioned, but not mine or Winfield's. The article said the fire was "under active investigation."

"Sleep well?" Kathy asked when we met in the lobby.

"Like a baby."

Inspector Grimby was somewhat surprised to see me accompanying Kathy to the police station. *Miss Cornwall, do you think it wise to keep company with this shifty American?* he should have said, but didn't. Instead, he simply told us about his progress—or lack of it. "We have been unable so far to locate either Winfield or Professor Cornwall," he admitted. "The London police checked the Guilford Hotel last night and this morning, but Winfield has not been seen there. They also checked the coach station. A man answering Professor Cornwall's description boarded a coach to Nottingham. The Nottingham police met the coach last night when it arrived, but Professor Cornwall was not on it."

"Did the Nottingham police talk to the driver?" I asked.

Grimby withered me with a glance. "Yes, they did think to talk to the driver, Mr. Sands. The driver remembered a passenger that answered Cornwall's description, but was not sure where he got off. He thought perhaps Leicester or Northampton. And yes, I have been in contact with the police there, and they will be watching for him. Any reason why he might have gone to one of those places, Miss Cornwall?"

Kathy shook her head. "I can't think of any. Maybe he just wanted to hide for a while from Winfield."

Grimby trained his gaze on her. "Miss Cornwall, your father's disappearance makes this case even more peculiar than it was to start with. Is there any information that you are withholding from me?"

Kathy was stunned. "Of course not. Why should I? I'm as puzzled as you are, Inspector. I don't know my father very well, you see. I haven't lived with him for years, and when I did he was quite secretive. I—I had the impression that he might not have been telling the entire truth when he spoke with Winfield. The resemblance was so strong there had to be some kind of relationship, yet my father denied everything. But I don't know why. I honestly don't know why."

Grimby rubbed his mustache and made a note. "Very well. Since this is Christmas Eve, I'm afraid little immediate progress will be made. But we shall keep on it. We don't like people burning down houses in our city. And if either of you finds out anything, I trust you'll let me know."

We promised.

"What next?" I asked when we left the station.

"I suppose we can return to London," Kathy said. She seemed distracted, ill-at-ease.

"Don't you want to check out your father's house? There might be valuables or something."

"Oh. Of course. How stupid of me." She shook her head. "I'm sorry. I'm still not quite right, I'm afraid. I spoke to my mother this morning, and that always puts me into a state."

We started walking toward her father's house. "You don't get along with your mother?"

Kathy shook her head. "It's as if we're from different planets, Walter. There's no common ground."

"What does she say about this business? Does she think Winfield could be a clone?"

"All she says is that she wouldn't put anything past my father. She knows even less about his work than I do."

"No idea where he might be?"

Kathy shook her head. "She thinks maybe—maybe he's off on a binge. My father drinks too much, you see."

"Strange that he'd take a bus to London and switch to another bus, just to go to some small town so he could get drunk."

"Yes, that's what I think."

"But if he knew somebody there—"

"I can't imagine who, and neither can my mother." Kathy said this with a finality that precluded further discussion. We were silent until we reached her father's house.

We smelled it before we saw it: the acrid, overpowering smell of destruction by fire. It brought back a few unwelcome memories. We fought off the smell and walked up to the remains of the house.

Two men were inside, poking through the icy rubble. "No trespassing, please," one of them said when he saw us. "It's quite dangerous in here."

"It's my father's house," Kathy said.

"Ah, of course," the man replied. "We're from the fire brigade, you see. Investigating. The fire appears to be of suspicious origin." He had one of those lower-class British accents that made bureaucratic clichés sound newly minted.

"May we come inside?" I asked.

"You may, but I don't recommend it. It's dirty and dangerous, and there's not much to be salvaged."

Nevertheless, we felt obliged to take a look around. The man from the fire brigade was right. The room where we had enacted our little scene the day before was just a pile of debris surrounding a lonely and useless chimney. "Any clues?" I asked the man.

"The official verdict will have to await our final report," he replied. "But I'd say an empty petrol can in the livin' room's a pretty good clue, wouldn't you, sir?"

"Not bad," I agreed.

Kathy reached into the wreckage and pulled out something dark and shapeless. It was the dressing gown she had given her father.

"You'll have to look into having the place pulled down,"

the man said. "It's a public menace right now. The kids'll be into it in no time, no matter how much it's boarded up."

Kathy nodded, still staring at the dressing gown. Then, abruptly, she dropped it and rushed outside. I followed.

"I'm sorry," she said when she reached the sidewalk. "I'm afraid the place was too much for me."

"That's all right," I replied. "Anyway, I think you should stop apologizing."

She attempted a smile. "I'll try." She took a couple of deep breaths. Two kids riding bicycles stopped on the opposite sidewalk and stared appraisingly at the house, trying to figure out a way to make it fall on top of them. I waited for Kathy to calm down. "Let's go," she said finally, and we headed off along the now-familiar route to the railway station.

The wait on the platform was short and pleasant this time; there were no interruptions, and the train arrived on schedule. We boarded it, found seats in an empty compartment, and left Oxford behind.

Kathy seemed enormously relieved.

"I get the feeling the past couple of days have not been among your favorites," I said.

She managed a real smile this time. "You're very perceptive." And, after a pause: "You've been a big help, Walter. Thank you."

I couldn't see that I'd done much of anything, but I shrugged graciously.

"I have to spend Christmas with my mother," she said, abruptly changing the subject. "It's not the sort of thing one can get out of. You know how it is."

I nodded in sympathy. I didn't really know how it was.

"But anyway, I have a feeling you've nowhere else to go, so I was wondering if you'd like to spend Christmas with us."

I must have been a very good boy. This was better than coal in my stocking. "That would be wonderful," I said, "but I'm sure your mother wouldn't want—"

"Oh, but you see she was the one who suggested it. I told her about you when I phoned this morning. She's rather sweet on Americans, actually. That's what attracted her to my father, I think. Anyway, she's frightfully dull and not a very good cook and the two of us are likely to have a fight before the day is through, but we'd both love to have you."

"Well," I said, "I suppose I could ask her about your father. Maybe I could help figure out what's going on."

"Yes, of course. Does that mean you'll come?"

I smiled. "Of course I'll come. I have always relied on the kindness of strangers."

Kathy looked puzzled for a moment, then grinned and squeezed my forearm, just a little.

CHAPTER 22

Kathy left me at Russell Square. Our plans were set for Christmas, but there was no mention of Christmas Eve, of the long, lonely day and night that stretched ahead of me. I guess you can't have everything.

Maybe she had a date, I thought with a pang. She had to have a boyfriend, of course. Maybe her Trigorin: I pictured a bearded, serious type who would use her for his pleasure, then discard her when he became bored. Well, we'd see how he would stack up against the dashing, enigmatic American.

But we wouldn't see today. I walked back to the hotel, alone.

"Wot's yer mate been up to, then?" the desk clerk demanded before I had a chance to ask for the room key.

I hadn't had to deal with the day clerk before. He was fat and had a crew cut and wore suspenders. He was reading a newly published dirty magazine that Art would have lusted after. "Dr. Winfield hasn't shown up here by any chance, has he?" I asked.

"No, and if 'e does the police wants to know about it too. We don't like 'avin' the police nosin' around."

"I understand, but I'm sorry, there's nothing I can do about it."

"There's sumfin' I can do about it, though, and that's to kick both of you out. You owe us forty quid anyway."

"Look," I tried to explain, "the police in Oxford want to speak with Winfield. He may have witnessed a crime there yesterday. But that's got nothing to do with me. Now could I have my room key, please?"

"Wot about the forty quid?"

"It's Christmas Eve, for God's sake! Would you give me a break?"

The desk clerk grimaced, but he handed the key over. "Americans," he muttered as I headed upstairs.

I felt almost as if I had returned home when I entered the dreary room. The first thing I did was to search Winfield's stuff to see if he had left any money. I wasn't going to steal it, understand, just pay the room bill and take the per diem he owed me.

My scruples didn't matter, in any event; there was no money to be found.

I began to feel depressed. And hungry. I counted up my money, and decided I should give myself a little treat. I went to a McDonald's and had a Big Mac. It was everything I had hoped it would be.

The restaurant was crowded with last-minute shoppers resting from their exertions. So much to buy. About all I could afford, in addition to the Big Mac, was a newspaper. I read it while I ate.

PM Promises Prompt Action on Budget. Two Tots Die in Brixton Blaze: Christmas Decorations Blamed. Sixteen-Year-Old Found Murdered in East Norton. Corruption Alleged in City Inspection Services. Sutton United Sack Manager.

To Have and Have Not and *The Petrified Forest* were playing at Notting Hill Gate. No money to see them.

There was no mention of a house burning down in Oxford. More important things going on in the world, I expect. They didn't particularly interest me at the moment, however. I counted up my remaining money, and tried to figure out how I was going to buy Christmas presents for Kathy and her mother.

I realized with a start that I had an untapped source of funds—considerable funds. But as soon as the realization came I pushed it away. I wasn't ready for it yet; I would know when I was. Meanwhile, I would make do. I would have to make do.

I left McDonald's and wandered the streets of London. So much to buy—and so little time. I thought of Dickens: "The brightness of the shops, where holly sprigs and berries crackled in the lamp heat of the windows, made pale faces ruddy as they passed. Poulterers' and grocers' trades became a splendid joke; a glorious pageant, with which it was impossible to believe that such dull principles as bargain and sale had anything to do." It was exciting and depressing. The shops were closing early. Time to go home, sit with your family around a roaring fire, sing carols, read Dickens, reminisce.

Ah, well. Using all my ingenuity, I picked out a couple of gifts finally, and I trudged back to my lonely hotel room with them.

The Indian desk clerk was on duty by then, thank goodness. He smiled knowingly at me, and his smile seemed to say: *Yes, you and I are two loners in an alien world.* I smiled back and went upstairs.

I took a bath. I reread the newspaper. I reread the Gideon Bible. I stared out the frosted window of my dreary room and gazed at the ruddy faces passing by in the dark, alien world. And I waited for a visitor.

It was the Ghost of Christmas Past. I knew he would come. He always came, so why should he make an exception now that I was in London, in his hometown?

"Rise, and walk with me!"

There was no refusing him, of course. Some nights, perhaps, but not on Christmas Eve.

Through the window, across the frigid London sky, over the fierce, churning ocean—to the awful abode of memories, still alive, still waiting to claim me…

"Why, it's old Fezziwig!"

Not likely. It was a solemn, gaunt man—too gaunt, far too solemn—his bony hand resting on my shoulder, light as a leaf. I was warm—the wood stove was kept well filled. But I was hungry. Always hungry. The man's eyes glittered, reflecting the oil lamp's flickering flame. "Tomorrow is Christmas," the man said. "Least, Mrs. Simpkins says so. I've kinda lost track myself. Thing is, well, there's nuthin' to give you. I've tried—you've seen how I've tried, haven't you? But everything's gone. The entire world is gone. Oh, I'm so sorry."

The man's glittering eyes turned liquid and overflowed, wetting his leathery skin, his gray beard. His hand moved down onto my back and pulled me toward him. He held me against his chest, and I heard the *ka-thump ka-thump* of his heart beneath the frayed flannel shirt. The intensity of the sound scared me. The sudden strength of the hand scared me. I stayed there, listening, and eventually the hand loosened its grip, and I stepped back. The man looked at me—looking (I know now) for forgiveness, and if not forgiveness, at least some sort of understanding. But he was looking for something I was far too young to offer.

"Daddy," I said, "what's Christmas?"

"These are but shadows of things that have been," said the Ghost.

"That's swell," I said. "That's really swell."

The Spirit pulled me along.

And I was chopping wood outside a familiar, broken-down barn. I was sweating, despite the cold, and my arms ached. A woman came out of the barn, carrying a scrawny chicken she had just killed. Her face was lined and wind-burned, her body shapeless under a heavy coat. She stopped and looked at me, and I kept on chopping. "Walter," she said, "things is tough."

"Yes, ma'am," I said. I kept on chopping.

"Mr. Simpkins says we'll have to leave here pretty soon if things don't get better. I don't know what we'll do if we leave, where we'll go, but there's got to be someplace better."

"I expect," I said. I put another log on the block.

"But we'll take care of you, Walter. We made a promise, and no matter how hard things get, we keep our promises. You understand?"

"Yes, ma'am. Thank you, ma'am."

The woman nodded, satisfied. "Christmas is coming, but I'm afraid there won't be any gifts. We can have a tree, though. You like them old ornaments, right? We can make the place real festive. Won't that be nice?"

I split the log neatly. "Very nice," I said. "Much obliged."

The woman nodded some more. Chicken blood dripped onto the snow. "It's the spirit that counts, that's what I always say. We don't have much in the way of things anymore, but we still have the spirit, don't we, Walter?"

"Yes, ma'am. We still have the spirit."

The woman smiled and went inside. I picked up another log and put it on the block.

"Spirit," I said, "show me no more! Conduct me home. Why do you delight to torture me?"

"One shadow more!" exclaimed the Ghost.

"No more!" I cried. "No more. I don't wish to see it. Show me no more!"

But the relentless Ghost pinioned me in both his arms, and forced me to observe what happened next.

The three of us were sitting in the parlor that first year together, and Stretch was expounding. "If we're going to preserve our civilization, we have to preserve its rituals. Rituals are what bind us together. They shelter us from the terror of loneliness and death. They give life meaning and shape."

"Christmas sucks," I said.

Gwen smiled.

"It isn't Christmas that sucks," Stretch explained earnestly, "it's your *experience* of Christmas. That's why it's so important to create our own experiences—to overcome those other experiences, to connect with the best of the old civilization, to keep us alive. Don't you see?"

Yeah, I saw.

And then it was Christmas Eve. The pine boughs had been strewn, the popcorn strung, the fire roared wastefully; and at midnight we all kissed and exchanged presents that we couldn't afford.

I gave Gwen a typewriter I had bought at the Salvage Market.

Gwen gave me a book from Art's special stock. It was called *The Maltese Falcon.*

"See?" Stretch said. "Isn't this good? Isn't this the way life should be lived?"

And then later, lying upstairs in each other's arms. "What do you think of Christmas?" I asked Gwen. "Is Stretch right?"

"I think," she said, "that I have never been happier in my life."

"Spirit," I said, in a broken voice, "remove me from this place."

"I told you these were shadows of the things that have been," said the Ghost. "That they are what they are, do not blame me!"

"Remove me!" I exclaimed. "I cannot bear it!"

He let me go finally—back to my bleak hotel room, back to my guilt, back to this present that I had so longed for all my life—while he went off, presumably, to torture some other undeserving soul. No other ghosts came to call—I didn't expect any—and eventually I drifted off to a tense and restless sleep.

When I awoke it was Christmas Day.

CHAPTER 23

It was a beautiful day. Even the desk clerk's dark comments about the money I owed couldn't spoil it. If I wasn't as happy as Scrooge on Christmas Day, at least I was nowhere near as depressed as the Sandman on Christmas Eve.

I met Kathy at Waterloo Station. She was wearing a forest-green wool skirt and a white blouse with a red plaid vest. She looked gorgeous. She was carrying a shopping bag that contained a gift-wrapped box. "A blouse," I said.

She smiled. "Absolutely correct this time. You're quite good."

"Elementary. You look very nice, by the way."

"Thanks. I hope my mother will approve, but I'm sure she'll find something to criticize."

"I can't imagine what."

Kathy took my arm when we went to board the train.

Mrs. Cornwall lived in a suburb south of London. The train ride wasn't very long, and there wasn't much to say. Kathy had called the Oxford police, and there were no new developments; Winfield and her father were still missing.

"Maybe if you and I and your mother put our heads together, we can figure out what's going on," I said.

"Good luck talking about my father with her," Kathy replied. "There's a lot of bitterness."

"But probably no one knows him better."

Kathy shrugged and was silent.

We walked from the station. The town was drearier than Oxford, but not unpleasant: the houses were all intact, all inhabited; there were no stray dogs lurking. People smiled and nodded to us as we passed.

"God, how I hate this place," Kathy murmured.

"Did you live here long?"

"Too long—from when my father and mother split up until last year, when I finally managed to escape. My mother got a job as a cashier in a bank after the divorce. She's good at it—she's very practical, very precise. But it's all so dull. She's never seen any Chekhov. I don't think anyone in this entire town has seen any Chekhov."

"Does your father like Chekhov?"

Kathy didn't respond. "Here we are," she said instead.

We had reached a semidetached brick house with about ten square feet of snow-covered garden and a stunted tree in front. There was a wreath on the door and little electric candles in the front window. "Well," I said, "I'm sure we'll have a lovely time."

Kathy didn't say anything. She led the way up to the door, and we walked inside without knocking. "Hullo," she hollered. "We're here."

There was a noise in the kitchen straight ahead, and Kathy's mother came out to meet us. "Katherine, Happy Christmas, dear."

"Hullo, Mum." They leaned toward each other and kissed, missing each other's cheek by about half an inch.

Then Mrs. Cornwall turned to me and held out her hand. "And you are Mr. Sands. So good of you to come."

I shook her hand. "Please call me Walter. It was awfully nice of you to invite me."

The pleasantries continued while we took off our coats. Mrs. Cornwall was in her mid-forties, I guessed, but her features were still handsome, her face unlined. Her black hair, turning to gray, was cut short. She was wearing a white lace blouse and a black skirt, covered at the moment by a gravy-stained apron. On the blouse was a plastic Christmas-tree pin.

She looked a little like Kathy grown older, but the style was obviously different. There was a severity in Mrs. Cornwall's looks, a no-nonsense plainness that I doubted Kathy would ever want to emulate. And Kathy had mastered the upper-class British accent in a way that her mother apparently couldn't. I could see why the two of them didn't get along, but still I was disposed to like Mrs. Cornwall. After all, she had produced Kathy—and she had invited me here for Christmas. It was hard to be critical with that in her favor.

She led us into the living room. "And here is our other guest, Mrs. Stumple."

I could feel Kathy suppress a groan. Apparently I was not the only stray that her mother had taken in for the holiday. Mrs. Stumple was a thin old lady with blue hair and a look of attentive idiocy. She smiled at us and started nodding, and she didn't stop.

"Mrs. Stumple has nowhere else to go on holidays, poor thing. But she's always welcome here." Mrs. Cornwall turned to her guest and raised her voice. "Mrs. Stumple, you know Kathy. And this is her friend Walter—from America."

Mrs. Stumple nodded and smiled. "America," she repeated.

"That's right," I said. "How do you do?"

"Boom!" Mrs. Stumple replied, throwing her arms over her head. Then she started to laugh. Understated British humor, I guess.

"Oh Lord," Kathy whispered.

"Would anyone like something to drink?" Mrs. Cornwall asked.

"Whiskey," Kathy said.

Her mother gave her a look but said nothing.

"Do you have any, uh, cider or apple juice?" I asked.

"Why, yes I do, Walter. Why don't you two sit down, and I'll bring the drinks."

I sat next to a plastic Christmas tree the color of Mrs. Stumple's hair.

"I'm so sorry," Kathy murmured, sitting on the other side of the tree.

I smiled. "Quit apologizing," I said. "I'm having a wonderful time."

She shook her head. "Maybe I overestimated you, then."

I kept smiling. How had she estimated me in the first place? I looked around the room. It was filled with knick-knacks and ugly plants. There wasn't a book in sight. But it was warm, and there were several photographs of Kathy on the mantel above the fake fireplace. It was a nice enough room.

Mrs. Cornwall brought in the drinks. Sherry for herself and Mrs. Stumple. Kathy's whiskey looked as if it had been watered down. We drank a toast to the holiday.

"How is your juice, Walter?" Mrs. Cornwall asked.

"Just wonderful, Mrs. Cornwall." It was lousy.

"Oh, good. May I ask: you don't drink alcohol?"

"Never developed a taste for it."

"I certainly approve."

Kathy swallowed half her whiskey. Mrs. Cornwall ignored her. "Walter, isn't this a terrible business with Kathy's father?"

"'E's an ass," Mrs. Stumple interjected.

"It certainly is terrible. And I'd like to apologize for—"

Mrs. Cornwall waved me silent. "Please. I understand. Kathy told me how helpful you've been."

"It was the least I could do, considering my part in all this. Anyway, I thought perhaps we could talk about what happened. Maybe the three of us could come up with some explanation—maybe figure out where Professor Cornwall might be."

"Well, of course, although I don't know—"

"Could we do it later?" Kathy broke in. "I'd like to relax for a while before we start dredging up the past."

"Why, of course, dear. Perhaps we can talk after dinner, Walter."

"That would be fine," I said. The last thing I wanted was to have Kathy angry at me. The two of them clearly had their problems with each other, and I wasn't going to be in the middle if I could help it.

Mrs. Cornwall politely changed the subject. "So tell me, Walter," she said, "how do you like England?"

"I feel as if I've died and gone to heaven," I said.

"But don't you miss the excitement in America—with the rebuilding and all?"

"No, ma'am. I find hot baths exciting enough."

Mrs. Cornwall smiled.

"I never bathe," Mrs. Stumple said. Everyone ignored her.

"I went to America once," Mrs. Cornwall said. "Just for a vacation—before the war, of course. It was so alive, so fascinating. It still seems hard to believe what happened."

"You get used to it," I remarked.

"You must have suffered a great deal, though."

"Not as much as a lot of people."

"Will you be going back?"

"Maybe someday—just for a vacation."

And we talked that way till dinner. I told just enough about my life to be polite. Kathy was sullen, and Mrs. Stumple pretended to be deaf until she had an opening to say something obnoxious. There was much to-ing and fro-ing to check on the progress of the meal. Whenever her mother was out of the room, Kathy whispered an apology. Whenever they were both out of the room, Mrs. Stumple and I smiled and nodded at each other.

When everything was ready, we sat down in the small dining room. There were times when I would have fainted to see a table heaped high with turkey and stuffing and mashed potatoes and bread and vegetables. I was getting acclimated, though; this time it simply took my breath away for a quick moment.

We bowed our heads while Mrs. Cornwall said grace. Then the serving dishes were passed, and the meal began.

"And what is the state of religion in America nowadays, Walter?" Mrs. Cornwall asked, resuming the interrogation. Across the table from me, Kathy stabbed at a piece of white meat.

I thought about Jesus Christ and his little son. "Confusing," I said.

"I would think many people would turn to God for solace."

I thought of Linc. "I suppose, but a lot of people believe God has a lot to answer for."

"Which group do you belong to—if I may ask?"

I smiled. "I'm in the group that thank God they got out. Could I have some more bread, please? Everything is wonderful." Everything was lousy. Kathy was right: her mother couldn't cook. Still, I wasn't complaining.

Mrs. Stumple wasn't complaining either: her skinny arm was a blur between plate and mouth. She was too busy eating to say anything at all, which was a blessing.

Kathy picked at her food and drank a lot of wine.

When the meal was over we all helped clean up except Mrs. Stumple, who was very tired from her exertions. Then Mrs. Cornwall poured everyone but me a brandy, and we returned to the living room to exchange gifts.

"Oh, it's lovely," Mrs. Cornwall said when she opened the box from Kathy and saw the mauve blouse. "I must wear it to work this week." I looked at Kathy, and her expression said: *She hates it. Shell never wear it.*

"Oh, how thoughtful," Kathy said, holding up the bathroom scale from her mother for everyone to admire.

"I noticed you didn't have one when I visited your flat," Mrs. Cornwall explained. "And I thought, in your profession you have to watch your weight, and—"

"Absolutely. Thank you so much." Kathy tried to look pleased, but she wasn't a good enough actress yet.

"Um," I said, "I have these little presents for you." Mother and daughter looked delighted not to have to say anything more about blouse and scale. I got the presents out of my coat. "You have to understand that since my ex-employer disappeared, I've had something of a cashflow problem. But you're being so good to me, I thought, just a token—"

Oh, you shouldn't have. Oh, you're too kind.

I gave Kathy hers. She tried not to look puzzled. "It's a notebook," I explained. "The same kind Trigorin uses. You can jot down insights about your characters."

Kathy smiled. "That's awfully thoughtful, Walter." I don't believe she was acting.

"Who's Trigorin?" Mrs. Cornwall asked.

"A friend of Kathy's," I said. I gave Mrs. Cornwall her present. It was just an envelope.

She opened it and smiled. "It's a gift voucher to McDonald's," she said.

"Kathy told me you were partial to America," I said. "This was the most American thing I could find."

"That's so sweet."

"I'm sorry I didn't know you were coming, Mrs. Stumple," I said, turning to her. "But perhaps you could go to McDonald's with Mrs. Cornwall."

"I threw up in McDonald's once," Mrs. Stumple said.

"Um."

"I read somewhere they found ratshit in them 'amburgers."

"So perhaps we could talk about Kathy's father now," I said to Mrs. Cornwall.

She eyed Kathy quickly to see if there was an objection, but Kathy was silent, sipping her brandy. "All right," she said. "Where shall we begin?"

"At the beginning, I suppose, if that's all right. How did you meet?"

"I was a secretary in the Ministry of Science, you see, and he started coming there quite often. This was shortly after he arrived in England."

"He was at the Ministry setting up the Bromford project?"

"I imagine so, but it was all very secret, and he didn't talk about it with a secretary, of course."

"But you met, and—"

Mrs. Cornwall smiled. "I was a bit of a flirt in those days, I must say. Especially with the Americans—I thought they were so glamorous and exciting. And tragic, too, what with all they had suffered. Robert responded to my flirting."

"And you got married and moved to Bromford?"

"Yes, to make a long story short. We lived there about ten years—Kathy was born there."

"Did you know what his work involved at Bromford?"

"Well, he was always rather vague about it—it was secret, of course, and I'm not very bright about such things. I knew it involved children, and he told me once it had something to do with studying genetic defects from radiation. But I never really learned any of the details—I wasn't all that interested, to tell you the truth. I had my own baby, and that was enough for me to worry about."

"Did you know about the surrogate mothers?"

Mrs. Cornwall shook her head. "Only at the end, when it came out in the papers."

"Did your husband ever talk about cloning?"

"No, I never heard that term until Kathy mentioned it on the phone yesterday. But it doesn't surprise me that he would—would clone himself, if he knew how to do it."

"Why do you say that?"

Mrs. Cornwall folded her hands in her lap and stared down at them. "My husband was—is—a very self-centered man," she said. "Not vain, exactly, but—but—"

"Solipsistic," I suggested. "As if he were the only person who really existed."

"Yes, that's it. Sometimes he scarcely noticed that the rest of us were alive, I think. That was all right for a while. I had my baby, and a roof over my head. I had no reason to complain. But after Bromford, well, things became quite bad."

"This was when he went to Oxford?"

"Yes. His project was canceled, and there was nothing he could do about it; it was all political. I don't think Oxford particularly wanted him—the Ministry pressured them to take him on. But at any rate, he was desperately unhappy, and he started to drink. Whatever had kept things working at Bromford was gone now, and everyone's life became intolerable. And so I took Kathy and left. I've never regretted it. It was the right thing to do."

We were all silent for a moment. Those last remarks had sounded sort of defensive. And I wondered if everything she said wasn't aimed at Kathy as well as me: Kathy, whom she had taken away from Oxford and her father to a dull life in a dull suburb. Who so obviously despised her mother. Kathy stared at her empty brandy snifter. Mrs. Stumple had fallen asleep.

"Perhaps you'd like to see a couple of letters Robert wrote me after I left," Mrs. Cornwall said.

"Sure," I replied. I was beginning to feel uncomfortable. She left the room and went upstairs. Kathy got up and poured herself some more brandy. "We don't have to keep talking about this," I said to her. "It doesn't sound like we're going to solve the case here."

"No, it's all right," she said. "I've never heard of these letters before. I'm fascinated." She sat back down and drank more of her brandy.

Mrs. Cornwall returned with the letters, which she handed to me. "He used to send me checks every month for Kathy. I must say he was very conscientious about that. At the beginning he would enclose a letter. I think he was drunk when he wrote them. I threw most of them away. These I saved."

I took a look. They were badly typed on yellow paper. There was no date or salutation. "Read them aloud, Walter," Kathy said. I read.

Here is the check for K. Do not waste it, as I am not made of money.

I've been wondering a lot lately why I ever married you. I've decided it was a momentary weakness on my part, pure and simple. I was lonely and maybe a little afraid back then, I admit it. I thought maybe I needed the old-fashioned domestic life as an anchor while I carried on my researches. Obviously I was wrong.

I have never "loved" you. Love is a strange word, and I have never understood it. How do you know when you are "in love"? Love is just another name for a momentary weakness. You weren't in love, either, you just wanted to get out of the Ministry, and you were scared because you were on your own, with your parents dying in the epidemic and all.

All right, we have made our lives, and that's that. Your problem is, this is the only life you can make.

Please do not call, as I have no wish to speak with you.
Robert

"I've got to go to the WC," Mrs. Stumple announced. We had awakened her.

"Read the next one," Kathy said when Mrs. Stumple had left the room. I read.

I deny that I have been a bad father. Granted, my research has given me less time to spend with Kathy than you've had, but that's unavoidable. My work has kept you both fed and sheltered at a time when a lot of people are starving. Enclosed is another check. How many bad fathers do this?

Your real point, of course, is that I don't "love" her the way you love her, because I said I don't believe in the word. This is just sentimentalism. I don't see why an offspring generated out of lust and loneliness is entitled to any special consideration. Kathy shares half my genes, and that makes her important to me. What word you apply to that is your business. In any case, she has no reason to complain, and neither do you.

I don't know why I have to spend so much time on these things. When I was at Bromford, everything was fine. Now, my life is dribbling away in teaching stupid seminars and writing angry letters to you. What's the point? You wouldn't understand, though. No one understands.

Robert

I looked up from the letter. Mrs. Cornwall was staring at her hands. Kathy was staring at her mother. I heard the muffled sound of a toilet flushing. I handed the letters back. "I'm not sure," I said carefully, "that these letters do much to explain what happened the other night. I think it's pretty likely that Winfield is in fact Professor Cornwall's clone. But

I can't understand why Cornwall would deny it. Everything I know about him seems to suggest that he'd be overjoyed to find his clone—and these letters seem to bear that out. What do you think, Mrs. Cornwall?"

"Oh, I don't know what to think, Walter. He was such a— What was that word?"

"Solipsist."

"Yes. He was such a solipsist that perhaps even a clone wouldn't matter to him. But I really never could understand him, you know, and your opinion is as good as mine, I'm sure."

"Kathy?" I asked. "What do you think?"

"I think it's time to go," she said. She stood up.

"And you have no idea where he'd be now, Mrs. Cornwall?" I asked, eager to finish the interrogation.

"I imagine that he's in some awful hotel somewhere, getting drunk and feeling sorry for himself. I'm sorry, Walter, but that's the kind of man he is."

Kathy went to get our coats. "One final question," I said. "Winfield insists that someone tried to kill him back in Boston when he started tracking down your ex-husband. Does that seem likely to you? Would you know any reason why someone would want to keep Winfield from finding Professor Cornwall?"

Mrs. Cornwall shook her head. "I haven't a clue, Walter. If he is Robert's clone, I wouldn't be surprised if he decided that people were out to get him. Robert certainly was like that—he saw a conspiracy in everything."

"Yeah, that's sort of the conclusion I came to myself." I stood up. "I guess I've got to go. Thank you for a wonderful Christmas, Mrs. Cornwall."

"Oh, we were very happy to have you." She stood up too. "Walter, are you going to keep looking into this? I mean, I'm not married to him anymore, but I don't think his house should be burned down and—"

"I'll do what I can, Mrs. Cornwall."

"Thank you. Now let me get you some leftovers before you rush off."

Mrs. Cornwall bustled out into the kitchen. I went into the little entrance hall, where Kathy was waiting impatiently with our coats.

Mrs. Stumple was standing on the stairs. "Can't wait to get 'ome, op between the sheets together, eh?" she cackled. "A little 'anky-panky, that's the idea."

Kathy looked as if she were about to explode.

"Here we are," Mrs. Cornwall said when she returned from the kitchen. She handed Kathy a brown paper bag. "It was so nice to see you, Kathy. It's so convenient that the trains run on Christmas nowadays, and you can come. I only wish you'd come home more often."

"I've been awfully busy lately," Kathy said, "what with classes and rehearsals and everything."

"Of course. I understand. But if you have a chance—you could bring Walter too. We could all go to McDonald's together."

"I'd like that," I said.

"Ratshit," Mrs. Stumple called out.

Kathy and her mother kissed the air around each other's cheeks, and we left the house.

"Thank God that's over with," Kathy murmured as we walked away.

But it wasn't. A minute later Mrs. Cornwall came running down the sidewalk, coatless in the cold. She held out a package to Kathy. "You forgot your scale," she gasped. "Happy Christmas."

"Happy Christmas," Kathy managed to reply.

Her mother attempted a smile, then turned and retreated to her home.

CHAPTER 24

The platform was deserted except for a couple necking at the far end. I tried not to look.

"I'm sorry," Kathy said.

"Quit apologizing," I replied. "I really had a wonderful time."

"I didn't mean to get you into all this—all this family stuff."

"That's okay. Believe me. I think your father is fascinating."

"He's really not as...*weird* as my mother makes him out, you know."

"Excuse me for saying so, Kathy, but those letters speak for themselves."

"I know, but what I mean to say is, I think he's changed since then. I don't think he'd say the same things now."

"What would he say?"

"Well, I think the things he'd say would be...normal."

The train pulled into the station. The necking couple, their arms around each other, got on the next car. Kathy and I had no difficulty finding an empty compartment. We sat next to each other, our arms almost touching.

"Are your parents alive, Walter?" Kathy asked as the train pulled away.

I shook my head. "In America, everyone's parents are dead, more or less."

"How awful."

"You get used to it."

And then she started to cry. I had been expecting it. "It's all so stupid," she said. "The world is falling apart, and I'm unhappy because I had a lousy childhood."

"Everyone's pain is real," I replied. I reached out and took her hand.

"I was just looking for love, and I never could seem to find it. Just looking for some...normal...love."

I thought of Cornwall's love, in quotation marks: a momentary weakness. "Your mother loves you," I said. "That's pretty obvious."

Kathy shook her head. She took her hand away from mine and fumbled for her handkerchief. "So stupid," she repeated. And then: "You know, he wasn't a bad father, he really wasn't. Just, you know, *private.* And the divorce was good for all of us, I think. When I came to visit, he would take an interest, we would do things together. I remember once—it was my thirteenth birthday—he gave me a gold necklace. I still have it. And he hired a car and we went for a drive. We stopped off in a village somewhere and we had lunch, and then we just walked about. We went by a playground, and we stayed for a while watching the children running around, enjoying themselves. And I don't think I had ever felt so happy—because I didn't envy those children their normality, you see. I was there with my father, holding his hand, and nothing else mattered.

"But even so, even then, I couldn't really...connect. Sometimes I think I'm studying to be an actress just so I can find the right role. 'Is this it? Is this what you want?' Just so I can connect with him. Oh, God."

Kathy sobbed some more. I was silent. The train rattled toward Waterloo.

When it came into the station, she quickly dried her eyes. "I'm sorry," she said, as usual.

"It's all right," I murmured.

"This is inexcusable, though. You, with your problems—"

"I left my problems behind when I came to England," I lied. "The only problem I have now is a desk clerk who thinks I should pay the hotel bill for Winfield and me."

She glanced at me. Her eyes were red, her expression uncertain. "You know," she said, "you could stay at my flat if you like. My roommate moved out a couple of months ago, so there's an extra bed." And then she added quickly: "You don't have to come, of course. It's not, you know, *that* sort of invitation."

Why would she think I'd object to *that* sort of invitation? Well, it didn't really matter. "I'd like to come very much, Kathy. Thank you for asking."

She smiled. I smiled. The train came to a stop.

When we got off, the affectionate couple we had seen at the beginning of our journey was ahead of us, walking slowly, hand in hand, through the vast empty concourse. We followed them to the exit, and then our paths diverged.

Kathy lived two flights up in an old brick building on a Soho side street. She was in better spirits as we took the brief Tube ride from Waterloo. We joked about Mrs. Stumple and her mother's cooking, and there was no crying, no mention of her father. She didn't apologize until we reached her building. "Sorry for the climb," she said. "The lift never works."

"I've lived in places like that," I replied.

And it wasn't until we were on the landing outside her flat that she gripped my arm, her eyes wide with fear.

She was looking at the door. It was open a couple of inches. "I'm sure I locked it this morning," she whispered.

I pried her hand loose and moved forward.

I looked inside. The flat was dark. I strained to hear any sounds. Nothing. I kicked the door all the way open and stepped to one side. No response. I walked in.

"Winfield?" I called out, guessing. "Cornwall?" No one answered. "Is there a light here, Kathy?" I asked. She came up behind me, reached to the right, and flipped a switch.

We were standing in a large living area. At the far end, three windows looked out onto the street. There was a kitchenette to the right, and three doors leading off to the left.

The living room looked all right, except that papers were scattered all over the floor around a rolltop desk next to the kitchenette. I quickly searched the two bedrooms and the bathroom on the left. Nobody under the beds, nobody in the closets or the shower. The drawers of Kathy's bureau had been emptied. Papers and makeup and jewelry and underwear and clothing covered the floor. I shuddered and returned to the living room.

Kathy was sitting by the rolltop desk, staring at the chaos. Her arms were folded tightly across her breasts, as if to protect herself from the unseen forces that were attacking her. She seemed too stunned to cry. "You think it was Winfield?" she asked.

"Maybe. Maybe he figured he'd find an address where he could find your father. Or maybe you just got robbed. Why don't you check to see if anything's—"

Kathy got up and rushed into her bedroom. She returned a few moments later with a gold chain, which she carefully placed around her neck. I knew without having to ask that it was the one her father had given her on the magical birthday she had talked about on the train.

She leaned against the wall and closed her eyes. "Everything's going to be all right," she repeated softly, as if it were a mantra. "Everything's going to be all right."

CHAPTER 25

"Shall we call the police?" I asked her.

She opened her eyes and shrugged. "I should tell Grimby, I suppose. But that can wait until morning."

"Okay. What about your mother, then? If Winfield is prowling around looking for your father, he might end up at her place."

"Oh, I can't imagine he would go that far. Anyway, I couldn't face talking to my mother again tonight. Let's just clean the place up and go to bed, shall we?"

She was wrong not to call her mother, but I figured it wasn't up to me to argue with her. "Whatever you say, Kathy."

We spent half an hour setting the flat to rights, and then Kathy made up the bed in the spare room. I tried, and failed, to fix the broken lock on the front door. "Have to get a new one, I'm afraid," I told her.

"I'll worry about it tomorrow," she said. She looked exhausted. "I'm glad you're here, Walter."

"So am I."

"Will you be staying up?"

"For a while, maybe."

"Well, you can read, of course." She motioned to a large bookcase next to the desk. "And the refrigerator—there's not much in it, but feel free."

"Don't worry about me. Get some sleep."

She smiled. "All right. Good night, then. And thanks."

"Good night, Kathy."

She went into her bedroom and closed the door. I went into the bare room on the other side of the bathroom and sat in an uncomfortable ladderback chair, trying, and failing, not to listen. Another night eavesdropping on Kathy preparing for bed. Where had I gone wrong?

I knew, of course. Kathy was not a private eye's fantasy. She was too real. When she cried, her nose ran like a little girl's. There was a cut on the index finger of her left hand. She was mean to her mother; she apologized too much. All of this made her infinitely more appealing than the sultry blondes in the novels I had read; but it also made me unwilling to try to make her part of my fantasy. This was life, for better or worse, and I had to learn how to live it, private eye or not.

After a while her sounds ceased. I wandered out of my room and into the kitchen. Photographs of skinny models were taped to the refrigerator door. Kathy was prettier than any of them. I looked inside: tomato juice, milk, cottage cheese, eggs. She was right—not much. I noticed the bag of leftovers on the counter, next to the scale. I took out half a turkey sandwich and put the rest of the bag into the refrigerator. Munching on the sandwich, I went back to the living room.

There were mostly plays in the bookcase. Too bad. What I needed was some fat, exciting novel I had never set eyes on before—something that would sweep me up in its plot and make the hours till dawn fly by.

I read *The Winters Tale* instead. Shakespeare would do.

And after I was finished, I sat in a rocking chair by the window and stared down at the silent street.

Too deep in my dreams, I didn't react at first to the sound behind me. The ever-alert private eye. I turned my head slightly and caught a glimpse of a white shape creaking toward the kitchen. "Kathy?" I whispered.

The shape gasped and stopped. "Walter?"

"I couldn't sleep."

"Neither could I."

"There's half a turkey sandwich in the refrigerator."

"Oh. Thanks." Kathy went out to the kitchen and turned on a light. A minute later she returned with the remains of the sandwich and a glass of milk. She came over and sat on the sofa to my left. I moved the rocker slightly to face her. She was wearing a plain white nightgown and fluffy slippers. She looked very real. "You like Shakespeare?" she asked, pointing to the play on the floor next to the rocker.

"'We shall not see his like again,'" I said.

She smiled. "You're an interesting fellow, Walter Sands."

I shrugged.

She stared at me. "You don't talk about yourself, do you? My mother certainly didn't get much information, for all her prying."

"There's not much to tell," I said. "Just the usual tale of mistaken identity, unrequited love, vengeful fairies, and feigned madness. Shakespeare wrote about it all the time."

Kathy laughed. "Come on, Walter." She paused. "I've told you a lot."

Had she? I suppose she had, although I still didn't feel as if I knew her very well. Would she know me if I recited the grim facts of my past? That wasn't the way I wanted her to know me, of course; but the way I wanted her to know me was fantasy, and this was real life. I didn't want to talk about my past, but I didn't have a strong reason not to, just a temperamental disinclination. And there was this in its favor: if I talked, Kathy would stay. I wanted very much for her to stay. "Well," I said tentatively, "what do you want to know?"

"Everything. Start at the beginning." She curled up in the corner of the sofa and waited for the story to start.

The beginning. "Chapter One: I Am Born," I said. "Eight months after the war. I like to think I was conceived on the day itself—you know, so that at least something good came out of it. But I don't really know."

"Where were you born?"

"On a farm in Maine—in the northeast corner of the country. The bombs didn't hit us, and most of the fallout missed us, too, so we were better off than a lot of people. But that's not saying much. The harvest was lousy, and the winter was bitter cold, and everyone was sick and hungry, and that's when I came into the world. My mother didn't survive the labor. People were surprised that I did; I guess I didn't know any better.

"A woman on another farm had lost her baby about the same time, so she nursed me, but then she died too. There was a lot of dying going on back then. My father and I were left to make it on our own—and, believe me, I wasn't much of a help.

"I don't expect he had much fun running the farm and taking care of me. The machinery would wear out and couldn't be replaced, of course, and the growing seasons were all screwed up for a while, and there were no pesticides, and I certainly didn't know enough not to complain when there wasn't enough to eat.

"The worst of it was, he seemed to think it was all his fault. Or maybe his only fault was that he had brought me into this world, when he should have known better. At any rate, you're a pretty good apologizer, Kathy, but you've got nothing on him. The most vivid memories of my childhood are of him saying he was sorry about something—no Christmas presents, no milk, no new shoes, too many chores to be done.

"And then, of course, he got sick."

"Oh, Walter," Kathy whispered. I felt uncomfortable, playing on her sympathy, but what else could I do? She had asked for the story, and here it was.

"He made some neighbors promise to take care of me," I went on. "I was almost old enough to be useful, so it wasn't a bad deal for them. And when he got too sick to work anymore, he went out and dug a grave—I don't know where he got the strength—and then he sat down beside it and shot himself in the head. I think if he could have gotten into the grave and shoveled the dirt in on top of himself he would have. He wanted to make it easy on us. He was sorry about having to die on me; he was sorry about everything."

Kathy had started to cry.

"You want to hear Chapter Two," I asked, "or have you had enough?"

"Is it…too painful, Walter?"

Well, it wasn't as much fun as eating a Big Mac, but it wasn't as bad as I had thought it would be. "It's okay," I said. "Mr. and Mrs. Simpkins took me in. They weren't bad people, I think, but times were too tough to let them be very nice. There was too much work to be done and too little food, and there was no hope of it ever getting any better. They would talk about moving to California or Florida, places where they'd heard life was still almost normal. But it was impossible to get to those faraway places—and besides, life was normal there because the people who lived there kept everyone else out. So finally they decided to try Boston. Someone told them Boston was all right, Boston had food and jobs; things were looking up. So they hitched their old wagon to their old horse and abandoned the farm they had lived on for thirty years.

"It was a mistake."

"My father lived near Boston," Kathy said. Her gaze never left my face.

"That's right. The city wasn't hit, but, like most places, order broke down pretty completely afterward. The British sent troops and supplies over to help out along the East Coast, but for some reason Boston treated the British as if they were the enemy. Maybe it was some racial memory of the American Revolution, or maybe it was the Irish and their memories of oppression—or maybe people were just plain crazy. At any rate, the residents gave the British soldiers a hard time, and eventually you folks pulled out and left the city to fend for itself.

"And then the Frenzy started. That's what people call it now. During the Frenzy, you didn't go out at night. Night belonged to the crazies—and maybe if you went out at night there was something in the air that made you crazy too. We were spared the Bomb, but the Frenzy did a pretty good job of destruction on its own—mostly libraries and laboratories and concert halls and colleges, the places where science and civilization had once been. The places that had created the world we now had to inhabit."

"How long did the Frenzy last?" Kathy asked.

"Depends on how you want to define it. The worst of it was over within a few months, from what I'm told. But then it became a sort of institutionalized anarchy that went on for years and years."

"How could anyone live through something like that?"

I shrugged. "You got used to it. There were rules of a sort, and you learned the rules. By day things were tolerable. There were all these petty kingdoms—those six blocks of Roxbury belong to Horrigan's people, that bridge is controlled by the Monument Square gang—and if you knew the turf, you'd be all right. Unfortunately, Mr. and Mrs. Simpkins didn't know the turf."

"What happened?"

"Well, they knew enough to come into the city during the day—or maybe that was just dumb luck. All I can remember is how excited I was when I saw the Boston skyline in the distance. I had never seen anything remotely like it, outside of old magazines. Life would be different here, I knew, and since life couldn't get any worse, that made me happy.

"Anyway, we clomped along the highway, and eventually the highway became the lower deck of this two-tiered elevated structure, and we all became pretty nervous—with good reason, since nobody had done any maintenance on structures like that in years. We became even more nervous when we saw three men standing at the far end, waiting for us. Mr. and Mrs. Simpkins muttered to each other about turning back and finding another way into the city, but in the end they just kept going, right up to where the men were standing. They were carrying shotguns. 'Toll road, pal,' one of them said.

"Mr. Simpkins asked what the toll was.

"The guy looked at us. He knew the sort of people we were. 'We'll take the horse,' he said.

"Mr. Simpkins looked at his wife. They wouldn't need the horse in the city. They were scared. They just wanted to get to the food and the jobs. Mr. Simpkins got down to unhitch the horse.

"Now, see, that was his mistake. If he had tried to bargain with those guys, everything would've been okay. They would've taken his old Timex watch or something and let us go. But agreeing to hand over the horse showed just how much of a rube he was. The men lost respect for him. So the guy raised his shotgun and said, 'We'll take the kid, too.'

"One of the men came over and pulled me down from the wagon. Mrs. Simpkins started screaming then about how you people can't take the kid, he's ours, we need him, but she didn't do anything to get me back, and neither did her husband. Finally the third guy clubbed her on the head with his shotgun. 'Get outta here before we pitch you over the side,' he said.

"So she got off the wagon, blood running down her face. Her husband just stood there. And finally the two of them started hauling the wagon into the city themselves. Once or twice they glanced back at me. I think they were crying, but I'm not sure. And that was the last I ever saw of them. I think maybe I'd like a glass of tomato juice."

"I'll get it for you," Kathy said, and she raced into the kitchen.

I rocked. It had been a long time since I had allowed myself to dredge up some of these memories. I hoped it would be a long time before I'd be forced to do it again. "Thanks," I said when Kathy handed the glass to me.

Her fingers lingered against mine. "Walter, please don't go on if it's too much for you," she said.

"Oh, maybe I'll just summarize the highlights. Believe me, none of it is really very interesting."

She sat back down. "But what did the men do with you?"

"They took me home. They were part of a gang, and they figured I'd be a good addition. Everyone lived in an old warehouse in Charlestown. It wasn't bad: there was food, and there were guards all around the place, so you felt safe. But I didn't like being kidnapped, so I felt obliged to escape and look for Mr. and Mrs. Simpkins. They were nowhere to be found, however, so I ended up on my own."

"Was it hard, being on your own?"

"Sure. But I learned fast. I had to."

"Weren't there—I don't know—orphanages or something?"

"Well, there were youth camps. Some were good, most weren't so good. When things got tough—in the middle of the winter, maybe, or when I was sick—I'd head for one of the good ones. But I never stayed. I'm not sure why—some sort of independent streak, I guess."

"But you're so well educated—Shakespeare, Chekhov—when did you have time to learn?"

I laughed and sipped my juice. "Time has never been my problem, Kathy. I often wish it was. See, I don't sleep very much. Maybe an hour or two a night. The rest of the time I've got nothing to do but read and learn and think. I'm a mutant, I suppose, but it's not the sort of thing one complains about to fellow mutants.

"One other mutation that I sometimes wish I didn't have: I don't forget. I read something, and it stays with me. My mind is stuffed full of all this useless information, like an attic where nothing ever gets thrown away. You wanna do a scene from *The Seagull?* How about the awful monologue Konstantin wrote for Nina: 'Men, lions, eagles, and partridges, horned deer, geese, spiders, silent fish that dwell in the water, starfishes and creatures that cannot be seen by the eye—all living things, all living things, all living things, having completed their cycle of sorrow, are extinct.' That about sums up modern life, huh?"

Kathy continued. "'In me the consciousness of men is blended with the instincts of the animals, and I remember all, all, all! And I live through every life over again in myself.'"

"That's me, all right. It's a sad little irony of my life, Kathy, that I would like nothing better than to forget my past, but I can't. I simply can't. It's all there, waiting for me every night when the rest of the world is asleep."

"I'm terribly sorry, Walter. I didn't know—"

"Quit apologizing. There's not much left, anyway. Eventually the government got working again, and I was drafted. I spent a couple of boring years as a soldier, and then I went back to Boston. I figured it was about time I did something with myself, and so I decided to give the private-eye business a try."

Kathy looked puzzled. "The private-eye business?"

I stared at her, and I realized that I had never exactly explained it to her. It wasn't all that obvious, apparently. "I'm a private investigator, Kathy—or at least I pretend to be. Lineal descendant of Sam Spade, Lew Archer, Philip Marlowe. Friend of the distressed, foe of the distressor. I ran an ad in the local paper, and I commandeered an office in an abandoned building, and I waited for clients. Winfield was the first one that came along."

I half expected her to laugh, but she didn't. "Do you think you'll be a good private eye?" she asked.

I considered. "I'm not doing very well so far, I'm afraid. A private eye should be in control of things, I think, and I sure haven't felt that way yet about this case. Instead, I feel as if something is taking its course, and I'm just standing around watching—or worse, as if I've been made a sort of unwitting agent in the thing, helping it along when required, shoved aside otherwise."

Kathy was crying again—abruptly, unexpectedly. She rubbed at the tears vainly with her fist. "I'm sure you're mistaken," she whispered.

I made a forlorn gesture. Her sorrow was catching. I stared at the tomato juice, stared out the window, bared my soul. "I decided to become a private eye because I figured a private eye could change things, could make a difference," I said. "Oh, he can't change history, he can't rebuild America, but who can? At least he can help a few people who need help. But I'm beginning to think even that's asking too much, that I've been deluding myself with fantasies out of popular fiction. Maybe the pull of events is as strong for people as it is for nations. Maybe what's going on between your father and Winfield is as uncontrollable as—as war, as fallout. You told me on the train that you had become an actress so you could find the right role. I think I'm acting, too, Kathy—looking for a role. But I'm also beginning to think maybe it isn't worth it, maybe there are no roles worth playing. Maybe all we should do is duck the fallout and try to stay alive."

Surprisingly, my speech did little to cheer Kathy up. "Oh, don't say that, Walter," she sobbed, "don't say that." And she came over from the sofa and buried her face in my lap. I put my tomato juice down. I stroked her black hair. I felt her body convulsing with an anguish I didn't understand. Reality was too complicated. I didn't know what to do, and so I waited.

And eventually Kathy got to her feet and took my hand, and we went into her bedroom together. She undid a button or two and pulled the nightgown over her head. She was naked except for the gold chain her father had given her, and her nakedness almost stopped my heart. She lay back on the bed and waited. I took off my clothes and lay next to her. We kissed, and our bodies came together.

My hands moved over and over her flesh, as if unwilling to believe that this awful world could produce such beauty—and that the world would let me touch that flesh, that the person inside that flesh would think me worthy. That the person would think my own flesh worth touching, her need as strong as my own.

And so another dream came true, more or less. In the dream I had never kissed away her tears—she was too perfect to cry. In the dream, entering her flesh was like entering a new world, a world of warmth and happiness and hope, where I could leave my past like a shed skin far, far behind. Reality, as always, was different, but reality had its own pleasures. I experienced them all that night, and I would not have traded that night, those pleasures, for any dream.

CHAPTER 26

I was staring at Kathy when she woke up. She smiled at me. "Were you awake all night?" she asked.

"I dozed off a bit, that's all."

"What did you think about?"

"I was thinking that I'm probably the luckiest guy in the world."

She kissed me on the cheek. "Why don't we go over to your hotel and get your things?"

"Okay, but there may be trouble. Winfield and I owe them a good bit of money by now."

"Oh, I forgot. How much?"

"I've lost track. Eighty pounds or so."

Kathy shook her head. "Haven't got it."

Thinking about that hotel room made me very uncomfortable. "I suppose I could at least check out and keep the bill from getting any higher," I said. "Maybe they'll let me have my clothes, anyway."

Kathy ran a hand over my chest. "Why don't we just forget about it for today? Let's just stay here and be happy. It's a holiday, after all."

That was certainly okay with me. "Great. Um, what holiday is it, by the way?"

She laughed. "Boxing Day, Walter. It used to be about

giving gifts to your household staff or the poor or something, but now it's just a way of surviving your Christmas hangover."

"Ah. Sounds like a wonderful holiday."

"It will be this year, anyway." She kissed me, and I kissed her back, and we forgot about the hotel bill and the holiday and everything else.

We went out and got some food and a newspaper, then returned to the flat and had a late breakfast. Christmas hadn't changed the world much:

TYPHOID EPIDEMIC SWEEPING MEDITERRANEAN STATES

NEW ULSTER ACCORD SEEN POSSIBLE BY SPRING

NERVE GAS REPORTEDLY USED IN MIDEAST CONFLICT

CHRISTMAS DAY SHOOTING IN SHREWSBURY: MURDER HUNT FOR YOUTH'S KILLER

TIPS ON USING THOSE CHRISTMAS LEFTOVERS

I wasn't interested in any of it, although Kathy appeared to be. She stared at the newspaper long after I had given up and returned to staring at her. "I saw those same headlines in a thirty-year-old paper once," I said finally. "They aren't worth memorizing."

Kathy looked up at me, startled, and then smiled. "I'm sorry, Walter. I was just daydreaming."

"About what?"

"Oh, about the future."

"Stick to the present. It's safer."

"I suppose you're right."

I reached out and caressed her hand.

There was a knock on the door. Kathy clutched at me. "I'm not expecting anyone," she whispered.

I got up from the table and went to open the door.

It was Inspector Grimby. He did not look pleased to see me. "Ah, Mr. Sands, I was wondering where I might find you," he said. "You haven't been at your hotel since yesterday."

"Has a crime been committed?" I asked. "I have an alibi."

He glanced at my rumpled clothes with distaste. "Indeed. May I come in? I'd like to speak to Miss Cornwall, if she's here."

I stepped aside, and Grimby entered. Kathy was standing by the door to the kitchenette, looking worried. "Have you found out anything, Inspector?"

"Nothing of great consequence, but I had to come in to London today, so I thought I'd look in on you and tell you what we know. I also called at the Guilford Hotel, but you are apparently aware of the situation there."

Kathy blushed. "Won't you sit down?"

Grimby sat on the sofa and accepted a cup of tea. I sat opposite him. He looked as if he were about to protest, but he said nothing.

"No word of my father, then?" Kathy asked when she brought in the tea.

"I'm afraid not, Miss Cornwall. The local police have conducted inquiries, but have turned up nothing. Unfortunately, it's difficult to say how thorough their inquiries have been. Since your father is not wanted for a crime and is not apparently the victim of foul play, I doubt that searching for him would rank high on their list of priorities."

"I see. What about Winfield?"

"Well, we've had a little more luck there, although actually it does seem to complicate matters." Grimby reached into his breast pocket and took out the photograph Kathy had given him. He handed it over to her. "The owner of a pub near your father's house recognized the snap," he said. "Winfield was at the pub on the night of the fire. Apparently the publican noted the resemblance to your father, who frequents the place."

"How does that complicate matters?" Kathy asked.

"Because Winfield didn't leave until after the fire began. The publican clearly remembers when people came in with news of the fire—it was a major occurrence, you may well understand. And he remembers that Winfield left immediately afterward—to watch the fire, or so the man thought."

"But that isn't much of an alibi," Kathy pointed out. "You say the pub is nearby. Winfield could have left and come back, and no one would be likely to notice."

"Possibly true, but the publican seems convinced otherwise. Apparently he kept his eye on Winfield, who was drinking heavily and being rather obnoxious. The publican tried to engage him in conversation, assuming that he was Professor Cornwall's son, and was apparently rebuffed in no uncertain terms."

"Ms. Cornwall mentioned that her father got a phone call shortly before the fire," I pointed out. "Did anyone see Winfield use the phone?"

Grimby shifted awkwardly. He hadn't thought to ask. "If Winfield was at the pub at the time of the fire, it doesn't matter if he made any calls or not, does it?" he demanded.

"If you don't think Winfield started the fire, who *do* you think started it?" Kathy demanded in turn.

Grimby's gaze moved in my direction.

"Oh, but that's absurd," she said. "The fire wasn't set when I left the house. I went to the railway station, got Walter, returned to the house, and it was on fire."

Grimby rubbed his finger alongside his mustache. "There is more to this case than meets the eye," he said. He had obviously been studying his lines.

"Well, here's something you should consider," Kathy said. "My flat was broken into sometime on Christmas Day. The lock's all twisted—you can see for yourself. It wasn't a robbery—nothing was stolen. And it couldn't have been Walter, because he was with me all day. We think it was Winfield, trying to find out where my father might be."

Grimby rubbed a little harder. "Difficult to prove that, though," he said.

"You could dust for fingerprints," I suggested, trying to be helpful.

Grimby glared at me. "And what would that prove?" he asked. "We don't have Winfield, so we don't have any prints to compare with whatever we might find here."

"Cornwall's prints are probably available somewhere, for his security clearance," I responded. "And Winfield's prints may actually be the same as Cornwall's. Be interesting to find out, anyway."

The idea was so absurd that Grimby couldn't bring himself to reply. He returned his attention to Kathy. "Miss Cornwall, we are still interested in finding this man Winfield, and I assure you that he will be questioned about all aspects of this affair when he is apprehended. Please try to be patient."

"I'm afraid that I might be in danger," Kathy said. "Winfield sounds as though he may be mentally unbalanced."

"I understand your concern. But believe me, we are doing all we can."

Kathy stood up. "Well, thank you for taking the time to visit me, Inspector. I appreciate it."

"Not at all." Grimby stood up too. "I'll be in touch if there are any new developments." He gave me a final glare for good measure, and then Kathy escorted him to the door.

She was smiling when she came back. "He warned me about you just now," she said. "He says he can spot a bad one right away. And you're clearly a bad one."

"It's true, I admit it. I was lurking in the bushes behind you when you left your father's house. I set the fire, then took a shortcut to the railway station so you could find me there. It was very clever of me, I thought."

"And I was just beginning to trust you." She took the empty teacups out to the kitchenette.

"You know," I said, "it sounds as if the police aren't looking very hard for your father. I was thinking—we could go look for him ourselves. I mean, I've spent my entire professional career tracking him down; there's no reason why I couldn't do it some more."

Kathy came back into the living room. She sat on the sofa and closed her eyes. "I just don't know," she said after a while. "I mean, how seriously should I take all this? Rehearsals start again tomorrow, and classes start the day after that. Should I disrupt my life looking for him, if he's just on a binge somewhere?"

"It's up to you. I could look for him by myself, I suppose."

She opened her eyes and shook her head. "Oh, please, Walter, don't go anywhere. Just stay here with me."

"Okay," I said, more than willing to do that. "I only thought—"

"Look," she said, "we'll enjoy our holiday, and then tomorrow you can see about the hotel, and after rehearsal we can decide what to do about my father. Maybe he'll have shown up by then. Maybe everything will be fine."

"All right," I agreed. I sat down next to her.

She leaned her head against my shoulder and looked enormously relieved. "What shall we do with our holiday?" she asked.

"Well, uh, you wouldn't by any chance be a Humphrey Bogart fan, would you?"

The Maltese Falcon and *Casablanca* were playing at Notting Hill Gate.

Kathy hadn't seen *The Maltese Falcon* before. "Oh, but *Casablanca*…" she sighed.

I admitted to being quite fond of *The Maltese Falcon* as a novel. I didn't know anything about *Casablanca.*

"Well, it will be fun to compare our opinions," she decided.

We went to a Chinese restaurant for dinner first. Strange, wonderful food. Wonderful companion. Kathy confessed that she had been attracted to me from the start. "I couldn't figure you out—still can't, I suppose. But I thought you were utterly charming, especially compared to Winfield."

"I wish I had known," I said. "We wasted some lonely nights."

Kathy nodded. "Christmas Eve, I sat at home by myself staring out the window. I thought it would be too forward to invite you over."

I groaned. "I was sure you were out having a wonderful time with your boyfriend."

She smiled. "No boyfriend, Walter. I've been working too hard at becoming an actress."

"Do you think you'll make it?"

"Oh, I expect I have the looks to get some work. But I want to be *good.* I'm hoping to apply to RADA next year—the Royal Academy, you know, very exclusive, and that's why I'm taking all these classes. I've got so much to learn. This Chekhov is only a student production, but it's my first really big role, and I want so much to do it well."

"You sound like Nina and Konstantin—desperate to be an artist."

Kathy stared into her wonton soup. "Maybe I'm just desperate."

Desperate to please her father, to prove her mother wrong? Maybe all of the above. I didn't want to press it. This was our holiday, after all. I covered her hand with mine, and eventually I got another smile.

Later, we held hands in the darkness as the double feature began.

The Maltese Falcon was every bit as good as the novel; the actors seemed to have been born to play those roles. Watching it, I felt the same old adolescent yearning I had felt when I first read the novel—the yearning to be tough and smart and honest, according to my code, and irresistible to good-looking women. The yearning to be in control of events. To have happy endings.

I had read the novel on Boxing Day, too, I realized with a pang. And Gwen, not Kathy, had been by my side. I decided not to think about that just now.

Kathy didn't share my enthusiasm for the movie. "I didn't expect the ending," she said quietly. "I kind of hoped—"

"It's your standard trick ending," I explained. "Private-eye stories have to have trick endings."

"They should have happy endings."

"Yeah," I agreed. "But I guess maybe it's tough to have both."

"I expect you're right."

The lights in the theater dimmed, and *Casablanca* began.

Casablanca did not have a particularly happy ending either—at least, boy did not get girl. But I thought it was a wonderful movie, and I fully concurred with Kathy's judgment. She was crying at the end. "They were in love," she sobbed. "They belonged together."

"I guess sometimes love doesn't amount to a hill o' beans in this crazy mixed-up world."

"Well, it should."

I couldn't disagree with her. I was thrilled by the movies, but they didn't exactly leave us in a jolly mood. We rode the Tube in silence back to Kathy's flat and made slow, almost pensive love. Kathy held me tight afterward, but she still had nothing to say, and eventually sleep claimed her. I stayed with her for a long while, and then I wandered out to the living room.

I sat in the rocker, naked, and stared out the window.

I was thinking about Gwen. What was she doing at this instant? Churning out a last-minute rewrite at the *Globe?* Playing the piano for Stretch and Linc? Or perhaps she was lying in bed, awake, wishing she had someone to hold her, someone to protect her from the dark.

Was she thinking of me?

Gwen would understand, I thought. Gwen understood everything.

But what did that matter? Gwen was an ocean, a lifetime away.

And yet…

I hadn't told Kathy about Gwen. I had told her a lot, but I hadn't told her about dancing in the fallout shelter, about Louisburg Square, about our little family. And that meant something.

But I wasn't sure what.

I stared out the window and rocked back and forth, back and forth, as I waited for the dawn.

CHAPTER 27

Kathy and I were both on edge the next morning. The holiday was over, and now life had to go on. We were excessively polite to one another, eager to avoid the pointless arguments that tension produces. Kathy spent a long time at breakfast silently reading the newspaper, as if afraid to leave her flat and face the world. I understood the feeling. Finally she got up from the table and prepared to go.

"Will rehearsal be all right?" I asked.

"I'm sure it'll be difficult," she said. "I haven't thought about my character for days." She paused. "You'll go to the hotel, then?"

"Right."

"I have some money in the bank," she said. "Not enough to pay the whole bill, but maybe—"

"That's okay, Kathy. Let me try reasoning with them first."

"Well, you know I'm happy to help."

"I know. Thank you. You'll be back…"

"In the middle of the afternoon, I expect. We can talk then about what to do, if you like."

"All right. We'll talk then."

We embraced stiffly, but after a few moments the

stiffness disappeared, and Kathy pressed herself against me, burying her face in my neck. I stroked her hair and held her tight. When she pulled back from me finally, her eyes were moist. "Well," she said. "See you later, then."

"See you later, Kathy."

She walked out the door with its broken lock. I listened to her footsteps on the stairs until I couldn't hear them. Then I cleaned up the breakfast dishes, read the paper some more, tried again to fix the lock. I wasn't eager to face the world, either.

Facing the world meant going to the hotel, and going to the hotel meant making a choice I did not want to make.

You see, in the hotel, in my room, in a pocket inside my old suitcase, was a return ticket to America. Land of Opportunity. If I cashed it in, I would have enough money to pay the hotel bill, with enough left over to take Kathy to as many movies as she liked.

If I cashed it in, America would become the dream, and England the reality. Maybe that's what I needed. Maybe then I would quit thinking the thoughts that had whirled around my brain as I rocked all night in front of Kathy's window. Make the choice. Shut the door. Start living my life.

I had to start sometime.

The day was cold and gray and windy. The leftover Christmas decorations looked tired and faded; so did the people I passed on the street; so did the Guilford Hotel. I stood outside it for a moment, then gathered up my courage and marched in.

The desk clerk was reading another dirty magazine. He lowered it when he noticed me. "Well," he said, "the cops've started looking for you too, mate."

"Yes, I spoke with the police yesterday. There's no problem."

"The only problem's wot you owe us, then."

"Yes, about the bill. If I could just get into the room for a moment, I could—"

"Oh, no, you don't. Settle up first."

"But I can't do that unless I can get into the room. The money's in the room—at least, what I need in order to get the money is in there. Someone can come with me, if you like."

The clerk looked at me with a mixture of suspicion and pugnacity. Finally he shrugged and said, "'old on till I talk to the manager." He picked up the phone and turned away.

I stared past him at the pigeonholes that held the keys. Where was mine? Second row, middle. Yes. So close I could almost reach over and grab it. Something different about that pigeonhole. What was it?

My brain needed a moment to wake up. There was a letter next to the key. Air mail stationery, American stamp. I couldn't make out who it was addressed to, but Winfield hadn't told anyone in America where he was staying. And I had. It hadn't taken them long to reply.

"The manager's comin' out to talk to you," the clerk said, hanging up.

"Fine. I wonder if I could have that letter in my slot there."

The clerk looked behind him, saw the letter, and laughed. "No chance, mate. Settle up first." A short fat man wearing a suit and tie came over to the desk. His sparse black hair glistened greasily. "'ere's the bloke," the clerk said, gesturing at me.

"Mr. Sands, my name is Ormsby," the fat man said. "I'm the manager of this hotel."

"Hi. I wonder if I could have that letter there that's addressed to me."

Ormsby raised a hand. "One moment. I understand that you have a large unpaid balance here, and you wish to enter your room to procure the money to pay it."

"Well, yes. Sort of."

"*Sort of?* Please be more specific."

"Listen, I'd really like to see that letter—"

"Mr. Sands, we shall be happy to give you the letter when you pay what you owe us. Not before. Now, how do you intend to settle your account?"

There was my dilemma, then. I could have the letter only

if I sold the ticket. But looking at the letter made me want very much to hold on to that ticket. At least for a while. At least until I had rocked some more. So what was I supposed to do?

"Mr. Sands? I repeat, how do you intend to settle your account?"

I looked at the manager. How had he gotten so fat? He must have worked at it. He must have wanted to be fat. I disliked him very much. "I don't know," I whispered.

"You don't know? Then why are you wasting my time?"

I looked at him. "I don't know."

Ormsby shook his head, exasperated with the stupid American. He advised me that he was evicting me from my room. He started explaining how and when he would sell my possessions for nonpayment. In the middle of the explanation I turned away and walked out of his hotel.

I stood outside for a while, not knowing what to do next. I had certainly been clever in dealing with Ormsby: now I had neither the letter nor the ticket. A gust of wind made me shiver, and I began walking. So much for making my choice, for starting my life. Whichever way the wind blows. What was the matter with—

Someone grabbed my coat collar and pulled me backward into an alley. The barrel of a gun pressed against the back of my head. *Geez, that Ormsby doesn't fool around,* I thought stupidly. But then my attacker spoke and brought me back to reality. "Sands, it's me. Don't pull anything, okay? I just wanna talk."

It was Winfield. He let go of me and lowered the gun. I turned around.

He looked awful: pale, unshaven, eyes feverish, black hair dirty and uncombed. The hand that held the gun was trembling—from liquor? from the cold? "Hi," I said. "Where've you been?"

"I could ask you the same thing," Winfield responded.

"I can't pay the hotel bill, so Kathy is letting me stay with her. I just came back here today to try and pick up my things."

"I've been waiting for you," he said. "The police are after me. Everyone's after me."

His voice was whiny, full of self-pity. I leaned back against a garbage can. "Did you spend the night out here?" I asked.

He gestured vaguely with his gun. "Flophouse. I couldn't stay anyplace where they could find me."

"Where'd you get the gun?"

"Someone in the flophouse. I still have enough money for stuff like this."

"Did you burn down Cornwall's house?"

Winfield shook his head violently. "No, can't you see? I was in a pub when I heard about it. I figured I'd be blamed, so I hitched a ride back to London. I saw the police going into the hotel when I got here, so I knew they were after me. That's when I decided to lie low. Is Cornwall all right?"

"I don't know. He disappeared the night of the fire too. Hasn't shown up since."

"Disappeared?" Winfield thought that over for a moment, and then nodded. "They must be after him, too, of course—if they haven't already got him."

"You have a theory to explain all this, I take it?"

"Isn't it obvious? It's the government—Hatton's antiscience government. They're out to get me because I'm a clone. Cornwall lied to me to try and protect me, but it was too late. So now they're after both of us."

"But who was trying to kill you back in Boston?" I asked. "And why would the government suddenly be out to get Cornwall after all these years?"

"It was—it was finding out that *he* had a clone that upset them. They were willing to leave Cornwall alone until that came up. They're afraid he'll pass his secrets on to me, and then there'll be more cloning taking place. My existence forced them to act, don't you see?"

I saw that his physical condition hadn't affected his ability to spin crazy theories. I didn't bother to argue with him anymore about this one. If the facts changed again, he would find a new theory, even if it totally contradicted his old one. There would always be another theory. "Did you break into Kathy's apartment?" I asked.

He looked puzzled. "No. When did that happen?"

"Sometime on Christmas Day. We figured it was you, trying to find out where Cornwall was."

"It wasn't me," he said quickly. "I was—well, I was having a few drinks on Christmas. It must have been the government, right? They're looking for him too." He saw the expression on my face and hurried on. "You've got to believe me, Sands. I'm innocent. I haven't done anything. I don't *know* what to do. That's why I've been waiting for you."

I felt a twinge of pity for him, like the one I had felt for him at Cornwall's house, as his dream died. Looking at his alcohol-drenched helplessness, I was inclined to believe that he was innocent.

But if he was innocent, who was guilty?

I hadn't a clue. "Well, what do you want from me, then?" I asked. "I can't make the police stop looking for you."

"Give me a place to stay," he said. "Just till I can straighten out. I'll pay you—I've still got money."

"What will you do once you've straightened out?" I asked. "Start looking for Cornwall again?"

He looked as if he were about to cry. "I don't know, Sands. I don't know. Just help me. Please."

I considered. Kathy's apartment was hardly mine to offer. But perhaps she wouldn't mind if a deal could be worked out. "Give me, say, a hundred and twenty pounds to check out of the hotel," I said. "Then we can go back to Kathy's, and you can rest up there for a day or so."

Winfield seemed dubious. "Why would she go along with that?" he asked. "She doesn't think I'm her father's clone. She probably blames me for everything."

"Oh, I think she's pretty well convinced you're a clone. It'll be up to you to make her trust you."

"All right." He fished into his pocket, counted out the bills, and handed them over. "You believe it, too, don't you?" he asked eagerly. "I am his clone, right? It's obvious."

"Yes," I said. "It's obvious." I left him standing in the alley and went back to the hotel.

The desk clerk was on the phone. His eyes narrowed when he saw me approach. I laid the money down in front of him and watched his eyes widen.

He hung up quickly. "Wot'd yer do, 'old up a bank?" he asked me.

"Precisely. Remarkable deduction. I'm checking out of Room 28. Kindly pass me the key. Oh, and I'd like any mail that may have come for me."

The clerk sullenly got the bill, counted out the money, and gave me my change. Then he handed over the key and the letter.

"Thank you so much." I looked at the letter. The return address said:

R. Gallagher
E Street
S. Boston, MA USA

I put the letter in my pocket and headed upstairs.

The room was exactly as I had left it on Christmas Day. I quickly packed everything and took a final look around. Would I miss the place? Not really. Every place has its memories. You do your best to ignore them. I lugged the bags back downstairs.

Mr. Ormsby was standing in the lobby, staring at me suspiciously. "Wanna search me for towels and soap?" I asked. He didn't respond. I put the bags down and took out a pound coin. "Listen," I said. "I just want to show that there are no hard feelings about all this." I stuffed the coin into the breast pocket of his suit. "You look a little peckish, Mr. Ormsby. Why don't you go have an ice-cream cone on me. And keep the change, okay?" I picked up the bags and walked out of the hotel.

I hailed a cab—never did that before in my life—and instructed the driver to stop in front of the alley. Winfield jumped in, and we were off to Kathy's. In the cab, Winfield kept twisting around and looking out the rear window.

"See anyone?" I asked.

"They're too clever to let themselves be noticed."

I didn't ask why they cared if we noticed them—if they wanted us, why not just capture us? Winfield's paranoia was too complete to be worth questioning.

Once inside Kathy's flat, I made him some tea and toast while he sat shivering on the sofa. He consumed both greedily, then leaned back and closed his eyes. The warmth and safety of the flat seemed to drain him of whatever energy he had left.

"Why don't you get some sleep?" I said. "There's a spare bedroom you can use."

"I s'pose." He stood up with an effort. He happened to glance out the window, and then turned away quickly. "There's someone out there," he said.

"Oh, I don't think so," I said.

He glared at me. "There's someone out there," he repeated.

"All right," I agreed. "But what can we do about it?"

He shrugged helplessly. "I don't know," he said. "I can't think anymore."

"Look," I said. "Go to bed and we'll talk about it later, okay? Maybe they're just hanging around, hoping you'll lead them to Cornwall."

He didn't have the strength to disagree. "Will you stay here?" he asked.

"I'll be here." I led him into the spare bedroom. He managed to take his shoes off, and then he fell back on the mattress, asleep.

I covered him with a blanket and took his gun away. Back in the living room, I glanced out the window. I couldn't see anyone. I took Winfield's dirty dishes out to the kitchenette and washed them.

I was beginning to think that helping Winfield was a stupid idea. I should just call Grimby and have the police cart him away, innocent or not. I didn't need him here, and neither did Kathy. Him and his paranoia, him and his solipsism. *They're out to get me because I'm a clone.... My existence forced them to act, don't you see?* If he hadn't offered me a way out of my dilemma at the hotel—

My dilemma. I took out the letter from Bobby and stared at it, smiling. At least something had worked out right. I started to open it, and then abruptly stopped.

My existence forced them to act, don't you see?

No, not quite, but—

The morning newspaper was sitting there on the counter in the kitchenette. I glanced through it quickly, confirming my memory of what I had already read. Then I went and got a map of England I had noticed in the rolltop desk when cleaning up Christmas night, and I studied it for a long while. Then I made a few phone calls.

I had a Theory, don't you see? The kind private eyes have all the time, I suppose, but I wasn't used to theories, and this one tantalized and bewildered me. A real private eye would know in his gut if his theory was right, I suppose, but all my gut told me was how much I didn't know, how much still didn't make sense. I thought and I thought and I thought. I was still thinking when Kathy returned to the flat late in the afternoon.

"Hi," she said.

"Hi." We kissed shyly. "Um, we have a visitor," I said. I showed her Winfield, still passed out in the spare bedroom.

Kathy gave me the puzzled look I had been anticipating.

"He was waiting for me outside the hotel," I explained. "I let him come here in exchange for paying the room bill." The truth, although not quite the whole truth. And anyway, there was something more important on my mind. "Listen," I said. "We can talk about him later. I want to talk about your father now."

Kathy's puzzled expression turned frightened. "What about him?"

"Come with me," I said softly. I brought her back to the living room, and we sat down on the sofa. "Did you happen to notice this story in the newspaper today?" I showed her

the headline: "CASTLE FROME TEEN MURDERED."
Kathy shook her head. "There have been two other stories
like that since—well, since the day before Christmas," I
went on. "I don't have the newspapers, but 'SIXTEEN-
YEAR-OLD FOUND MURDERED IN EAST NORTON'
was the headline for the first story, and the next one was
'CHRISTMAS DAY SHOOTING IN SHREWSBURY:
MURDER HUNT FOR YOUTH'S KILLER.' I remember
stuff like that."

"I don't understand," Kathy whispered. "What does this
have to do with my father?"

I showed Kathy the map, on which I had marked the
three murder sites. They formed a rough semicircle around
Oxford. "East Norton is a little ways off the Ml," I pointed
out. "That looks to me to be the route a bus would take
between London and Nottingham. I called around this
afternoon, Kathy. None of the murders have been solved."

"Are you saying my father committed these murders?"
Kathy asked, her voice rising. She thrust the map back at
me with barely a glance.

"I think it's a possibility we have to consider," I replied.
"I think the victims may be the clones he created at
Bromford. They were probably scattered all over the
country when his project ended, but it wouldn't have been
that difficult for him to keep track of where they were."

I paused, frightened by the coldness in Kathy's
expression. I had known this wouldn't be easy. "Go on,"
she said.

"Seeing Winfield affected your father terribly, Kathy. We
both saw that. But why would he deny that Winfield was
his clone? It's obvious that he is. I think your father must
have become profoundly disenchanted with his work over
the years—a lot of people seem to think cloning is terribly
immoral. You yourself said he's changed, become more
normal. And maybe that explains why he's drinking so
much. The shock of finding out that an adult clone of his
has survived might have triggered something in him—
might have made him decide once and for all that he should

rid the world of these creatures. And maybe that's what he's doing now."

Kathy was shaking her head. "This is so absurd. I'm sitting here listening to you accuse my father of murdering children in cold blood. That's hardly 'normal,' is it? Walter, weren't you there the other night? Didn't you see the same person I saw? He's an old man, Walter. He's changed, but he hasn't become a murderer. You don't have any evidence, you just have—have newspaper headlines."

"I understand that," I said softly. And I didn't mention the one other piece of evidence I had: Winfield himself. Winfield, I knew, was willing to steal, and, in his solipsistic universe, I was pretty sure he'd be willing to murder too. He probably would have murdered Cornwall that night in Oxford, if I hadn't stopped him. If Winfield could do it, why not the man who had cloned him?

But of course the argument didn't quite make it. How did I know that they would behave the same way? I wasn't going to convince Kathy if I couldn't do a better job of convincing myself. "Look," I said, "I'm not at all sure I'm right, Kathy. But if I am, then we have to do something immediately, before someone else dies."

She suddenly closed her eyes. I don't think she liked the mention of death. "Do what?" she whispered.

"Well, go to the police, I guess. Tell Grimby. The Ministry of Science must have some record of the clones and what was done with them. The police could at least get a hold of that list and find out if I'm right. If I'm wrong, then I owe you a very deep apology."

Tears leaked from beneath her eyelids. "Don't go to the police, Walter," she said. "I beg you. I don't think I could stand that."

"But we've got to do something, Kathy. I know it's only a theory, and maybe not a very good one, but lives may be at stake."

Her nose was running. Her face looked like it was about to be washed away. "Find that list of clones, Walter," she said when she had regained a little control. "I know you can do it. And if you're right, do whatever you like. I'll help you. Just don't go to the police with nothing but this. Okay?"

It seemed pointless to me, and I wasn't at all sure I'd be able to find the list, but how could I argue with her—how could I make her go against her love and loyalty?

"Okay, Kathy," I said. "Grimby probably wouldn't believe me any more than you did. I guess I'll have to find the list."

It was an awkward afternoon. It didn't become any less awkward a couple of hours later when Winfield came out of the bedroom, yawning and scratching at his beard.

He nodded to Kathy; she nodded back. "I didn't do it—any of it," he said to her.

"That's what Walter has been telling me," Kathy replied.

"Do you believe me?"

"I don't really know what to believe anymore."

"I think this is more complicated than any of us can imagine," Winfield went on. "Did Sands tell you that I'm being followed?"

She shook her head.

Winfield glared at me.

"I didn't want to worry her," I said. I shrugged at Kathy while he went to the window and stared out.

"Still there," he announced. "He's the one who broke into your apartment—him or one of his cronies."

"I guess we're safe here," I said, "if they haven't come in to get us yet."

Winfield sat down and drummed his fingers on his thigh. "What are we going to do? What are we going to do?" he murmured.

I didn't even consider telling him about my theory. But I figured I had to say something to shut him up for a while. If I found Cornwall, after all, the case would be over, and I wouldn't have to worry about Winfield again. "I'm going to look into this government conspiracy tomorrow," I said.

"We can plan a course of action once I've learned a little more."

Winfield nodded. "Good idea. What exactly are you going to do?"

"Um, well, I haven't formulated it too clearly yet, but I'll be starting at the Ministry of Science."

"Yeah. That's the place to start. Be careful, though."

"I'll be careful," I said, surprised at his solicitude.

Winfield drummed his fingers some more. "Got any liquor here?" he asked. The question was apparently directed at Kathy, although he was gazing off into space when he asked it.

"No. I'm sorry," Kathy said.

He looked around, bored and thirsty, but saw nothing that interested him. "Guess I'll get cleaned up," he muttered. "Bathroom?"

Kathy pointed the way, and he left us.

"Does he remind you of your father?" I asked her.

She shook her head. "I love my father."

Later, the three of us ate a silent meal together; then Winfield (after a quick glance out the window) retreated to his room.

"I suppose I should go to bed too," Kathy said.

"Do you have another rehearsal tomorrow?"

She nodded. "I was quite awful today. I expect I won't be much better tomorrow." She paused a moment, then said, "Will you be staying up?"

A little awkwardness here. "Yes," I replied. "I guess I'll be staying up."

"All right. Well, good night, then."

"Good night, Kathy."

And she left me alone in the living room. It didn't seem quite right to sleep with her, with my theory looming over us. We both seemed to understand that. And I had another reason for wanting to stay up. I got the letter from Bobby and took it over to the rocking chair. I sat down and stared at it for a moment, savoring my expectation, and then I opened it. It was laboriously printed in black ink on white lined paper.

Dear Wally,

Season's Greetings from your freinds in America! Gwen and all showed your postcard to me, so I decided to respond thru my trusty secketary ** Doctor J** (Hi!— **Doctor J**) as my eyes aren't what they used to be. It's good to hear your doing well and the case is coming along. We all have great faith in your ability. Have you managed to kill any Brits yet?

We are all fine. Well, that is not exackly true, Linc has been feeling pretty bad as you know and we are all worried about him. Maybe if he can make it thru the winter everything will be ok. Stretch is the same as always. He is feeling pretty important as he is in line for a promotion. Someone should cut him down to size (ha ha). He has put a sign up at your office like he promised.

Gwen is working hard. She doesn't say anything but of course she misses you. She isn't writing because she says your coming back soon once you wrap up your case so why bother?

As far as Gallagher Enterprises Inc. is concerned we are doing great. We made another run up to Mr. Fitch's place the other night. Some nice porselin, a grandfather clock, even another Sarjent. The things that are still out their! He was awful disappointed that you weren't with us but he understood when I told him about England. He started resiting Shakspear and it was all pretty boring, altho Im sure you would have liked it.

Speaking of paintings, I have been waiting for your Renwars to come back from the shop. I think they'll look great in my office don't you?

Anyway we all hope you are well and doing fine. Write to us again and let us know what you are up to. And dont forget to go to **Ireland** which Im sure is a lot nicer than crummy old England.

Happy New Year!
Bobby

(and **Doctor J**!)

I read the letter about fourteen times, even though I had memorized it the first time through. It made me feel slightly dizzy—the way I had felt my last night in Boston, standing by the statue of Columbus—as if I or the world were spinning too fast.

I wanted to concentrate on the news—on Linc's sickness and Stretch's promotion and all the rest. But I couldn't. I could only think about one thing: my case.

I had another Theory.

Strange that it should arrive in such an offhand manner, via a casual letter from an old friend. But my first theory had arrived in much the same way, from casual reading of a few newspapers. Not the way it's written up in the private-eye textbooks, certainly. Maybe both theories were wrong—maybe they were as absurd as Winfield's. I just didn't know, and my gut didn't tell me.

But I knew that I would find out tomorrow.

I stood up and stared out the window. The street was empty; the world was asleep. *Tomorrow*, I thought. *Tomorrow.* I sat back down, folded up the letter, and started rocking, thankful for once that I had the long sleepless night in which to think and plan.

CHAPTER 28

In the morning I went out early and bought a newspaper. There was nothing in it about a teenager being killed. Good. And no one followed me. Bad. I was very nervous.

Kathy looked just as nervous when she got up, and I felt obliged to reassure her. "How are you going to find the list?" she asked.

"Oh, we private eyes have our ways. Can I borrow the notebook I gave you?"

"Of course." It was on her night table. She handed it to me. "I'm afraid I haven't had any insights about my character to put in it yet."

"That's all right. They'll come."

She sat on the bed and stared down at an old scatter rug. "What shall we do," she asked, "if you don't find out anything?"

"Don't worry," I said. "We private eyes always find out something."

"I think you've read too many novels, Walter."

"Funny, you're not the first person to tell me that."

For some reason I felt obliged to reassure Winfield too. He was bleary-eyed but apparently rational when he came out of his room looking for breakfast. "It's going to be dangerous," he warned. "These people burned down Cornwall's house. No telling what they'll do to you."

"I can handle them," I said. "Everything's under control."

"I don't like the idea of being left alone," he said when he found out Kathy was also leaving.

"No one's going to bother you. I'm going to take care of that too."

He shook his head. "I hope you know what you're doing."

I smiled and nodded confidently. I hoped so too.

I left Kathy getting dressed and Winfield sitting by the desk, staring nervously at the unlocked door.

This was it, then. Time to show what I could do. Time to show that I was more than a novel reader. When I reached the street, I stopped for a moment and looked around casually. I thought I saw him, but I wasn't sure. The day was cold and clear. I walked slowly to the right, feeling the faint rays of the sun on my face. I started to speed up as I turned the corner. Then I stopped abruptly and bent over to tie a shoelace that did not need tying. I caught a glimpse of a gray-overcoated man across the street, struggling to keep up. That was all I needed. I stood up and kept walking.

I could have raced across the street and confronted the man, and in the process tested Theory 2 in all its particulars, but there would be time enough for that. Theory 1 was more important right now; I just needed to know that the gray-overcoated man was with me.

I walked through Soho, the theater district, and Trafalgar Square, then down the starchily official length of Whitehall. The Ministry of Science was in a little courtyard in a little side street. Its location was commensurate with its status in the government, I supposed. I walked inside. The gray-overcoated man would not follow me here, I knew; instead he would be forced to linger outside in the cold, curious and impatient, while I did my business. I hoped he would not have to linger long.

I was standing in an oppressively ornate foyer. Grim portraits of royalty and stuffy ministers stared down at me. A tiny fire smoked in a marble fireplace. The place was as cold as any building in Boston.

A couple of bobbies stood guard next to a large reception desk, where an old and cranky-looking woman was talking on the telephone. She was wearing a black dress, and looked like she was in perpetual mourning. I stood in front of her until she put the receiver down. "May I help you?" she asked. Her tone suggested that a positive response would be the greatest of impositions.

"I'd like to see Mr. Carstairs, please. Mr. J. T. Carstairs."

"No Mr. Carstairs here." A hint of triumph in her voice this time: complete victory on the first exchange.

I was prepared for the response. It had been a long time, after all, and I hadn't come across the name in any of the stuff I had read about the place at the newspaper library. "Perhaps I could speak to his successor, then," I suggested.

She stared in amazement at my persistence—and my idiocy. "There's *never* been a Mr. Carstairs here," she said. "Eighteen years I've worked here in this Ministry and never a Mr. Carstairs."

I wasn't prepared for that. I don't forget things. The letter had been signed "J. T. Carstairs." He had been from the Ministry of Science. *I have enclosed a list of those scientists whom our American Relief Expedition accommodated with air transportation to England....* The secretary could have been senile, but she certainly didn't sound it.

Not an auspicious start. But I couldn't stop to puzzle it out; I had to talk to *somebody*. And, after all, Carstairs was just a name: he was no more likely to have the information I needed than anyone else.

I smiled my most winning smile. "I wonder if you could help me, then. Someone gave me the name of this Carstairs person, but obviously it's a mistake. I'm a reporter—for *The Boston Globe*, back in America. Perhaps you've heard of it? No? Well, I'm researching an article on American scientists working in England, you see, and I wanted to talk to someone in this Ministry. Perhaps you could suggest the appropriate person."

"You'll want the Public Information Department, then," she said accusatorily. "I'll ring Mr. Finch-Thistle. Your name?"

"I would certainly appreciate that. The name is Sands. Walter Sands."

She rang, held a brief conversation, then hung up. "Mr. Finch-Thistle will be with you presently," she announced, and she gestured dismissively toward an uncomfortable-looking straight-backed chair. I sat and awaited Mr. Finch-Thistle.

The name conjured up images of some epicene British bureaucrat, sallow and supercilious. The person who finally came for me was quite different—young, florid-faced, and with the mischievous eyes of a schoolboy. He looked as if he enjoyed his pints of bitter. "Mr. Sands? Arthur Finch-Thistle here."

I stood up, and we shook hands.

"We don't get many reporters from the States," he said as he escorted me up a grand staircase. "In fact, I believe you're the first I've encountered."

"Things are starting to pick up over there," I said.

"Glad to hear it. Glad to hear it." He led me through a frosted-glass door into a tiny office that bulged with stacks of paper. The window behind his desk was filthy; one pane was broken and had been replaced with plywood. "Excuse the squalor, if you would. Budget cuts, you understand."

"I understand." I sat on a chair with a cracked plastic seat that had been poorly repaired with strips of tape. I began to feel comfortable; the place reminded me of my own office.

"Now, how can the Public Information Department help you, Mr. Sands?"

My story had to be adapted slightly for my new audience, but basically it was the same one I had prepared for the mysterious J. T. Carstairs. "Are you aware, Mr. Finch-Thistle, that the British forces brought many

American scientists back to England after the war?"

"Um, certainly sounds familiar. Before my time, of course."

"Well, I'm interested in one of these scientists: a biologist by the name of Robert Cornwall. When he lived in America, Cornwall was involved in cloning. Do you know what cloning is, Mr. Finch-Thistle?"

"Copying a frog or something, right? Never was very good in biology. Call me Arthur, incidentally. Saves a lot of energy."

"Great. Call me Walter. You're right about copying frogs—but Cornwall was interested in copying people too. And that's what I believe he's been doing here in England."

"I daresay this Ministry isn't involved with anything like that, Walter."

"I'm not so sure about that, Arthur," I said. I took a breath. *Here goes.* "Cornwall ran a research center at Bromford up until about ten years ago, when this Ministry shut it down. It was shut down, apparently, because people started raising questions about what was going on there. Cornwall then went to Oxford, and he retired a few years ago."

"But this is all ancient history," Arthur said, smiling. "It was the old government."

"True, but if my information is correct, and Cornwall was cloning human beings at Bromford, the question remains: *What happened to the clones?* Is it possible that the Hatton government, while it might not actually support cloning, might be willing to enjoy the fruits of the previous government's efforts? I'm not saying that's true, I'm just raising the possibility. It's one I raised with Cornwall, incidentally, when I interviewed him recently."

"And what did he say?"

"He told me a lot," I lied. "He said, for example, that he had been cloning military leaders, mathematical geniuses, and the like at Bromford. He said that Hatton's government had stopped further cloning, but they certainly intended to use the existing clones for the government's own purposes when the time was right. And immediately after the interview he did a curious thing."

"What's that?"

"He disappeared. He hasn't been seen since. Stimulates the curiosity, wouldn't you say?"

Arthur's good humor seemed to be fading. "Why would American readers be interested in a story like this?" he asked.

"Oh, lots of reasons. They might want to know how sincere our ally's commitment is to ridding itself of this kind of godless science, for example. Or they might wonder about who exactly got cloned, and why. What would England do with a bunch of brilliant young military leaders, for example?"

Arthur picked at a pimple on his neck. He hadn't shaved very well. It occurred to me that he was here because he was a loser. The sallow, supercilious bureaucrats were in more important ministries. "What specifically is it that you want from us, Walter?" he asked. His tone had become rather formal.

"I want to know about the clones, Arthur—where they are, who they are, what the government is doing with them. Can you help me?"

Arthur stared at the ceiling for a long moment. It was dirty and water-stained. "Supposing such information were available," he said, "it would certainly be secret, and we would therefore be unable to share it with you."

"Then I'll have to write the story as I see it," I replied self-righteously, "and let my readers draw their own conclusions. Of course, if the information clears the government of any—oh, how shall I put it?—impropriety, I would think you might want to share it with me, secret or not."

"How would it 'clear the government,' as you put it?"

"Well, what would you do if you came into power as a humane, antiscience government, and you found out you had inherited this bunch of young clones?"

"I'd put them up for adoption, I daresay."

"Of course you would. You'd try to give them as normal a life as possible and hope they'd forget about whatever happened at Bromford. Now maybe your government did that and maybe it didn't. Maybe Cornwall has an ax to grind with the government and is lying about everything. Maybe the government had nothing to do with his disappearance. I don't know, but I'm hoping someone will tell me."

Arthur sighed and stood up. He had not bargained on this when he came to work this morning. "Would you kindly wait here for a few moments, Walter?"

"Of course."

He left the office, and I leaned back in my chair. Could have been worse. Of course, I hadn't accomplished anything yet, just made a junior bureaucrat a little nervous. I picked up a press release from his desk. It was full of misspellings.

He was gone a long time. When he returned, it was with the brisk step of a junior bureaucrat who has been told what to do. "Sorry for the delay, Mr. Sands. I was wondering if I might examine your press credentials—purely a formality, of course. I should have done it to start with. An oversight on my part. Please excuse."

I smiled at him and noted that we were back on a last-name basis. "I haven't got any credentials, Mr. Finch-Thistle. We've lost some of those formalities back in the States."

Arthur smiled apologetically. "Well, I'm sure you can understand that we can't do anything without the proper credentials."

"I can understand. But that means I'll have to write the story as it stands. How shall I word it? 'A spokesman for the British government refused to comment on the allegations.' Does that sound about right?"

"Oh, now, Mr. Sands, surely you can understand the need for—"

"I can understand. But I've got a story to write, whether or not the British government wants to help."

Arthur pondered. *Oh, come on, give in.* "I suppose we could write to your newspaper," he suggested. "That would establish your *bona fides.*"

"I don't have time for that," I responded. "I'm leaving the country tomorrow. The *Globe* is influential, but it doesn't have a lot of money to send its reporters overseas. I'm way over budget as it stands."

"But surely, Mr. Sands, you didn't expect us to provide you with this kind of information immediately," Arthur objected. "Even if it exists, it strikes me as being quite obscure. And with the security issues to be dealt—"

Time to get mean. "Mr. Finch-Thistle, I don't expect anything. You will either help me today or you won't help me at all. The choice is yours. Either way, the story is going to get written."

Arthur tried to suppress a glare. He did not entirely succeed. "Would you excuse me again?" he asked, and he strode out of the room without waiting for a reply. He was away somewhat longer this time, and he returned looking decidedly harried. He didn't sit down. "We are attempting to locate the information you have requested, Mr. Sands," he announced. "This is certainly against our policies, but we have decided to make an exception. Even so, we cannot guarantee that we will find this information today. If you would like to call us, or leave a number where you can be reached, we will be happy to—"

"I'll wait, if that's okay with you." Arthur shook his head. "Perhaps you don't understand. This may take hours, or we may not even find it."

"I've got nothing better to do. I'll wait."

Arthur tried to suppress a look of total exasperation. He did not succeed. "Very well," he said. "You will have to wait downstairs, however. You'll be sent for when—if—we find what you are looking for."

"Terrific."

Arthur escorted me back down to the lobby, where I sat in the uncomfortable chair across from the cranky old receptionist. People came and went; the phone buzzed;

morning turned into afternoon. I chatted with one of the bobbies. I listened to my stomach growl. I thought about the man who was waiting for me outside in the cold. Should I go out there and get it over with? No, this was more important.

I tried not to look as tense as I felt. Arthur Finch-Thistle approached. I stood up.

He looked embarrassed. "Sorry," he said. "Only going to lunch. Be back shortly."

I sat down and waited.

He returned within an hour. His florid face was a little more florid than when he had left. Had his pint, probably, to help him make it through the afternoon. He nodded to me. "Working on it," he said.

"Waiting," I said.

He came downstairs again an hour later. "Mr. Sands, would you come with me, please?"

"Success?" I asked.

"I'm taking you to speak to the Deputy Minister."

We went to a different floor this time. The offices looked larger and less dingy. There were portraits of sallow, supercilious men on the walls. Arthur knocked on an oak door. The sign on it said simply: "D. Cahill."

"Come," a deep voice said. Arthur opened the door and ushered me in.

D. Cahill was a large, silver-haired man wearing an expensive suit. His eyebrows were so bushy they looked as if birds could have nested in them. The dark eyes beneath the eyebrows stared at me curiously. "Mr. Sands," he said. It sounded like a statement, not a question or a greeting.

I nodded. He gestured to a seat. I sat. Arthur sat too. Cahill ignored him.

"I understand you are preparing to write some sort of exposé of the government for an American newspaper," Cahill said to me. He had a beautifully intimidating upper-crust accent. He made the phrase "American newspaper" sound faintly obscene.

"I'm just trying to write a story," I responded. "I've told Mr. Finch-Thistle the facts as I know them so far. If you have more facts, I'd love to know them too."

"Some facts are more newsworthy than others," Cahill observed. "In my experience, reporters tend to ignore the facts that aren't newsworthy."

"Facts are a lot easier to ignore if you don't know them," I observed in turn.

Cahill made the faintest of movements with his shoulders. It could have been a shrug. There was a terminal on his desk. He switched it on and typed something on the keyboard. "You are investigating Robert Cornwall's activities at Bromford, and what happened after Bromford was closed," he informed me unnecessarily. "You think it had to do with the cloning of human beings, and you think the experiments are continuing under the present government. I am now going to tell you the truth. It will be interesting to see if you believe it as readily as you believed a somewhat more sensational fiction."

I didn't argue. I took out Kathy's notebook and a pencil and smiled expectantly.

"In fact," Cahill went on, "Cornwall told you the truth about the cloning. That is what he was doing at Bromford. The previous government were interested in its potential for perpetuating useful genetic traits, especially in view of the somewhat doubtful future of the human race back then. This is precisely the kind of meddling with nature that our present government find reprehensible, of course.

"The other assertions that you claim he made to you are incorrect, however. When Bromford was closed, there was an attempt to continue Cornwall's study in some fashion. The new government put an end to that as soon as they learned of it. The children involved were placed in suitable homes and have not been bothered since. And I sincerely hope that this article of yours does not cause them to be bothered now. They are not freaks, Mr. Sands. They are human beings, and we have treated them that way."

I pretended to scribble a few notes. "Well, that's just terrific, sir. Believe me, I think it's eminently newsworthy. I wonder if you have any proof, though."

Cahill raised one of his immense eyebrows.

"Right now I have your assertion and Cornwall's assertion," I explained. "How am I to choose between them without proof?"

Arthur cleared his throat. "As I suggested to you might be the case, Mr. Sands, the relevant documents are secret."

"All right," I said. "I don't need copies of them. Just let me take a peek, to satisfy myself that they exist."

I stared at Cahill and tried to maintain an expression of detached journalistic interest. Wasn't easy. Cahill returned my stare, and then gave another one of his almost-shrugs. "I expected as much," he said, and he typed something else on the keyboard of his terminal. "This is only for purposes of verification," he added. "If you say that I showed this to you, I shall deny it."

He swiveled the screen halfway toward me. I leaned forward.

On the screen was the beginning of a memo dated nine years ago. I didn't recognize the name of its writer or recipient. Its title was "Disposition of Subjects in Research Program 014-6125." It was what I wanted.

It began by sketching in vague bureaucratic terms the background of the situation. The children were always "subjects," never "clones." The Ministry had determined that the research program was to be terminated and the subjects put up for adoption. The adoptive parents were informed in a general way about the research, but it was not felt necessary to go into detail. The Ministry was prepared to deal with the appropriate social welfare agencies if problems were to develop, but it was not expected that any would.

The list of adoptive parents follows:

I thought of the government office in Boston and the other list, slid across the desk to me for one magic moment. "May I page down?" I asked.

Cahill reached forward and pressed a key. A new page appeared. When he noticed that it showed the list, he quickly pressed the key again. "There's no need for you to see the names," he said. "I don't want you bothering any of those people."

Too late. "You're absolutely right," I said. "I've seen all I need to see." I stood up. "I want to thank you both for taking the time to provide me with this information. I'm sorry for any inconvenience I've caused. I can't imagine why Cornwall would have said the things he did."

"We'd appreciate a copy of the article when published," Cahill said gruffly.

"Of course, of course." I headed for the door. I didn't have time to waste on pleasantries.

Arthur followed me, clearly delighted that everything had turned out all right. "So glad we could help, Walter. We do try to oblige, you see. The Deputy Minister is a crusty sort, but he—"

I didn't listen. I had to think. "Pay phone?" I interrupted.

"Oh, well, you could use my phone."

"Thanks. I need privacy, though."

"Of course."

We returned to his office. He showed me how to make an outside call, and then tactfully departed. I dialed long distance directory inquiries and got a number. I dialed it. No answer. I cursed and hung up. I thought for a moment, then got the number for BritRail information and called it. The person who answered told me what I needed to know. Finally, I dialed Kathy's number, hoping she'd be home from rehearsal.

She was.

"Hi, Kathy, it's me."

"Hello, Walter. Did you—were you successful?"

"Yeah. I saw the list. I'm sorry, Kathy. I was right. The kids in East Norton and Castle Frome were on it. The other kid didn't have an address in Shrewsbury, but the list was old and his family could've moved there."

She was silent for a moment. I looked at Arthur's grimy ceiling. This couldn't be easy for her. "What do you want me to do, Walter?" she asked in a whisper.

"Well, the obvious next candidate on the list lives in Bath. I got the phone number from directory inquiries and called, but there's no answer. I'm going to Bath—it's only an hour and a quarter from Paddington. Do you want to come?"

"Yes."

"Good. Meet me under the message board as soon as possible. What's Winfield doing?"

"I'm afraid he found my bottle of whiskey. He's passed out."

"Good. Listen, it might not be a bad idea if you brought his gun. I hid it in the top drawer of your bureau."

"Oh, Walter."

"Just in case, Kathy. Would you rather we just called the police?"

"No. I'll be there. And Walter?"

"Yes?"

"Thank you."

"Okay, Kathy."

I hung up and hurried out of the office. Arthur was lingering in the corridor. I smiled at him. "Thanks. Gotta run."

He smiled back. "Don't mention it. I'll escort you out." He brought me downstairs and left me at the doorway, expressing warmest regards that I absently returned.

I opened the door and walked outside. The day had turned overcast and raw; the late-afternoon sky looked heavy with snow. I took a deep breath. Theory 1 was on its way to being proved correct; I didn't feel particularly good about that, but at least it showed my thinking wasn't completely crazy.

And that left Theory 2. Was the man in the gray overcoat still waiting for me? Had to be. And now was the time to meet him.

CHAPTER 29

I sauntered away from the Ministry. I turned a corner and sauntered down a busy street. There was too much traffic to hear any footsteps behind me. I sauntered for about a hundred yards, and then turned abruptly. Was that his gray overcoat disappearing into a doorway? I walked back and stopped in front of the doorway. He was standing there. A newspaper hid his face. The hands holding the newspaper were trembling slightly.

I took a deep breath. "Don't you think it's time we had a talk, Professor Hemphill?" I said.

The newspaper slowly descended.

I studied the thin, nervous features that I had last seen in the corridor at Northeastern. The man looked old and tired and very frightened.

The door behind him opened, and I caught the aroma of french fries as a couple of teenagers pushed past us. We were standing in front of a McDonald's, and I was suddenly very hungry. "Let's go inside," I said.

He obeyed.

We sat in a booth. "Want coffee or something?" I asked.

He nodded. I got him his coffee, and a Big Mac and french fries for myself. I set the cup down in front of him. He put both hands around it and lifted it slowly to his lips, trying not to slosh the coffee onto the table. I took a bite of my Big Mac. There was time before the train for Bath. Time to straighten out a lot of things.

"I should have figured out days ago that you had lied to me back in Cambridge," I began. "First of all, you were so certain that Cornwall was dead—and he is so obviously alive. Second, you said he couldn't have created a clone of himself—and he obviously did. But I didn't really think about you—I had more important things to worry about—until I received a letter yesterday from a friend of mine named Bobby Gallagher."

I paused. Hemphill looked at me silently over the coffee cup.

"Bobby mentioned that he'd sold a painting by Sargent to one of his customers," I went on. "Ain't that many Sargents kicking around nowadays, I figure. I remember the one you had hanging over your mantel, though. And I remember telling you how valuable it was. I probably even mentioned Bobby's name. But you weren't eager to sell it—and with that dog of yours, no one was likely to steal it. So I thought: if it was your painting that Bobby sold, what made you sell it to Bobby? And the answer I came up with was: to get airfare to England."

Hemphill didn't respond. I realized that he hadn't said anything so far. And I realized what I had let myself in for: the big scene where the private eye explains it all to the culprit and forces him to break down and confess. Trouble was, I wasn't at all sure I had everything straight. And what if the culprit didn't cooperate—just sat there drinking his coffee and listening? Couldn't be helped. I plunged ahead.

"Here's how I figure it, Professor. You hate Cornwall—I don't know why, and I don't know what sort of hatred can last for twenty-two years after a nuclear war, but there it is. When you saw his clone at Northeastern, you tried to kill him—maybe as a kind of posthumous revenge, maybe because you went a little crazy and thought Winfield really was Cornwall. But the situation changed when you found out Cornwall was still alive—or maybe you knew all along.

I don't know. Doesn't matter. Anyway, your hatred made you sell your most prized possession and come to England in search of Cornwall. You found Winfield and me and followed us to Oxford. You waited for him to be alone. You went in, the two of you quarreled, but he escaped. So you set fire to his house, and then kept after him. You broke into his daughter's flat, hoping to find out where he might be hiding. Then you staked out her flat, hoping one of us would lead you to him. And here you are."

I paused again. It wasn't going particularly well so far. Theory 2 was obviously correct in outline—here was Hemphill to prove it—but its specifics sounded a little thin when recited like that. And the culprit wasn't breaking down.

"Do you know where Cornwall is?" he asked, finally speaking. His voice was a thin rasp.

"If I know where he is, why should I tell you?"

"If you tell me, then I'll tell you the real story," Hemphill whispered.

I ate some more of my Big Mac and considered. I held the upper hand here. "Tell me the story," I said, "then I'll tell you where Cornwall is—if I think you ought to know."

Hemphill nodded. "All right." He stared at his coffee, as if trying to find inspiration there, or a key to the past. His eyes glazed over a little, as they had in Cambridge when the memories came. "You've got it all wrong," he began, and my heart sank. "Well, most of it, anyway. Yes, I lied to you when we spoke in America. Cornwall and I had in fact figured out a method for cloning adult human cells. Tensions were high back then, of course, and we wanted to try it out as soon as possible. We found a volunteer to be the surrogate mother, and then we had to decide who to clone. The choice was obvious. Me.

"You see, even before the war made it a popular condition, I was sterile. So cloning was my only chance for reproducing my genes. Cornwall was unmarried, but as far as we knew he wasn't sterile. We agreed, then, that I would be the one. *We agreed.*"

Hemphill said those last words as if they were carved into his soul. He had started to twitch. "I take it Cornwall had other ideas, though," I said.

Hemphill took a deep breath before continuing, as if he were steeling himself to finish the most horrible story he knew. "Cornwall handled the actual procedure, you see. He must have used one of his own cells. And he never told me. Tensions kept getting worse, and the mother-to-be went home to Florida, carrying what I assumed was my clone. We couldn't find any more volunteers; people had other things on their minds. And then the world exploded."

Hemphill paused. People tend to pause when their stories reach this point. After a few moments I decided to prompt him. I didn't have all day. "So for twenty-two years you thought that maybe, down in Florida—"

"Until I saw the clone in a corridor at Northeastern," Hemphill continued, "and I knew instantly what Cornwall had done to me. I should have suspected all along, of course. He never cared about anyone but himself. But I wanted so much to believe. I wanted that clone to exist. There was nothing else left for me: my wife had died, my friends were gone, there was nothing left but hunger and disease and fear. I dreamed of him coming to Boston one day and finding me, and I could teach him what I knew, and despite all the world's problems, his life would be better than mine. It was a dream, Mr. Sands, that helped me make it through many hard days and nights."

"So the clone showed up, and you went crazy."

"My dream turned to dust when I saw—what did you call him? Winfield? Can you understand what that feels like, Mr. Sands?"

"Maybe not. I've never tried to kill an unarmed stranger who meant me no harm."

Hemphill looked appropriately chastened. "I admit it was wrong. I realized that right away. My quarrel wasn't with Winfield."

"Did you really think Cornwall was dead?"

He shrugged. "I didn't want the clone to find him. I didn't want the wonderful reunion I dreamed of to come true for Cornwall. But it didn't matter, I guess. You found him on your own."

I thought of Winfield and *his* dream. Everyone was having trouble with his dreams, it seemed. That's life. Isn't it? Hemphill's dream hardly seemed to justify all he had gone through lately, but what did I know? *Everyone's pain is real,* I had told Kathy. And I supposed I believed it. "So you decided to follow us to England," I said, "and make sure Cornwall's dream didn't come true."

"Yes. But I didn't follow you to Oxford. I found Cornwall on my own."

"How did you do that?"

"Well, I thought he might be associated with a university, so I simply called up information in Oxford and asked. It took me five minutes."

Five minutes. It was all I could do to keep from banging my head against the table. "Go on," I managed to say.

"When I got to Oxford, I went to a pub to gather up my courage. And while I was there the clone came in, obviously in a terrible mood. Seeing him made all my anger come back, but I still couldn't bring myself to face Cornwall. So finally I simply called him up."

"Oh," I said. "It was your phone call that got him so upset."

"Yes, well, the call didn't last very long, and it wasn't very satisfactory. It's easy for someone to hang up on you."

"So you went there—and maybe he had gone by that time, afraid to face you—and you set fire to his house, out of anger and frustration."

Hemphill shook his head. "No. That's the part you've got wrong. I didn't do anything. I swear it. I left the pub after I made the call and I went back to my hotel. I didn't find out about the fire until I read the newspaper the next day."

"Oh, come on. You sell your painting to get to England so you can find Cornwall, then you talk to him on the phone for a minute and that's it?"

"I agree with you. It was stupid. I realized it was stupid when I read about the fire—when I found out that Cornwall was missing, and I had lost my chance. I am not a brave man, Mr. Sands. I learned that long ago. I had my chance, and I was too afraid to take advantage of it."

I tried to figure it out. If Winfield didn't do it and Hemphill didn't do it, then who did? Cornwall himself? But why? There was a lot I still didn't understand about Cornwall, and maybe Hemphill could help me there. But another question took precedence. "Did I at least get it right about you breaking into Kathy's flat?" I asked.

"Yes. Her name was in the article about the fire. I couldn't think what else to do if I was going to find Cornwall. But of course he wasn't there, and there was nothing in the apartment to help me. I found her mother's address, and I went and hung around there the day after Christmas, but that was a waste of time. So I came back to the daughter's place, and then I saw Winfield and you, and I thought maybe you were all up to something—maybe you knew where Cornwall was. Was I right?"

He looked at me hopefully. I shrugged. I wasn't ready to give him what he wanted just yet. "The reason the clone was in such a terrible mood at the pub was that Cornwall denied knowing him," I said. "Can you think of any reason why Cornwall would do that?"

Hemphill shook his head. "It doesn't make any sense to me. Why would Cornwall have gone to the trouble of double-crossing me and using one of his own cells back before the war unless the clone—unless the *idea* of a clone—meant a great deal to him?"

"Maybe he's changed his mind. Any reason why he might want to kill clones?"

Hemphill look puzzled and a little frightened. "Kill clones? I don't understand. What's going on?"

What was going on? Good question. Cornwall was killing clones, but I didn't know why. Hemphill was in England, but he denied burning down Cornwall's house. The case was there for the solving, but I couldn't solve it.

And I had a train to catch. The solution would be there, perhaps, at the end of the train ride. "What would you do if you were to meet Cornwall now?" I asked Hemphill.

"I just want him to talk to me," he replied eagerly. "I don't want to kill him or even to harm him. Killing solves nothing—I understand that now. I'm an old man, Mr. Sands. Cornwall has caused me enormous suffering, and I should at least have the chance to confront him before I die, to make him explain. Is that asking too much out of life?"

I wasn't sure you could ask anything out of life—and I wasn't convinced that what Cornwall had done was such a big deal. The reason I decided to bring Hemphill along, finally, was that it seemed right—right to have him there at the climax. He was part of the case, and perhaps he would even help solve it.

I gulped down the rest of my Big Mac and fries, and then stood up. "Let's go," I said.

"Where?" Hemphill asked.

To the climax. "I'll tell you on the way. Hurry up."

When we reached Paddington Station, it didn't surprise me a bit to see Winfield standing next to Kathy beneath the message board. "He woke up and got the gun away from me," Kathy whispered. "I couldn't stop him from coming."

I nodded. It was okay. Each of us was obsessed with the same man, and now it was time to go find him.

I stared at them all; they all stared at each other. "Who wants to lend me money to buy a ticket?" I asked finally.

CHAPTER 30

We made an odd band: Winfield drunk and paranoid, Hemphill twitching with excitement and fear, Kathy silent, distant, always apparently on the verge of tears that never came. And me.

Courtesy of Art's guidebook, I thought of others who had gone to Bath: Roman soldiers seeking relief from the harsh foreign climate in the hot baths; monks coming to chant their prayers in the abbey; elegant ladies out of Jane Austen novels eager to promenade in the Pump Room. Layers upon layers of history. We fit in as well as the rest of them, I supposed.

The journey was quiet, once Winfield was convinced that Hemphill was not a government agent out to trick him. We all found windows to stare out of and thought our own thoughts. Snowflakes spattered the windows as we approached our destination. It was going to be a cold climax.

We roused ourselves when the train pulled into the station. "Now what?" Winfield asked groggily.

"Let's find the clone," I said. "I have the address. We should make sure he's safe before we do anything else."

No one disagreed. As soon as the train came to a stop, we

hurried off and found a taxi. Everyone piled in, I gave the driver the address, and we headed out into the snow.

It was slow going. The snowfall made everything seem vaguely unreal. Time felt as if it were standing still—or, no, as if it had stepped aside, leaving us adrift, directionless, in the ancient city.

"What do we do when we find the clone?" Hemphill asked.

"Let me take care of that," I said in my best private-eye tone. I had no idea what we should do.

The taxi wended its way up a steep hill overlooking the city and finally pulled up in front of a block of flats. "Everyone stay here," I said. No one argued. I got out. The dream-city lay spread out before me, serene and virginal in the snow. I looked around for Cornwall, in case he was staking the place out. No sign of him. I trudged up the steps of the building.

The outer and inner doors were both unlocked. I walked slowly inside, still looking for Cornwall. The flat was on the ground floor. I walked along a dingy corridor. A baby was screaming behind a thin wall. Someone was cooking cabbage. I knocked on a door.

It opened, and a man peered out. He was short and bald and wore a gray sweater with a hole in one shoulder. He eyed me suspiciously.

"Mr. Pritchard?"

"Yes?"

"Is your son Michael at home?"

"Who wants to know?"

I reached into my coat pocket and took out the badge that Mickey had given me once upon a time, long, long ago. I flashed it at the man quickly and put it away. "My name is Sands, Mr. Pritchard, and I'm from the Investigative Division of the Ministry of Science. Let me try to explain briefly. As you know, your adopted son spent the first few years of his life at our Bromford Research Center, where he was a subject in a secret research project. We have reason to believe he may now be in danger from people who were involved in that project."

"Danger? What do you mean? What sort of danger?"

"Let me be blunt, Mr. Pritchard. I mean that other subjects have been murdered. Please, sir, there's no time to waste. Where is Michael?"

"Murdered? But why?"

"That's what we're trying to find out."

The man scratched his fringe of gray hair. A woman appeared behind him. "Who is it, Alf?"

"Says he's an investigator from the Ministry of Science," Alf told her. "Says Michael's in danger."

"Danger?" The woman's eyes watered reflexively at the mention of the word. She was thin and plain and wore her grayish hair in a bun from which a couple of strands had come loose.

"There may be a problem, ma'am, and we want to check it out. Can you tell me where Michael is at this moment?"

She looked at her husband. "You sound like an American," he said to me. "Why would an American be working for—"

"Your son's life is in danger!" I shouted. "Please help us."

"He's at the mall, I'm sure," Mrs. Pritchard said. "On Southgate, near the Abbey Green. That's where he usually goes this time of night."

"Can you describe him for me?"

"Well, you know, black hair, dark eyes, average height. Wears a black leather jacket and them damn hoop earrings."

"Thanks very much," I said. "I'll be in touch."

"Now wait a minute—" Mr. Pritchard started to say, but I wasn't waiting. I left them standing in the doorway and hurried back to the taxi. I got in and told the driver where to go.

Everyone looked at me. "His mother says he's hanging out at the mall," I said. "I don't think he'll be hard to find."

"We've got to be on the lookout for government agents," Winfield said, but he didn't sound very sure of himself, and I wondered if reality was starting to sink in.

The taxi made its way through the snowy streets. The four of us were silent. Kathy leaned heavily against me; her eyes gazed out into the darkness.

When the taxi pulled up in front of the mall, I was the first one out, "Pay him!" I shouted. I don't know if anyone obeyed. I rushed inside the mall.

Strange to be in one that wasn't a ruin. Smashed windows, caved-in walls, and bare shelves were all that remained of those I had seen in America. Still, I had a feeling this wasn't much of a mall. The people were working class, and the stores, with their banners advertising after-Christmas sales, looked worn and tawdry. This wasn't the tourist section of Bath.

I looked for teenagers hanging out. They weren't difficult to find. In the middle of the mall there was a group of thugs draped over some benches next to a sick-looking tree. I approached them.

"Is he there?" Winfield demanded in a low voice as the others came up next to me. "What does he look like?"

It seemed impossible to me that Winfield couldn't see. One glance at Kathy told me that she saw. The boy with the long black hair and wispy mustache and acne—the boy in the leather jacket, wearing black hoop earrings and smoking a cigarette and talking to the crew-cut girl in the fuchsia miniskirt. The boy who looked as much like Winfield as Winfield looked like Cornwall.

"So I says to the fuckin' teacher, I says…"

Another generation, another world for those brilliant genes to inhabit.

Cornwall was killing his own clones. Had he tricked the Ministry the same way he had tricked Hemphill? Were they expecting mathematical geniuses, when all they got was Cornwall himself, again and again and again? It didn't matter.

But why was he killing himself, again and again and again?

I scanned the shadows and the store entrances and the passersby. He had to be here somewhere.

An old man, his back to us, was sitting on a bench eating an ice-cream cone. Hemphill went up to him, but he was bearded and toothless. A fellow in a pea jacket came out of the shadows and stared at Kathy, but he was in his twenties and brown-haired; he admired her for a moment, and then walked away.

"So then I says, 'Hey, you stupid sod, I know this fuckin' stuff better than you do, so leave me the fuck alone.' And you know what the fuckhead says?..."

The boy turned and noticed Winfield, who was now staring at him, suspicious and maybe a little afraid. "What the fuck are you lookin' at, arsehole?" the boy demanded, but his tone was a little hesitant, and maybe a little afraid too.

And then I saw Cornwall. He was coming out of McDonald's, a Big Mac in his hand. Did it ease his homesickness, remind him of the good old days? Or did he just need some quick sustenance? Stalking victims builds your appetite.

He saw me an instant after I saw him. He saw Winfield, saw Hemphill, saw Kathy. Saw everything. He dropped the Big Mac and started to run.

I ran after him. We all ran after him. Out of the mall and into the night, the snow swirling like memories around us.

Cornwall was fast for an old man. He ran with the speed of someone whose entire past was pursuing him. Time had disappeared once again, and as I pursued him through the ancient streets, everything became jumbled—everything became real. A car skidded to avoid hitting a pair of togaed Romans; a procession of monks made its way past a leather-clad young couple kissing in a doorway; Beau Nash doffed his hat and bowed to me, laughing. And I thought— if I could look at things from the proper angle, then the future—if there was a future—would be here, too, as real as the five of us running through the night, as real as the past that surrounded us.

Then I slipped and cracked my knee against a curb. Now *that* was real. Pain is part of the job, I forced myself to think. I scrambled to my feet, visions fled, and kept running.

Cornwall was heading away from the center of the city. He crossed a bridge over a frozen river, then disappeared into an underpass on the other side. I was catching up. I entered the underpass just seconds after him.

He was standing at the far end, gun in hand. The gun was aimed at me. He fired.

Death is part of the job, too, I suppose, but I wasn't ready for it just yet. I hit the ground. The bullet made an awful roar, but it missed. I looked up. Cornwall was aiming again.

"Daddy!"

Kathy was standing above me, trying to catch her breath. Her cheeks were wet with snow and with tears that had finally come. She looked very young. She walked slowly toward her father. "Daddy?" she said, and her voice was low and frightened and pleading. "No, Daddy. Please."

He didn't respond, didn't lower the gun, but she was between me and her father now, and I was safe for the moment. Kathy kept talking.

"You should have told me, Daddy. I would have understood. Why couldn't we ever talk? Why was there only anger and tears and silence?" She stepped closer, and she was right in front of him. "Do *you* understand now?" she went on. "These others, they aren't you, they don't know you, they don't love you. I'm the one who loves you—who has always loved you. Remember the day you gave me the necklace—standing outside the playground together? Couldn't you feel the love then? Couldn't you understand? I'm the one who's real. I'm the one." She held out her hand to him. "But you've got to stop. You don't need to do this. It's not right, Daddy. You've got to stop. For me."

I looked at her, and I thought of my own father, a skeleton buried next to an abandoned farmhouse far, far from here, and the thought made me catch my breath and close my eyes. The bond remains, beyond time and war and murder and neglect. The bond remains.

I opened my eyes. Cornwall grabbed Kathy's hand, twisted her around, and placed the gun to her temple.

I stood up cautiously. Hemphill and Winfield had arrived, and they stopped next to me. No one spoke. The only sounds were the muffled roar of traffic passing over our heads, Hemphill's wheezing effort to catch his breath, and Kathy's helpless crying.

Hemphill finally broke the silence. "Too many people have died, Robert," he said. "Let the girl go."

"If so many people have died," Cornwall replied, "what do one or two more matter?"

"She's your daughter, Robert. Not everyone is lucky enough to have a daughter."

"Luck? The lucky ones were in Washington or driving past a missile silo twenty-two years ago. The lucky ones died being born or, better yet, weren't even conceived. Don't talk to me about luck." He stared at each of us in turn, as if daring us to mention the word. His gaze fixed on Winfield.

"The lucky ones have the genius to overcome everything—even life itself," Winfield said to the older version of himself. He was sober now, and he seemed angry. "Why are you wasting your luck?"

Cornwall shook his head. "Can't I make you see how it is?" he said. "Can't I make you see that you're wasting everything, wasting your life—*your* life—chasing this dream? I suppose I can't. You are me, and nothing is going to change that.

"I came to England chasing the same dream. I let them put me in that awful military base for three months after I arrived because I thought I had it within my grasp, and I didn't want to lose it because of a goddamn nuclear war. I worked for years setting everything up at Bromford, and I lied and lied, to make the dream come true.

"I know what you are thinking, because I thought the same thoughts. There's got to be happiness somewhere, sometime. If not in America, then in England. If not in this life, then another life. But that's so stupid, don't you see?" He was whispering now, on the verge of tears. "There is only me, and I am what I have always been—a wretched, lost soul in a wretched, lost world. I know nothing, I have nothing, I am nothing. And that won't change—in America or in England, now or in the future."

His grip on Kathy had loosened. She stared at me, pleading. What was I supposed to do? "You have your daughter," I said to Cornwall.

He looked at her and shook his head. "It's not enough," he whispered. And suddenly the gun moved from Kathy's head to his own. She was free, and she slumped to the ground.

"No," she cried.

"It took me so long to discover," he said, and he was speaking to Winfield again. "But you'll discover it, too, as you live through this awful life that I've forced upon you. The dream is crazy and evil. I cheated Hemphill, I turned my back on America, I failed as a husband and a father. For what? So that you can do these things all over again? So that you can face the same disappointments I've faced? I saw you in Oxford, and it was just too much, finally. I couldn't stand to look at you, couldn't stand thinking of you and the others having to suffer the way I've suffered, having to cause the suffering I know you will cause. And I knew I couldn't let it go on. It's time to stop. If you people had any sense you'd let me finish the job, let me wipe out every last vestige of my genes before they cause more harm, more unhappiness." He stared at the gun. "I'm so tired."

Kathy was sobbing at his feet, her hands clutching his leg. He looked down at her, and I like to think that maybe in that instant he changed his mind; maybe he decided she was enough, that the love of a daughter like her could make up for a great deal of evil in a world like this, in a man like him. But I suppose it doesn't matter.

When the instant was over, the tunnel roared with the sound of a bullet, and there was blood everywhere, and he fell beside her.

It took me a moment to realize that the roar had not come from Cornwall's gun. I turned, and Winfield was standing next to me, gun in hand, staring at the man he had killed.

"There will be another life," he whispered, his face wet with tears. "It will be a perfect life. And it will be mine." Then he turned and ran from the underpass.

—ran past a long-haired boy in a leather jacket, who stood at the entrance to the underpass, trembling uncontrollably. I followed. Winfield made it to the bridge, where he suddenly fell to his knees and rocked back and forth as he stared at the frozen river below.

He wasn't going anywhere. I returned to the underpass and looked at the boy; the boy looked at me. I didn't know if he understood what he had witnessed, but I knew that his life would not be the perfect one that Winfield sought so desperately, and I pitied him. "Call the police, Michael," I said, and I went back into the underpass.

CHAPTER 31

Cornwall was there, somber and polite. And Hemphill. And me.

Afterward, I found myself standing next to Hemphill in the crusty snow of the cemetery. "A long way to come, for this," he murmured.

"Was it worth it?"

He shrugged. "It doesn't matter at this point. I thought it did, but I was wrong."

"Are you going back?" I asked.

"I suppose. I have a life in America. There's nothing for me here. There could have been, once, but I missed my chance a long time ago."

I tried to think of something encouraging to say, but couldn't come up with anything. Some people are doomed to be unhappy, I guess, and even the best private eye can't help them. "Well, good luck," I said. "And Happy New Year."

"Happy New Year," Hemphill repeated, and he made the words sound like a sick joke. Then he shuffled off through the snow, the weight of the world on his stooped shoulders.

I walked over to where Kathy and her mother were waiting in their hired car. "Ready?" Kathy asked.

I scrunched into the back seat of the little three-wheeler. "Ready."

We drove silently out of the cemetery.

Kathy was taking her mother home before returning to London. It was not a pleasant trip. Mrs. Cornwall, I thought, was doing her best in what must have been a terrible situation. She tried hard to be pleasant and sympathetic to Kathy, but Kathy was having none of it. "Wasn't it a lovely ceremony?" was met with "Someone should shoot those reporters." "You must be quite tired, dear" provoked a "Just tired of talking, that's all." Eventually Mrs. Cornwall took the hint, and the journey ended as it began, in silence.

Kathy reluctantly agreed to stay for a while at the house. A few of Mrs. Cornwall's friends were there, ready with tea and sandwiches and sympathy. Mrs. Stumple was on her best behavior, except for one brief moment, when she caught me alone in the kitchen. "What are they going to do with that one?" she asked me.

"Which one is that one?"

"You know." She pretended to shoot me with her index finger.

"Oh. Winfield. Well, I expect they'll send him to prison for a while, don't you?"

Mrs. Stumple shook her head emphatically. "Oughta rip his guts out and stuff 'em in his mouth," she said. Then she got the mustard from the refrigerator and returned to the living room.

Just before Kathy and I left, Mrs. Cornwall also managed to have a brief conversation with me in private. "It was good of you to come, Walter," she said.

"I wanted to," I replied. I noticed she was wearing the mauve blouse Kathy had given her for Christmas.

"What will you do now?"

I shrugged. "Hard to say. I have plenty of options."

Mrs. Cornwall nodded. "You know, this has been quite hard on Kathy," she said.

"Yes, I know."

She gazed at me. "I think that Kathy could use a friend," she said.

I could see the longing and the love in her eyes, and I felt very sorry for her. She wanted to be that friend, but Kathy wasn't going to let her. "I think you're right," I said.

She pressed my hand in hers for a quick moment. Then Kathy called for me, and the conversation was over.

We drove to London in silence. It was early evening by the time we had dropped off the car and walked back to her flat.

Winfield's belongings were still scattered in the second bedroom. "I suppose I should ring the police and see about getting rid of these things," Kathy murmured as we looked at them.

"Plenty of time for that."

Kathy wandered into the kitchen without replying. She got out her bottle of whiskey, but Winfield had drunk most of it. She finished it off and threw the empty bottle into the trash. "I'm so tired," she whispered.

"Why don't you just go to bed?" I said. "Not much point in trying to keep awake to see the new year in."

She nodded. "What about you?"

"I guess I'll stay up for a while. You know how I am."

She smiled weakly. "Okay. I know how you are."

She was too tired to bother putting her nightgown on. I watched her strip down to her bra and panties, then fall into bed. She was wearing the necklace her father had given her. She looked very beautiful. She was asleep instantly. I shut the bedroom door and went over to the rocking chair.

I suppose the Ghost of New Year's Past should have come for me then, but he didn't. Perhaps he was otherwise engaged, or perhaps I had become stronger in the past few days. Or perhaps I had other things on my mind besides reminiscences. Whatever the reason, I rocked silently, hour after hour, and my memories stayed where they were supposed to.

Eventually a crowd of drunken teenagers came down the street, singing "Auld Lang Syne" at the top of their lungs. I glanced at my watch: they were jumping the gun by a few minutes. Probably couldn't wait. Some people in America were like that. They went wild on New Year's Eve, so happy to have survived another year, so certain that next year would be better. I wasn't one of them. I could never understand why the passage of time was a cause for celebration.

"Walter?" Kathy came out of the bedroom, wrapping her white robe around her nakedness.

"Hi."

"Hi." She sat on the sofa. "Rather noisy out there, isn't it?"

"Yeah."

"This isn't the best neighborhood if you want to sleep on New Year's Eve."

"Yeah."

We were silent for a moment, and then she reached out and put her hand on my knee. "Walter," she said, "I wanted to tell you how much I appreciate all you've done for me the past few days. I don't know how I could have kept on without you. You're a very special person."

I waited. She was silent. I started rocking slowly, staring out the window. Eventually she took her hand away.

"Walter?"

I turned to her. If not now, when? She was very beautiful. "You know," I said, "it bothers me that you didn't like the ending of *The Maltese Falcon.*"

"What do you mean?" she whispered.

"Remember it?" I said. "The surprise ending, when we find out that Sam Spade's beautiful client had set him up all along. Why didn't you like that ending?"

"It wasn't a happy ending," she replied. "We talked about that. Besides, it's only a movie. What does a movie have to do with anything?"

"Absolutely nothing. Except it gets a private eye to thinking. And when a private eye thinks, sometimes he comes up with a theory."

Silence. "And what's your theory?" she asked finally. Her voice sounded miles and miles away.

"Just what went on at your father's house after I left?" I asked in turn. "Who burned the damn thing down? Winfield has an alibi, Hemphill says he didn't do it—and I believe him. He just doesn't seem the type. I can't figure out a reason why your father would have done it. And that leaves just one person."

Kathy stared at me, wide-eyed, and then shook her head violently. "But that's crazy," she said. "Why would I rush over to the railway station to get you if I'd just burned my father's house down?"

"For the simplest reason in the private eye's textbook," I replied. "So you could ask that very question. 'Patsy' is the word that springs to mind."

"But why would I burn the house down, Walter? Hemphill at least had a reason, if what you told me about him is true. What reason would I have?"

"I'm not exactly sure, Kathy," I said truthfully. "Human beings are a little too complex for me to figure out. I guess I just need more experience in this business. But I've figured out this much: you knew. Knew about the clones, knew about your father's obsession. And the knowledge must have tormented you. Maybe you found out on that special birthday when he gave you your necklace—you even brought it up when you were talking to him in that underpass in Bath. Where was that playground you stopped in front of? East Norton? Castle Frome? He brought you to see one of the clones, didn't he? On your birthday, on the day that seemed so beautiful, so perfect. You were the one that loved him, you were the one that was real. But the clone was the one that mattered to him. And that was enough, eventually, to make you burn down your father's house."

Kathy was crying now, desperate sobs, each one an admission of guilt. It was all straight from the textbook. But it didn't give me any satisfaction. I pushed on.

"Burning down a house—who cares, besides Inspector Grimby? But you knew something else, Kathy: you knew your father was killing those clones. It doesn't really matter when you found out. Maybe it wasn't right away. Maybe it was one of those mornings when we sat together at the breakfast table, reading the newspaper like an old married couple. Maybe you saw one of those articles that I saw, and you recognized the town, or the boy's name, and you understood what your father was up to.

"What matters is that you didn't say anything—out of love? Because he was finally showing that he loved you? I don't know. And when I finally figured out about the killing of the clones, you fought it, you made me waste a day lying to people at the Ministry of Science while your father stalked another victim. That's the bad thing you did, Kathy. That's the thing you're going to have to live with."

Kathy's face twisted with the effort to control the emotions she had tried to control for so long. And when she finally failed, the words that came pouring out sounded hoarse and feral, as if she hadn't used her voice in a long, long time. "Goddamn him. Goddamn those...things. *I* should have killed them. And I should have killed him, too, and then maybe I could live like everyone else. *Why wouldn't he love me?* How could he have been so stupid? Even at the end, when there was nothing left, even then...goddamn him...."

And then abruptly she stopped, and the tears returned. "Oh Walter, I'm so sorry," she sobbed. "So sorry. Can you—can you ever—" She couldn't finish the question, but I suppose she didn't need to.

I went and got her a glass of water. She drank it down greedily, and she looked at me, and she realized the time had come. Time to tell it all. "Where do I start?" she asked softly.

"The clones," I said, just as softly.

She nodded. "I knew about them all along. I wasn't quite as stupid as my mother about such things. But in spite of them, I tried so hard to make him love me. I kept thinking I was succeeding, and then it would all turn to ashes. Like the birthday. So beautiful, so perfect, and then I realize that he's scarcely even thinking of me—he's just using me as an excuse to check up on one of his creatures."

"Then you must have known Winfield was a clone as soon as you saw him," I said.

"Yes, but as usual I decided to give my father one more chance. He had seemed so depressed lately by all he had done, so worn out, that I had begun to hope. I rang him up and begged him—if he loved me—to deny the clone. I was offering him a choice—do you see?—between real life, real love, and his—his solipsism. And it worked, Walter. He had his choice, and he chose me. I was so happy.

"But as usual it turned, out badly. He had made his choice, but he was angry with me for forcing him to do it. After Winfield and you had left he said, 'I denied him—my own flesh and blood, my own genes. What more do you want?' And I said what I have said so many times: 'I want you to love me.' And then the phone rang."

"Hemphill," I said.

"I didn't know it at the time, but it makes sense—more pressure, more fear for my father. It pushed him over the edge, I think. When he hung up, he started screaming: 'Just leave me alone. All of you. I don't care. I don't care about anything.' And he took his coat and stormed out.

"Can you understand, Walter? That pushed *me* over the edge. I suppose I share my father's temper. If he wouldn't give me his love, if I couldn't make him care, then I wanted to destroy everything that was his. And that's what I did."

Silence. Kathy's eyes were closed. Her hands were folded in her lap, and she was squeezing them spasmodically together. I had seen the gesture before—her father had done it, in Oxford, with Kathy and Winfield both staring at him, both demanding his love. I didn't feel much like it, but I had to push the story along. That was my job. "And then you got me involved," I said.

She opened her eyes and looked at me, pleading. "I didn't mean to make you a patsy, Walter. I was confused and alone and frightened, and you were the only person I could turn to—but I couldn't tell you the truth. I just couldn't. I suppose I knew Winfield would get blamed, and that was all right with me, but I honestly didn't think anything would come of it.

"And the killing of the clones: yes, you're right. I should have told you straightaway. But can you see that it was the same thing all over again—the same old hope that this time it would happen, this time he would show his love? Only this was the ultimate act that would show his love. Denying Winfield—all right, that's something. But killing them…what more could he do?"

"They were real people that he was killing, Kathy," I said.

She nodded. "I know, but I suppose I've never thought of them as being quite human—they have always been simply this *force* that opposed me, that possessed what was rightfully mine. Even seeing Winfield didn't change that. But in the end—in Bath, seeing that boy—it was different. The boy was real. Why should he have to die? And then in the subway, I told my father to stop. Don't you remember? I told him it wasn't right; I tried to make him understand.

"But finally, of course, it turned to ashes again. He knew that what he had done was wrong; he understood everything. But all that understanding, all that guilt couldn't make him love me. And that's what I wanted, Walter. That's all I ever wanted."

Kathy looked at me, but she didn't see what she wanted to see, and then she covered her face with her hands. She wasn't crying now. Her tears, perhaps, were exhausted. I heard a distant cheering and looked at my watch: Happy New Year. From the flat below came the sound of happy voices singing:

"Should auld acquaintance be forgot…"

"I'm sorry it had to end like this, Kathy," I said.

She looked up at me. She seemed terribly vulnerable. "What are you going to do?"

"I'm going to leave you with your memories," I replied softly. "Do what you want with them. I'm heading back to Boston."

She reacted as if I had punched her. "Oh, no, Walter. Please. You can't go. You hate America."

I shrugged. "I guess I don't hate it as much as I thought."

"But—but you've got to stay. You have to testify at Winfield's trial, right?"

"I gave my statement to the police yesterday. They said it would be sufficient. It's not like this is a difficult case. They were actually quite eager to have me leave."

Then Kathy did something awful. She got down on her knees in front of me, her hands clasped as if in prayer. "Please, Walter. Please. I'm sorry. I'll do anything. I'm so sorry. You're all I've got now. I love you, Walter. Can't you see that? I love you." And she buried her face in my lap, her hands clutching at my sides, her body shaking with grief and despair.

This wasn't the way it happened in books, in movies. This emptiness wasn't what I was supposed to be feeling. In movies, in books, you chucked people under the chin and said what needed to be said, and the scene faded out. The hysterics took place between chapters, the regret and the uncertainty were merely glints in the hero's steely eyes.

What could I say to her? I had to go back. Even if she were innocent—and she wasn't. Even if she loved me— and I wasn't sure she did, wasn't sure this wasn't a final, desperate performance. Even if I loved her—and I didn't want to think about that.

I had to go back, you see, because the case, such as it was, was not quite over. And the final chapters would have to take place in Boston.

CHAPTER 32

Hello good-bye hello good-bye.

The shotgun was trained on me from the time I turned the corner. I smiled.

The shotgun was slowly lowered, and the person holding it started to smile too. "Wally?"

"Hey, Doctor J."

Doctor J shook my hand solemnly. "What you doin' here, Wally?"

"Come to call on your boss. Is he in?"

"Course." He pounded on the door. "Got a visitor," Doctor J informed Mickey nonchalantly when he opened it; Doctor J looked pleased at Mickey's astonished reaction. Inside, Brutus started barking furiously. Nothing had changed.

I exchanged pleasantries with Mickey, then went upstairs and knocked on Bobby's door.

"Yeah?" he called out.

"Delivery from Harrods for a Mr. R. Gallagher," I said. "Fish and chips and shepherd's pie and a pint of bitter, eh what?"

Bobby opened the door in a hurry. "Jesus fucking Christ," he said cleverly.

"Hiya." I walked inside and sat on the couch beneath the photograph of John F. Kennedy. "How's things?"

He shut the door and went back to his desk. "Fine, I guess. I sent you another letter yesterday."

"Waste of postage. Sorry."

He sat down. "What happened, Wally? They kick you out?"

I shook my head. "I finished the case, more or less, so I figured I should come back here and get another one."

"You finished the case?"

"Yup. Tracked down Cornwall just the way I was supposed to. Of course, my client then proceeded to murder him, which isn't the way it's written up in the textbooks, but that wasn't my fault. So here I am, back at my home base, ready for anything."

Bobby looked nonplussed. "Jesus, Wally. You wanna elaborate on all that?"

"Oh, not just now. Maybe I'll write it down someday, get Art to publish it. But listen, there's this one aspect of the case I thought you might be interested in."

"Yeah?" He sounded more suspicious than interested.

I took a breath. I was getting to be an old hand at this. "It was just this minor point, you know, but it's been sort of nagging at me, and we experienced private eyes like to tie up all the loose ends. See, when I visited the Ministry of Science to find out about Cornwall, I asked for Mr. J. T. Carstairs. He was the guy who signed the letter that your friend in the JFK Building showed me, remember? Well, they had never heard of this guy at the Ministry. Okay, so big deal. But then I found Cornwall anyway, and he was talking about this and that before my client killed him, and he mentioned the months he spent at a military base after his arrival in England. But the letter said that all the scientists were put up at college dorms in London. Okay, big deal again. But it made me think about the letter and, you know, it was on this plain white stationery, and you'd think the Ministry of Science could afford their own letterhead. Well, I kind of juggled all of this around in my mind and came up with a theory. Just a theory, mind you."

I shut up. Bobby's customary smirk had disappeared. He looked very unhappy. "I confess," he whispered.

There. That was easy enough. But I hadn't expected him to take it this seriously. "You forged the letter?"

He nodded. "You needed proof to give your client so you could go to England. You weren't getting any. So I made it up."

"And the guy at the JFK Building just pretended it was a real letter?"

"Sure. What harm did it do?"

"I don't know," I said, quite honestly. "Um, why are you crying, Bobby?"

"Ah, shit," he said. He groped for a handkerchief and blew his nose. "Ah, shit."

Watching Bobby cry was very unsettling; that wasn't the way the world was supposed to operate. I tried to figure it out. "Bobby, the other scientists on the list—they were real, they went to England. I came across their names while I was tracking down Cornwall." He stared at me, cheeks wet with tears, not disagreeing. I plunged ahead. "Bobby, you told me once you worked at MIT. Did you know something about all this?"

He slowly nodded. "I worked at MIT. Until there was no more MIT, until there was just one long nightmare you never woke up from. Remember those days?"

"A little," I said.

"Yeah. You try to forget, like me. But they don't go away, Wally, they're gonna stay with you to the grave. No food, disease everywhere, people going nuts. And all you try to do is stay alive, even though you can't figure out why that seems so important. You know?"

"I know," I said. "Bobby, did you—"

"I worked for the fucking Brits," he shouted, loud enough to rattle the crucifix behind him. "There," he said, in a normal tone. "Satisfied, Wally? I heard they were rounding up the scientists. Shit, I knew what all those MIT guys looked like, I even knew their fucking addresses. So I offered my services to the Brits. And they put me on.

Piecework. They gave me food for every scientist I brought in. And they gave me a gun. I suppose they told you over there it was all voluntary. Bullshit. Ask your friend Professor Hemphill."

Hemphill wasn't there, so I asked Bobby instead. "What happened?"

Bobby leaned back in his chair and folded his hands over his large stomach. He wasn't crying anymore, but his eyes had that distant, misty look I knew all too well. "I went to get him, over in Cambridge. Cornwall was with him. That was great—saved me a trip, and the Brits were real interested in biologists like them.

"Cornwall was dying to go. I didn't have to do any convincing with him. Most of them, I think they wanted to get out, but they wouldn't look too eager, they felt like they should pretend they wanted to stay, help the suffering, shit like that. So I had to do a little persuading, maybe pull the gun on them, and that would do the trick. But I didn't have to bother for Cornwall.

"Hemphill was a different story, the stupid shit. He wasn't going. Couldn't convince him—I don't know why. I took out the gun finally and I pointed it at him and I said, 'You're taking food out of my mouth, asshole, so you'd better come with me or you're a dead man.'

"And he wouldn't come, Wally. And Cornwall starts laughing and says something to him like, 'You've only got one life, pal. Don't waste it.' But he wouldn't budge. I never killed anyone before in my life—shit, I never even fired a gun. But I figured it was now or never. A guy has to eat, right?

"But I couldn't do it. Not in cold blood, Wally. I left him there and took Cornwall to the Brits. And that was the last I heard of either of them, until you started asking your damn questions on the way back from New Hampshire. Didn't feel like going into it then. Don't much feel like it now, for that matter."

"And then Hemphill showed up out of the blue a couple of weeks ago with a business proposition," I murmured.

Bobby looked at me, wondering how I knew that, but he let it pass. "Yeah," he said. "We recognized each other right away. And we got to talking, and I said, 'You know, I've thought a lot over the years about that time I almost killed you, and I've decided I was stupid. I shoulda killed you.' And you know what he said, Wally?"

I shook my head.

"He said, 'I wish you had. I wish you had.' How do you figure people, huh, Wally?"

Beats me. *I am not a brave man, Mr. Sands.* That's what Hemphill had said to me in McDonald's. He had managed to be brave once, with Bobby's gun pointed at him and Cornwall's laughter ringing in his ears, so that he could be there if his clone ever returned. But the joke was on him. Was that the real reason he hated Cornwall so much?

Beats me. The more I knew, the more I knew I didn't know. Hemphill, Cornwall, Winfield—their dreams and passions would always be slightly beyond my grasp. Now my fat friend Bobby was turning out to be a lot more complex than I could have imagined. And Kathy—if I had stayed with her, would I ever have really understood her? She probably didn't understand herself. Maybe real private eyes had a better handle on these things. But I was beginning to doubt it.

"I'm sorry to bring all this up, Bobby," I said. "You did a big favor for me—bigger than I realized—and I appreciate it."

Bobby shrugged. "Shit, what are friends for? It's good to have you back."

"It's good to be back." I stood up, hesitated for a moment, and then spoke. "Bobby, there's just one thing that still bothers me about this case."

Bobby looked at me, and I looked at him, and then he started to laugh.

I laughed too.

Bobby stood up and stuck out his hand. "So long, Sherlock."

I shook his hand. "Thanks, Bobby."

CHAPTER 33

Rush hour outside Park Street Station. Not much of a rush. By the cemetery, Ground Zero was sitting on a milk crate in the slush, playing his accordion. A few people were waiting, like me, for the train to come in. "Haven't seen you around lately, Walter," a casual acquaintance said.

"Been on a business trip."

"Oh? How's business?"

"Never been better."

I waited, and Jesus Christ came walking across the plaza, dragging his cross. His little boy handed out scraps of yellow paper to anyone who would take them. I reached into the pockets of my parka and felt around. Yes, it was there. I took it out. "Still have mine," I said when the boy came up to me. I showed it to him:

The End Is At Hand

"Do you heed the message, Walter?" Jesus Christ asked me.

"Sure do," I said. "Thanks for reminding me."

He nodded solemnly and walked on through the Common with his cross and his child. I heard the train rumble into the station below. After a few moments, the commuters started straggling out of the exit. Gwen was one of the last of them.

She almost walked past me, head down, intent on making her way home through the slush. "Happy New Year," I murmured.

She stopped. "Walter?"

"Hi."

She reached out and touched my arm, as if to make sure I was real. "What happened?" she asked.

"Long story. Maybe I'll write it all down someday."

"Is the case over?"

"Well, not exactly."

She stared at me. I had looked at that face so many times—those hollow cheeks, those deep, wise eyes. We were so young; we were so old. I remembered. "Then why are you here?" she asked. "The case is in England."

I shook my head. "That wasn't the real case. It took me a while to figure out, but I finally understood. The real case was back here in Boston. I just finished extracting a confession from one Robert Gallagher."

Gwen was silent.

One last, spectacular summary of the evidence. "He admitted forging the letter that sent me off to England," I went on. "But see, that couldn't be the whole story. Bobby can't write letters like that. And besides, he's almost blind, and he has to dictate to Doctor J, who's a fine fellow but can't spell for shit. No, there's only one person Bobby could turn to who could've written that letter. Only one person," I repeated. "And I taught her everything she knows."

Gwen tilted her head just a little. She denied nothing, she admitted nothing. "You came back," was all she said.

"I came back. Linc will call me a fool, but I came back."

I took her arm, and we started to walk away from the station. Gwen stopped after a few steps and stood facing me. "There's no good time to tell you," she said, "so I'll just say it. Linc killed himself New Year's Eve."

I stared at her, unwilling to believe it. "No."

"He was in terrible pain, Walter. It was only a matter of time."

Time," I repeated dumbly. Memories of Linc rushed through me. I know I'm dying, he said, but you're dying, too, everyone is dying. All that matters is what you do before you take that last breath. Time. I wanted to turn it around and go back and see him just one more time, but that's not the way things work around here. Linc was gone. "I wish I could've said good-bye to him."

"He loved you," Gwen said. "He loved all of us."

We walked a little farther, and then I stopped in front of Ground Zero. "You know 'As Time Goes By'?" I asked him.

His scarred face lit up. *"Cathablanca.* Nineteen-forty-three."

I tossed a nickel into his soggy hat. "Play it, Ground Zero. Play 'As Time Goes By.' "

He hit a few chords on his accordion and started to sing. It was awful. I listened for a verse, and then I turned to Gwen. "Shall we dance?"

She gave a little smile. "I'd like that very much."

And when two loverth woo…

"Did you get to all those places on Art's list?" Gwen asked as we danced. "Stratford-on-Avon, Dover Beach…?"

I shook my head. "Not a one."

"Do you regret it?"

"No, I guess I don't." And then I smiled. I had my title, just in the nick of time.

They thtill thay "I love you." On that you can rely…

"Did you know I'd come back?" I asked.

"I don't know anything about the future," she said. "I try not to think about it."

No matter what the future bringth…

And I thought of Linc and of Cornwall, of Hemphill and Winfield and Bobby and Kathy and Stretch and Art, of all of us dead and dying, the past that clings to us and the future that terrifies us. And there is nothing we can do but hold on to each other on that darkling plain.

And dance.

Ath time goth by.

So that's what Gwen and I did. As we had in the fallout shelter so long ago, as we would again (perhaps) in some unimaginable future.

We danced—in the slush, amid the ghosts of the ruined city.

*Turn the page for an
excerpt from*

THE
DISTANCE
BEACONS

The Last P.I. Series
Book Two

Richard Bowker

It was one of those May days that make you wonder what's so bad about being alive. Sun shining, birds singing, flowers blooming—the Earth seemed to have shrugged off the awful things we had done to her, and she was offering the same old beauty and warmth and hope that had always been her gift to us. It was the kind of day that could make you half-believe that nothing awful had happened. It was the kind of day you had to take advantage of, in case the Earth changed her mind.

So why, I wondered, was I sitting in a dingy office on lower Washington Street, staring out into the sunshine and feeling sorry for myself?

Here are the answers I came up with:

~Because I am a responsible professional, and anyone responding to my ad in the *Globe* would expect to find me here.

~Because I don't have an answering machine to take a message, should anyone try to call. Don't have a telephone either, for that matter, so calling would not be easy.

~Because I am a dreamer, still trying to live my dream.

~Because I'm a fool.

That seemed to about cover it.

This is the life of the private eye, I told myself—the long stretches of boredom punctuated by the occasional burst of excitement. But this particular stretch was beginning to seem like a life sentence. I had arrived back in Boston from England in early January, having muddled through my first case, and there was nothing to do but set up shop once again. So I put a log in the wood stove and picked out a book from one of the many tottering stacks that littered the office. Then I said a prayer to the poster of Humphrey Bogart, my patron saint, who smiled a crooked but encouraging smile at me from the opposite wall, and I waited for the sound of footsteps on the dim staircase, the tentative rapping on the frosted glass door of my office.

And I waited. I ran out of books. I used the wood stove less and less as the weather grudgingly improved. I went home every night and faced the uncomfortable silences as my friends tried not to ask me why I was wasting my life. And now a beautiful spring day was drifting away from me and my money was all but gone, but still I sat in my office, and stared out my window, and hoped.

And eventually something happened.

It wasn't exactly what I was hoping for, of course: the mysterious blonde, dressed in black, desperate for my help; the dying man with a priceless figurine he could entrust to no one but me; the eccentric millionaire whose strange predicament only I could solve. Not this time, anyway. This time it was two young soldiers driving up in an ancient jeep. They parked and looked dubiously up at the building I occupied. I pulled back from the window. Wouldn't do to appear too eager. I hurriedly tossed aside the book I was rereading and spread some papers on my desk in what I hoped was impressive-looking disarray.

It occurred to me as they clomped up the stairs that these guys probably weren't interested in my professional services. Why would soldiers need a private eye? I tried to think if I had broken any laws lately that would merit an official visit. I was hardly a model citizen, but surely the government had more important things to do than bother with an insignificant private eye. Besides, the local police, not Federal troops, would be the ones to arrest the likes of me. But you never can tell.

They rapped on the frosted glass door.

"Come in," I said in a busy but welcoming tone.

The door opened, and the two soldiers entered. The first one in was short and had a spray of acne on his face. The other was lantern-jawed and hung back a little, as if loath to deal with the strange creature sitting behind the desk. Both had the requisite army haircut, so short they might just as well have been bald.

"Good afternoon," the short one said. "Walter Sands?"

"That's me. Have a seat."

"No thank you, sir," he replied. He had a flat Midwestern accent. He used the official tone of a soldier who is carrying out his orders and is therefore not required to think. "Mr. Sands, we'd like you to come with us, sir."

"Am I being arrested?"

"No, sir."

"Then what's up?"

"There is someone who wants to see you."

"Who?"

"We're not at liberty to say, sir."

"What about?"

"Don't know, sir."

I could have continued the interrogation indefinitely, but it would have been pointless. I had been a soldier once, not so very long ago, and I knew the situation he was in. He was supposed to be as polite as possible but say nothing. And he was to come back with me. No excuses accepted.

I decided to ask one more question. "What's your name?" I asked.

The question caused a flicker of indecision to cross the short soldier's face. He hadn't received orders about this. "Smith, sir," he said finally. "Private Daniel Smith."

I smiled. "Hi, Danny. And you?" I asked the lantern-jawed fellow.

His comrade's response had given him courage. "P-p-private Gus Ziegler, sir."

I kept smiling. "Pleased to meet you." They didn't smile back, but I think maybe they wanted to. It never hurts to be friendly. I stood up. "Shall we go, then?"

"Yes, sir," Danny replied.

I winked at Saint Humphrey as I followed the soldiers out the door.

I was a little excited as I got into the jeep. Anyone who could send troops to fetch me had to be a big shot. A government big shot, to be sure, but even dealing with the Feds was better than staring out the window.

We headed up Washington Street, with Gus doing the driving. Except for another government jeep or two, and a couple of cop cars, we were in the only motor vehicle to be seen. Not that we had the streets to ourselves. Gus had to bully his way past the pedestrians and the cyclists and the horses and even a few pigs; traffic was actually pretty thick around Downtown Crossing and the Salvage Market. No one seemed particularly interested in getting out of our way; there were the usual sullen stares, and the occasional utterly hostile ones. But still we made progress.

VOTE YES, the red, white, and blue posters urged us from the otherwise useless telephone poles and mailboxes.

I did my best to ignore the posters. "Where are you guys from?" I asked.

"Out of state, sir," Danny replied.

"Ah." That was hardly news. The Feds don't let their troops serve in their native states; they also don't like for them to fraternize with the locals. If there's an uprising of some sort, they don't want a soldier facing friends and relatives at the other end of his rifle. Much easier to kill a stranger. "You like it here?"

"It's fine."

They hated it. They were scared and lonely and not used to being around people who didn't like or trust them. They couldn't figure out why they were being forced to do this, and they just wanted to get it over with and go home. At least, if they were anything like me when I was a soldier, that's the way they felt. "Write letters," I suggested.

"Huh?"

"Write long letters home. Describe everything you see and do. Even if it's all so boring you can't stand it. Even if you never send the letters. That's what I did. It helped."

Danny stared at me, then nodded silently. It occurred to me that he might not know how to write.

Gus took us to Government Center, on the far side of Beacon Hill. I wasn't surprised. We stopped in front of the John Fitzgerald Kennedy Federal Building, and the two soldiers escorted me inside. There were more VOTE YES signs in the lobby. Seemed like a waste of time to me: preaching to the converted.

The lobby was air-conditioned; soft fluorescent lights shone down on us; the elevator that we waited for actually worked. Sometimes I've thought that it would have been better if all the elevators had stopped working forever after the War, if there were no more touch-tone telephones and laptop computers and stick-shift sedans and CAT scans. If all of that stuff was just a temporary aberration of a society that didn't quite work out, then we could maybe shrug our shoulders and go back to living the way human beings had lived for thousands of years before such wonders existed. But the wonders still existed, damn them. You could get almost anything you wanted (short of a nuclear reactor, maybe) if you had enough money or ingenuity or luck; I had certainly proved that, when I jetted over to England for my first case, then jetted back in triumph (more or less). And that meant we had to live with these constant reminders of what had been lost, of what was once so common and now shimmered just out of our reach, and it was almost impossible to go through life without a daily dose of self-pity.

Dealing with the Feds was a sure way to keep the dose high; they treated themselves pretty well, and were not inclined to hide it. To keep us all striving to regain what had been lost, their supporters might explain. Because they have the power and use it for their own benefit, their opponents would retort.

Whatever the explanation, the elevator arrived and smoothly lifted us ten stories into the building. The doors opened onto a corridor. On the opposite side of the corridor, a soldier stood guard in front of a glass door. The sign on the door said:

Francis Bolton

Governor of the Commonwealth

My, my, I thought. A big shot indeed.

The guard gave a nod to my two pals. He frisked me, but I was clean—I had left my revolver back at the office. "You can go inside now, Mr. Sands," Danny said when the frisking had been completed.

"Thank you. And thanks for the ride." I smiled.

Danny looked uncomfortable for a moment, and then said, "Good luck." Then he and Gus walked off down the corridor.

Why did I need luck? I wondered. I went inside.

I was in a large reception area: potted plants, framed paintings, air conditioning, and a view of the city that you just don't get one story up on lower Washington Street. There was also the unavoidable VOTE YES poster. I walked over to a woman seated behind a large oak desk. "Hi," I said. "My name is Sands. I was summoned."

"Yes," she agreed. "Please have a seat."

She was a pleasant-looking blond, maybe a bit old for my taste, and maybe with a bit too much makeup on—nobody wore makeup anymore. But she had the kind of figure you can only get when you you're allowed to shop at the Feds' own grocery store. I smiled at her. "What's your name?" I asked.

She stared at me as if I were a particularly disgusting mutant.

Friendliness doesn't always work. I let the smile fade, and I wandered over to a leather couch, where I parked myself while the secretary ignored me and I awaited the governor's pleasure.

I tried to imagine what he wanted with me. Something to do with the VOTE YES posters? Security at the polls, maybe. I'd rather be staring out my office window, I thought. But surely Governor Bolton didn't bother himself with details like who to hire for security. Maybe he had a priceless figurine....

Whatever he wanted, I knew that this was going to be an interview. So I tried to prepare. I considered Governor Bolton.

He had been around for a long time now—about eight years, I figured. The Feds had appointed him governor of the New England region shortly after their troops came up from Atlanta and put a stop to the anarchy that had been plaguing us for years. And in the time since then he had become the symbol of the Federal presence here: tough, distant, and a little bit mysterious—at least to me, who didn't spend a great deal of time thinking about such things. What did the Feds want from us? What was in the occupation for them? The taxes they managed to collect didn't pay their expenses; the men and women they drafted (like me) didn't make up for the number of troops they had to commit to the region. So why bother?

In a way, the most mysterious thing about Bolton was that he was a local. Somebody—probably my buddy Stretch—had told me that Bolton had sold real estate before the War. Not a lot of call for real estate salesmen in this new world, where mansions were free—all you had to do was be able to defend them. But somehow he had landed on his feet. And somehow he had made the Feds trust him enough to put him in charge of the region where he had grown up. And somehow it didn't bother him that many— perhaps most—of his fellow locals thought of him as a semi-traitor, zealously carrying out the edicts of the well-fed rulers from down south.

Or maybe it did bother him. How would I know? To me, he was just a photo in the *Globe* and a bunch of rumors.

After a while I began to wonder if he would ever be anything more. Men wearing suits and ties came and went.

The blond secretary had a smile for most of them. No one paid any attention to me, except perhaps to glance at my Salvage-Market jersey and jeans and wonder how I had gotten past the guard. This was not much better than being in my office. I didn't even have a book to read.

Finally the summons came. "The governor will see you now," the secretary said.

I got up and smiled at her. "Thanks a lot," I said.

She pointed silently to a door. I walked over to it and knocked. "Come in," a loud voice responded. I went in.

Governor Bolton was sitting behind a huge mahogany desk, flanked by the American flag and some other flag with what looked like a Native American on it. It took me a second to retrieve the flag's identification from my freakishly complete memory. It was the Massachusetts state flag. This struck me as somewhat incongruous, since Massachusetts didn't really exist as a separate political entity in the Feds' scheme of things.

There were no VOTE YES posters.

Bolton was scribbling on a piece of paper—or maybe, I thought, he was pretending to scribble, so I could see he was a busy man and a great deal more important than me. I was willing to concede the point. "Have a seat," he said, continuing to scribble. I sat. The chair was a little too low; I found myself staring up at the governor. He had gray hair, cut short, and a long scar next to his right eye. I hadn't noticed the scar in the photos I had seen of him; it made him look even tougher than my image of him—he was a man who took risks, the scar said, a man who understood physical danger. He was wearing a white shirt. His tie was loose; his shirtsleeves were rolled up. He was ready for action.

After an appropriate interval he put his pen down and looked at me. "Walter Sands," he said. His voice was deep and powerful. It sounded out of place in a private conversation; it should have been addressing a political rally.

"Pleased to meet you," I said. I smiled.

The governor didn't smile back. "Did my bodyguards treat you well?" he asked.

"They were perfect gentlemen. They both deserve promotions."

He nodded, although I got the impression he hadn't heard my answer. "I talked to Charles Moseby about you," he went on. "Mr. Moseby recommends you quite highly."

I nodded in turn. Mr. Moseby is my pal Stretch, and I would have killed him if he hadn't recommended me quite highly. "How did you get my name?" I asked.

"From that article in the *Globe* a few weeks back. Interesting business over there in England. Although why anyone would want to be a private detective nowadays is beyond me."

"Uh-huh." The article in the *Globe* had been written by another friend, named Gwen Phillips. I have a lot of friends. Gwen and Stretch are the ones I live with.

"Still, there might be circumstances where a person with your skills and contacts might be useful." He was dithering, I could tell. A common problem with clients, my extensive reading of private eye novels had told me. It's tough to tell someone you've got a problem. Maybe his wife is cheating on him, I thought. But no—I'd heard he was a widower.

"Perhaps you could tell me what your particular circumstances are," I said in that smooth professional tone I had mastered over the course of my single case, "and then we can decide if I'm the man for the job."

Bolton gazed at me. "Tell me," he said, still dithering, "what's your position on the referendum?"

My heart sank. He *did* want me to guard some damn voting booth. The referendum was the latest development in the Federal government's relationship with its fractious stepchild. It was a simple enough question that the Feds wanted us New Englanders to answer: "Do you support the government of the United States of America?" But the ramifications of their asking the question, and our answering it, had kept a lot of people in a tizzy all spring.

I knew what Bolton wanted me to say: *I'm proud to be an American. I'm going to VOTE YES, and I don't care who knows it.* But I figured we would both be better off if I didn't try to mislead him. "I haven't given it a great deal of thought," I said. "I'm an apolitical kind of guy."

"Now is no time to be apolitical!" Bolton thundered.

It seemed to me to be as good a time as any to be apolitical. "Why not?" I asked.

Bolton gave me a disgusted look. "At least you're not one of those sniveling isolationist types who prefer savagery to civilization—are you?"

Well, when you put it like that...I shook my head. "No sir, I'm not one of those."

"And you have no objection to working for the Federal government?"

That was a little trickier. "Um, perhaps if you could give me a few more details..."

Bolton tapped the fingers of his right hand on his desk. The dithering was about to come to an end, I figured. Either he'd give me the case, or he'd throw me out of the office. "Mr. Sands," he intoned, "the president of the United States of America is corning to Boston."

He sounded as if he was expecting a round of applause from his audience. "That's great," I said.

"It's the first time since before—" He waved his hand. I knew what the wave of the hand meant. People still had difficulty mentioning the War. Maybe if we were all very quiet about it, it would retroactively go away.

"She's coming here to get us to vote for the referendum?" I guessed.

"Precisely." Bolton stood up and stared out his window. He was shorter than I expected. Maybe that's why my chair was so low. All of a sudden he looked a little silly to me as he stood next to the American flag—as if he were playing at being governor. And I wondered just how tough he really was. Maybe he still thought of himself as a real estate agent, and couldn't really believe where life had brought him. I wondered if, in his heart of hearts, he thanked God for the War and the opportunity it had granted him. There had to be a few people around who thought like that.

My mind was wandering. It returned when Bolton started to speak. "This referendum is important, Sands," he said. "New England is part of America. People have to understand this—they have to *believe* this. They complain about the emigration controls and the out-of-state troops and the privileges for government workers, but they forget about what the government saved them from—and they forget about their *heritage.* We can't just let our heritage slip away from us.

"So that's why President Kramer proposed the referendum. She believes that, if people can be made to focus on the positives, they will understand what we're trying to do, and they will support us. And once she has New England's support, she can lead America back to the forefront of the world's nations once again. So she is coming to Boston to give a speech a few days before the voting—a speech that will make people realize just what is at stake here, that will convince them to give her the vote of confidence she needs."

Bolton sounded as if he were giving a speech himself. But his delivery was curiously rushed, as if this was a speech he was rehearsing for a different audience. I didn't mind, but I was still trying to figure out what all this had to do with me. "You want me to protect the president while she's here?" I guessed.

"Not quite." He returned to his desk. He took a piece of paper out of the top drawer and handed it to me. I read the message typed on it.

We know Kramer plans to come.

Boston is ours. If she comes, she faces our wrath.

THE FEDS MUST GO!

The Second American Revolution

The Second American Revolution: TSAR. I didn't like the sound of that acronym. I studied the message, and then returned the sheet of paper to Bolton.

"Have you heard of this group?" he asked.

I shook my head.

"Neither have I. This sheet appeared on the outer door to my office this morning. I need to know who's behind it."

"And that's my job?"

Bolton nodded. "We have to find The Second American Revolution and prevent them from doing anything to President Kramer."

I thought about it. "Why me?" I asked finally. "You've got your troops, you've got the local police—and the president has her own security people, I imagine. Can't they take care of this?"

"Maybe. They'll be on the case too. But I thought a local might bring something to it that they can't. You know what I'm talking about, Sands. Contacts. Sources of information. No one around here talks to the Feds; that's part of our problem. But they'll talk to someone like you."

Quite true. But...Bolton studied me as I tried to think it through. People weren't standing in line to obtain my services. Maybe they never would be. But I didn't like this case. Didn't like the way I got it, didn't like what I'd have to do to solve it. "I'm sorry," I said finally. "I don't think I'm right for this."

"Why not?" Bolton demanded. "We'll pay you your usual rate. Moseby told me you're not working on anything else at the moment."

Thanks, Stretch. I tried to explain. "If I work for you, I become just like the troops and the police." *And just like you,* I managed to avoid saying. "People may talk to me now because I'm a local, but then they won't be sure in the future whether or not I'm one of you. And then they'll stop talking."

"Doesn't the safety of the president of the United States matter to you, Sands?"

I wasn't sure it mattered to me more than the safety of any other poor soul in this godforsaken world, but I guessed that wasn't worth getting into. "Of course," I replied. "But I've got my career to think of."

Bolton gave me a look that told me what he thought of my career.

"Why not just have her stay in Atlanta?" I suggested. "That's the best way to keep her safe. And I doubt her speech is going to make much difference to the referendum, one way or the other."

"And give in to the terrorists' demands? That's precisely what we can't do. So are you with us, Sands?"

I took a deep breath and shook my head.

Bolton picked up his phone. "Lisa, get me General Cowens," he said, and he replaced the receiver.

Lisa, I thought. The blond secretary, presumably. Nice name. And then I thought: I'm not sure I like having General Cowens in on this.

The phone rang almost immediately, and Bolton picked it up again. "Bob, this is Frank," he said. "That private detective I was telling you about is here. He needs some persuasion. Can you come? Thanks."

The governor hung up and glared at me some more. "This is serious business, Sands," he said, "and you are a part of it, whether you want to be or not."

The governor's scar seemed to throb. He looked much more impressive sitting down; he looked like the kind of man who could make threats and carry them out. I decided it was time to start worrying.

———◆———

THE DISTANCE BEACONS

available in print and ebook

Richard Bowker is the author of *Replica*, *Senator*, and other novels. He lives near Boston with his wife and two sons.

You can contact Richard through his website: www.richardbowker.com

www.ingramcontent.com/pod-product-compliance
Lightning Source LLC
Chambersburg PA
CBHW031208020726
47499CB00002B/526